SUNSET KISS

BAYTOWN BOYS

MARYANN JORDAN

Cover by Graphics by Stacy

ISBN ebook: 978-1-956588-12-5

ISBN print: 978-1-956588-13-2

❀ Created with Vellum

Author's Note

Please remember that this is a work of fiction. I have lived in numerous states as well as overseas, but for the last thirty years have called Virginia my home. I often choose to use fictional city names with some geographical accuracies.

These fictionally named cities allow me to use my creativity and not feel constricted by attempting to accurately portray the areas.

It is my hope that my readers will allow me this creative license and understand my fictional world.

I also do quite a bit of research on my books and try to write on subjects with accuracy. There will always be points where creative license will be used in order to create scenes or plots.

LUKE (AGE SIXTEEN)

"There you go, Mrs. Galinski," Luke said. He smiled at her as he placed her bag of groceries into her cart even though he knew she usually complained. He was careful with her eggs and milk, but she always remembered his first day of bagging groceries a year ago when the bread became squished and several eggs broke.

"Were you careful with the eggs?" she asked, peering into the cart with such intensity he felt sure she would find something to fuss about.

"Yes, ma'am."

She pushed her glasses up on her nose and peered toward him. Then, much to his shock, she smiled. "Looks like you're finally learning."

Knowing that was the closest to a compliment he was going to get from her, he nodded. "Yes, ma'am." As she pushed her cart out of the grocery store, he noticed the store owner, Mr. Robbins, walking toward him.

Chuckling as he approached, Mr. Robbins said,

"Luke, my boy, you just earned a smile from Mrs. Galinski. I think that's worth a promotion."

Assuming Mr. Robbins was joking, he chuckled along with the older man.

Mr. Robbins clapped him on the back. "I'm not kidding, Luke. You've been working here for a year, never missed a day even though I know that's been hard with your mom. So, starting tomorrow, if you want, I'm moving you up to help with the stock in the back. You're strong, smart, and I know I can trust you to work without someone having to stand over you all the time." Before Luke had a chance to respond, Mr. Robbins continued. "And it comes with a raise."

Unable to keep the smile off his face, Luke grinned widely. "Thank you, sir! This means a lot to me. The responsibility. And the money."

"I like to reward hard work." Then, not wanting to hold up the line, Mr. Robbins said, "Come and see me when you get to work tomorrow after school, and I'll go over your new job."

Quickly agreeing, Luke shook the outstretched hand, then turned to accept the congratulations from Betty Lou, the long-time cashier at Robbins' Grocery. Feeling on top of the world, he couldn't imagine anything bringing him down. That was, until he looked up and saw his fourteen-year-old brother walking into the store.

Lowering his voice, he stalked over to Larry. "What are you doing here?"

"What? Can't I even come into a grocery store like anybody else?"

Luke glanced at the two other boys who'd walked in with Larry. He recognized them from school, and whenever they came in, he knew they were trouble. Looking back to his brother, he replied, "Unless you've got money I don't know about, then you don't need to be here."

Larry leaned in close, his young face harder than it should have been for someone his age. "Be cool, bro. When my friends found out that you worked here, they figured we could get something to eat."

Narrowing his eyes, Luke shook his head. "If you mean you came in here to steal something, think again. I'm not losing my job because of you."

Larry sneered, but Luke knew it was more for show. His brother wasn't a small kid, but Luke was bigger. Much bigger. He never liked to use his bulk to intimidate but straightened to his full height, crossing his arms over his chest. He and Larry shared a lot. Dark hair. Blue eyes. A deadbeat dad that ran off four years ago. And a mom that could never seem to pull herself together enough to hold down a job, always blaming someone else for her life not turning out the way she wanted. But that was where the similarities ended.

Whereas Luke studied hard in school, knowing that was going to be his way out of the inner-city neighborhood they lived in, and had worked hard ever since he'd gotten a part-time job, Larry had decided school was for suckers and the easy money found on the streets was the way of his future. It wasn't that he wasn't smart, but Larry definitely took after their parents in wanting things to come his way without working for them.

3

Now, staring down at Larry and the two weaselly friends who'd slinked in with him, they sneered in unison before turning and walking out.

"Know you're worried about him," Betty Lou said, drawing his attention over to her. "You've been a good big brother, tried to be a dad, and half the time been a mom, as well. But that boy's taken after your parents. Wouldn't know hard work if it jumped up and bit him."

She was right, of course, but it still rankled to hear. "He's not bad," he defended. "He just makes bad choices."

"Luke, you listen to me. You're right. He does make bad choices. But that doesn't excuse those choices. He chooses to hang with the wrong people. He chooses to ditch school. He chooses to steal rather than work. You've done your best to do what you can. But you have to take care of yourself."

He nodded slowly, his shoulders slumping. "Yes, ma'am." Glancing at several people in line waiting patiently to have their groceries bagged, he saw the sympathetic gazes on their faces and sighed. There were few secrets in this neighborhood, and most knew his family. With his head held high, he nodded at the next person in line and started bagging. Digging deep, he knew Betty Lou was right. Two more years of high school. Two more years of trying to be a good influence on Larry. Two more years of trying to get his mom to stop drowning her sorrows in a bottle. He had no idea what he'd do after graduation, but somehow, he was going to get out.

(Two years later)

"I don't know how you can do this to us!"

Luke kept his head down toward his bed where he was packing a small bag to take to boot camp but twisted his neck to look at his mom. He remained quiet, finding it best to let her complain since nothing he said would make a difference—not to her nor to his plans.

"Larry's in juvie, and you know he needs you to take him stuff so he's not so miserable in there. I just started a new job and need you to help out around here." When he didn't respond, she finally huffed loudly. "You just don't care, Luke! You're like your father running out at the first chance—"

"No, Ma… don't you dare say that to me," he bit out, his voice harsh but not raised. "You don't get to say that to me."

Her face twisted as she slumped down on the edge of the bed. "I know, Luke, I'm sorry. You're nothing like him." Her hands were clasped in her lap, knuckles white. She lifted her gaze back to him, drawing in a deep breath. "You've always been such a good boy. I know that. You helped me around the house when things were hard. I know you stepped in your daddy's shoes when you should have been running around playing. And I know Larry screws up, gettin' away with all kinds of stuff before he finally got caught. I'm just going to miss you. It's going to be hard being here on my own."

Zipping his bag closed, he peered down at her. Softening his tone, he said, "Ma, you know I love you. And I'm proud of you. You haven't been drinking in a while, and I think you're going to do fine in the new job. I figure juvie is the best place for Larry right now. He can work on his GED and get away from those fuckers in the neighborhood that got him selling drugs for them. If he can get his act together, he can get out of juvie and make something of himself. But this, right here, Ma, is for me. Joining the Army gets me out of this city, gives me a job, trains me in a career. This is my chance, and I'm gonna take it."

She stood, nodding, and reached out to place her hand on his arm. "I get that, Luke. I do. But what if they send you off somewhere far away? What if something happens to you?"

"Life doesn't come with guarantees, Ma, you know that. But I'll learn to take care of myself like I always have. I'd like you to be happy for me."

She stepped closer, wrapping her thin arms around him, hugging him tightly. "I am, honey. I wish I could have been a better mom. I wish I could have done more for you."

She barely came to his shoulders, and he held her in a warm embrace. "A man makes his own choices, makes his own destiny."

She chuckled as she leaned back and looked up at him. "That sounds like something Mr. Robbins told you."

His mom was right. Over the last two years, Mr. Robbins had not only continually promoted Luke at the store but had also talked to him about his future. With his grades, Luke could have qualified for scholarships, but in order to be his own man, Luke was ready for full-time employment and training. Mr. Robbins always talked about his time in the service, and after talking to recruiters, Luke was excited to sign on the dotted line with the Army. His ASVAB scores qualified him for medical training and, after boot camp, he was heading off for Combat Medic Specialist Training.

"You'll write? Or call whenever you can?" she asked, her eyes pleading.

"Absolutely. It won't be much during boot camp, but once I graduate and head off to medic school, I'll be in touch. Remember, Ma... take care of yourself, and let Larry get his head out of his own ass while in juvie."

She nodded, then stepped back so that he could grab his bag from the floor. They walked downstairs together, hugging goodbye at the door.

As he stepped into the sunshine, he stopped at the end of their driveway and turned to see her standing in the doorway, waving to him. A flash of memory from years before when she would wave goodbye as he went off to school and be there to greet him when he returned flooded his mind. She was a good woman and good mom brought low by a man who'd rather drink and carouse than hold a job or care for his family. If his father had taught him anything, it was what *not* to do, and Luke was determined that if he was ever lucky enough to be a husband and dad, he would never be like his old man.

With a last wave, he walked down the street toward the closest bus station that would take him to where he needed to go. He breathed easier and felt lighter, knowing he was heading toward his future.

2

(TWELVE YEARS LATER - BAYTOWN)

Sitting at the end of the bar in Finn's Pub, Luke offered a chin lift to those around that he knew. Surprisingly, other than the autumn tourists, he recognized quite a few faces. He'd only been in the Baytown area a few months, but having joined the local chapter of the American Legion and attended several meetings as well as joining their youth baseball coaching staff, he'd been welcomed into the small community.

"Jesus, I thought the tourists would be gone by now," Zac Hamilton grumbled.

On the other side of him, Joseph Newman laughed. "I swear a group of them were out kayaking off the beach the other night, so drunk they couldn't figure out which way was the shore. Ryan and I were rounding them up. Mitch had the Baytown Police out there once they hit the shore."

Zac shook his head. "And I had to make sure no one was injured. I know Baytown needs the input of cash from tourists, but the ones that go off the rails are a pain in the ass."

Luke nodded, sipping his beer as he listened to the conversation around him. Zac was the captain of the rescue squad. Ryan was the captain of the local Virginia Marine Police, and Mitch was the Baytown Police chief. And Joseph, a man who'd become a good friend, worked for the VMP, also. Many of the new friends he'd made were first responders, not surprising since most had a military background and were also in the American Legion.

Turning to Zac, he said, "Been meaning to talk to you when you've got a moment."

Zac halted in mid-bite, set his hamburger onto his plate, and turned his attention toward Luke. "I've got more than a moment now. What's on your mind?"

"My job is full-time, but I'd like to volunteer for the rescue squad if you need—"

"Fuck, yeah, man!" Zac enthused, his smile wide. "We can always use volunteers, and to have someone who's a medic… that'd be amazing."

A low chuckle rumbled from deep within his chest. "Well, all right then. Just let me know what I need to do, and I can start anytime."

Before Zac had a chance to reply, a couple of visiting patrons who'd overstayed their welcome and their drinking were being escorted to the door by Brogan MacFarlane, one of the owners of Finn's Pub. He, along with his siblings, ran the family business.

"Christ, shut the fuck up," Brogan was overheard

saying. "If you don't like this one-horse town, then stay the hell out."

"You tell 'em, bro," Aiden MacFarlane yelled, his laughter ringing out over the pub.

Joseph and Luke shared a grin. Brogan was gruff on the outside and didn't take any shit off anyone, but his wife and children had him wrapped around their fingers. Turning back to their beer and burgers, Luke soon finished, tossed money onto the bar, and offered another chin lift to those he knew.

Once outside the pub, he headed toward the beach where he'd parked, but with the sun just starting to set, he was drawn to the town pier that jutted out into the Chesapeake Bay. It appeared empty, and he walked along, his booted footsteps on the wooden planks mingled with the call of the seagulls as they flew over-head, diving into the water for their last meal of the day.

Reaching the end, he leaned his forearms on the fishermen's angled railing and stared out over the water. The vista in front of him was stunning. Not a man to wax poetic, he was still able to appreciate the beautiful scenery. The water reflected the blues, oranges, and yellows of the sunset sky. Having spent the first eighteen years of his life growing up in an inner-city concrete jungle and then ten years in the Army, including several tours to Afghanistan, he couldn't believe that this was now his life. While he didn't socialize often, he had friends. His job was full-time with benefits. His small, one-bedroom apartment was just for him.

Sucking in a deep breath of briny air, he let it out slowly. *Best place I've ever lived.* While he hadn't planned on a full military career, he'd left after ten years when his mom was diagnosed with cancer. He'd moved in with her and nursed her until hospice took over. After she died, he'd spent several months settling her minimal affairs, fixing up the tiny house that he'd grown up in, and selling it. He'd taken half the money and put it in the bank specifically for Larry, who hadn't bothered to come to the small service he'd had for their mom.

They'd talked on the phone, and Larry had claimed he'd get the paltry sum the next time he was coming through town but didn't know when that would be. Considering Luke wasn't sure Larry had ever held a legitimate job, he knew Larry would show up eventually.

When Luke had started to look for a new place to settle, he'd seen an advertisement for a medic at the North Heron Regional Jail. It wouldn't be the first time he'd held a position like that. He'd taken a trip down to interview and immediately fell for the rural county at the southern tip of the Eastern Shore of Virginia's peninsula. Crossing from the mainland of Virginia by the seventeen-mile bridge-tunnel over the Chesapeake Bay, he'd immediately decided this was where he wanted to live.

The sound of a woman's voice and laughter met his ears. Looking back down the pier with the sunset in the distance, a woman came into view as she wandered along casually, her phone pressed to her ear. Seemingly unaware of her surroundings, she chatted and laughed, her voice lighthearted. Thick, dark hair fell around her shoulders, the waves blowing gently in the breeze. Her jeans were molded to her body, and underneath her jean jacket, her purple T-shirt matched her purple sneakers. Even from a distance, he could tell that she was beautiful.

A strange longing filled his chest. The only thing in his life that was missing was someone to share it with. But in truth, he wasn't sure he was cut out for a relationship. He sure as hell hadn't witnessed a healthy one growing up. And if the smile on the beautiful woman's face was anything to go by, he figured she must be talking to someone special in her life.

Movement behind her caught his attention, and he recognized the two men Brogan had booted out of the bar, following the woman as she meandered down the pier—and she appeared to be unaware of her surroundings. "Bye, Mom. I'll talk to you tomorrow," she said, lowering her phone.

She was talking to her mom. A warm feeling moved through him at the realization that the bright smile on her face and light tone of her voice was while on the phone with her mom. That simple act was something he'd never experienced, at least not in years. He'd thought it would have been a lucky man to have been on the other end of the call and couldn't explain why he was glad it hadn't been. *Not like she doesn't have someone waiting for her at home.* But for a moment, he'd allowed himself the fantasy that she would have had that smile on her face while talking to him.

The two men were approaching rapidly from behind

her. They'd had too much to drink, and with the way their attention was locked onto her, he had no doubt their intentions weren't good.

Bolting into action, he jogged toward her, watching the instant her blue eyes lifted and met his, widening in apparent surprise. He saw the men stop, their gazes still riveted on her. "Hey, babe. I wondered when you'd get here," he said, placing his arm around her shoulders, pulling her in for a hug while trying not to frighten her, something he wasn't sure he could pull off. He was a large man, and now that she was close to him, the top of her head only came to his shoulders. Wanting to imply intimacy without overstepping his bounds, he shifted her to his side.

She blinked as her body stiffened and she stared up at him. "Um... I think you have me mixed up with someone else—"

"Fuck... didn't see him," one of the men cursed, stumbling into the other.

Her head swung around to stare at the men behind her, a slight gasp leaving her lips. Her long hair brushed against Luke's arm, and he choked back a gasp at the feel of the silky softness. Glad to have something else to focus on, he glared toward the men as they turned and walked back down the pier toward town.

She watched for a few seconds, then jerked her head back toward Luke, eyes still wide. "Were they following me?" she squeaked.

He hated that her evening was marred with the actions of a couple of assholes. Dropping his arm from her shoulder, he immediately missed the feel of her tucked close to him. Stepping back, he nodded. "Yes, they were. I'm sorry for startling you, but it was the easiest way to get them to move on."

"I didn't even realize they were there!"

He leveled a hard gaze toward her, lifting his brow. "A woman walking alone in the evening? Talking on the phone? Not paying attention to her surroundings?"

Her mouth opened, and then she snapped it closed, huffing. After a few seconds, her shoulders slumped, and she nodded. "You're right. That was incredibly stupid, and I know better." As though realizing she was still on the pier with a large man she didn't know, she took a step back.

"I'll escort you to your car if you'd like," he said. "I can stay behind you so that you don't feel crowded with someone you don't know."

She looked as though she might argue, then nodded again. Turning, she walked back down the pier toward town. She occasionally glanced over her shoulder, and he made sure he stayed far enough back that she wouldn't feel threatened.

His gaze occasionally dropped to her ass, unable to keep from appreciating the attractive woman. But to be honest, it was her face that had captured his full attention when she'd blinked up at him.

The walk down the pier didn't last long enough for him—he could have appreciated the view for a much longer time. She stopped at the end of the pier and turned, and he was glad he had the chance to lift his gaze so she wouldn't catch him admiring her assets.

She offered a little smile and jerked her head toward a small car parked nearby. "That's me, over there."

He shoved his hands into his jean pockets. "I'll stay here and watch that you get in safely."

She nodded, then hesitated before walking straight toward him, her hand out. "Thank you. What you did was very kind."

He lifted his hand and gently clasped his fingers around hers, immediately feeling the warmth of her touch and a slight tingle that moved up his arm. "I just did what anyone should do."

"I agree, but obviously, not everyone does that, or there wouldn't have been a need in the first place."

He regretfully let go of her hand and chuckled. "That's true, ma'am."

She laughed, and with the sunset casting a glow over her beautiful face, he wasn't sure he'd ever seen anything more stunning. "I'm Allie, by the way." She cocked her head to the side and waited.

"Luke."

They stared at each other for a moment, neither speaking as the sun began to sink lower over the water. Finally, she stepped forward and placed her hand on his shoulder as she lifted on her toes. He bent his head toward her, thinking she was going to say something, but instead, her lips touched the very corner of his mouth before she lowered her heels back to the ground. "It's nice to meet you, Luke." With that, she turned and jogged across the street, climbing into her little car after tossing him a wave.

He stared until her taillights disappeared. His lips

tingled where hers had been, and heat seared through his chest. Glancing up at the brilliant colors of the sky, he found it hard to catch his breath. Finally drawing oxygen into his lungs, his heart pounded at the memory of that gentle, almost-not-there sunset kiss.

3

"Okay, let's get ready for lunch!" Allie clapped her hands, gaining the attention of her third graders. School had been in session for over a month, and the classroom routine was well-established. The children who brought their lunch walked over to their cubbies to pull out their paper sacks or brightly colored lunch boxes. Those who were getting their lunch from the cafeteria lined up at the door.

She soon had her students settled in the cafeteria and smiled at the lunchroom aide before hurrying off to the teacher's lounge for her twenty minutes of adult time. The scent of pizza from the cafeteria had tempted, but the chicken salad sandwich she'd brought with her from home was a much more economical choice. With a master's degree, her salary with the North Heron School System certainly paid for her expenses, but she'd been saving for a house, praying that her car would keep running long enough for her to have the down payment necessary.

When she first came to the area, she'd rented a house with a couple of other teachers. She'd gotten along well with them, but it somehow felt like a continuation of college, and she longed to have her privacy. A fortuitous meeting at the local American Legion Auxiliary with Hannah Freeman, the police chief of the tiny, nearby town of Easton, had led to her being able to rent Hannah's cottage. Hannah had moved in with her fiancé, Dylan Hunt, another police chief in the area. As soon as she'd overheard Hannah telling someone she wanted to find a renter, Allie had jumped at the opportunity. The rent was little more than what she was paying for a shared house so she was still able to save money each month to go into her buy-my-own-house fund.

Prices of houses were at a low with the economy just then, and she felt sure she would be able to find something to buy soon. In fact, she'd just been talking to her mom about it the previous night.

Last night. That thought had her stop outside the teacher's lounge door, remembering the strange turn of events while walking on the pier and talking to her parents—and meeting the stoic Luke. Pressing her lips together, she could still feel the tingle from the light kiss. *I kissed a perfect stranger.* Feeling her cheeks heat, she shook her head to dislodge the embarrassment. *Oh, good grief! It was hardly a kiss! More like I simply pressed my lips to his cheek. Okay, maybe his cheek and the edge of his mouth. Still, not worth thinking about again.*

Pushing open the door, she walked into the lounge,

knowing that she was definitely going to be thinking about him again.

"Hey, girl," Shonna called out, patting the seat next to her. "Take a load off."

She plopped down into the chair and opened her lunch bag. Pulling out her wrapped sandwich and water bottle, she looked over at Shonna's soda. "Oh, God, that caffeine looks good right now."

"I've got some unsweetened tea," Terry said, standing at the refrigerator. "Want a glass?"

She twisted around and smiled at him. "Do you have enough?"

"Absolutely."

"Then yes. I think I'm going to need it to get through the afternoon."

"No specials?" Jade asked, finishing her lunch.

Allie glanced over at Jade's plastic container lunch, which smelled like delicious tomato-garlic sauce over some kind of pasta, and her stomach rumbled. "No. No music, no art, no PE. Just me and twenty-six eight-year-olds as we make our way through science, then math. What's nuts is that on Tuesdays, they have a morning and an afternoon special, so those days give me a breather."

"How are you doing on saving for a house?" Shonna asked.

"I'm getting there. I know I'm lucky to have such a cute cottage to rent, and Hannah is a wonderful land-lord. But I want something to call my own."

"How big do you want?" Terry asked.

"Three bedrooms. I'd like to have one for guests and

one for an office. It doesn't need to be huge but a place where I can entertain some friends without feeling like we're stepping on each other. And a nice, spacious kitchen. Oh, and a soaking tub in the master bathroom!"

The others laughed. "You should be able to find something like that within your budget," Terry said.

"Well, almost. But my budget could use a little boost right about now."

"Did you see the ad up on the board?" Jade asked, inclining her head toward the bulletin board on the wall. Even though most of their school information came through their email, the secretary would still post some announcements on the wall of the teacher's lounge. "It's for a part-time reading specialist job. That's right up your alley."

Shonna jumped up. "Damn, I've got to get to my class and hardly have time to run to the bathroom."

The others quickly tossed their trash and headed out the door. Looking at the board, Allie snapped a picture of the announcement with her phone. *I'll look at it later,* she thought, hurrying out the door to get to her class.

Sitting at her small kitchen table, Allie groaned in delight over her buttery, toasted garlic bread. Jade's lunch had been too tempting to ignore, so Allie had fixed spaghetti and meatballs for dinner, adding in the garlic bread along with her salad.

While fixing dinner, her calendar app had beeped, reminding her that she needed to pay rent. Trying to figure out when she could drive to Easton to hand a check to Hannah, or at least leave it at the police station for her, she remembered she hadn't looked at the picture she'd taken of the announcement for part-time work for a reading specialist.

Allie was not only certified in elementary education but also as a reading specialist. Curious to see what the position was, she clicked to the picture, her eyes skimming over the information.

Part-time job: Reading Specialist is needed at the North Heron Regional Jail. Hours flexible. Evenings or weekends as available. Duties would include individual and small group tutoring for men and women. References required. Background investigation required. For more information, go to the NHRJ website. Warden William Neely.

A part-time job at the jail. Working with adults. Leaning back in her chair as she continued to eat, she thought of the possibilities. *Flexible hours, which means I could determine when I work. Adults would certainly be a change from my third graders.* Taking a sip of wine, her mind jumped to the setting. *The jail.* While she had worked with adults before, she'd never even been inside of a jail. *Probably most people haven't unless they had to be there.*

When she finished eating, she washed off her dishes and put them away, placing the leftovers in a plastic container to take to school for her lunch the next day. Grabbing her laptop, she quickly looked up the website, knowing she needed more information before she could consider applying for the position.

The North Heron Regional Jail served not only

North Heron County but also the only other Virginia county on the Eastern Shore, Acawmacke, as well as taking prisoners from other districts if the room was available. She discovered that several of the small towns' police stations contained a few holding cells, but the main jail was housed in Easton. *Oh, Hannah will be the perfect person to ask about the jail since she works at the Easton police station.* The Sheriff's Department was responsible for the 250-bed facility. Housing both men and women, the jail had its own kitchen, laundry, library, and medical clinic. *Hmmm, wonder how that works with both men and women?*

Her phone rang, and she smiled, seeing her mom's picture pop up on caller ID. "Hey, Mom," she greeted.

"Hi, sweetie. You got off the phone so quickly last night, I didn't have a chance to tell you about Aunt Maggie and Uncle Henry."

As soon as her mom mentioned last night, her mind immediately went back to Luke... not that he'd been far off all day. Normally, she loved listening to her mother's anecdotes about family members, but tonight, she barely heard a word she said, instead thinking of the handsome man who'd come to her rescue on the sunset-lit pier.

He'd reminded her of her brother's friends in the Marines—muscular, handsome, hair trimmed shorter on the sides. His eyes were a mesmerizing shade of blue, a blue that both caught the light from the reflection off the water and was dark with intensity. When his arm had curled around her shoulder, she could feel the strength in his biceps that strained at the material of his T-shirt.

And he was tall. She'd had to lift way up on her toes and hope that he'd lean down so that she could kiss his cheek. She didn't consider herself to be short at five-foot-five but knew that to most people, she was. And while she was aiming for his cheek, she'd angled her mouth slightly at the last second to place her kiss on the edge of his lips. It was a split-second change, one that she'd given no thought to before it happened. And the feel of his firm, full lips and the softness of his trimmed beard had caused her to battle the urge to stay on her toes and take the kiss all the way to his mouth.

"Are you listening to me?"

Allie jolted at her mother's tone. "Uh... yeah. Sure. Of course!" Laughter greeted her, and she grinned. "Okay, fine. You caught me daydreaming."

"Oh, it doesn't matter," her mom laughed. "I was just telling you about the new sofa they bought that has to be one of the most hideous colors of mustard yellow I've ever seen."

"Well, now you've got me curious. I hate to make you repeat the story, but why did they end up with the sofa like that?"

"He bought it from some online sale without looking at it first. Then, when it got delivered, Maggie had a fit, but the store wouldn't take it back. She told him he can keep it out in the garage!" After a pause, her mother said, "What I'm interested in is what you were thinking about."

Not about to confess to her mother that she'd kissed

a stranger, she said, "I found out about a part-time position for a reading specialist today, and I'm thinking about applying. I don't know anything about it yet, so I don't know how much time it would take or how much it would pay."

"That is interesting! Is it with the school system?"

"No, it's actually at the county jail."

"Oh, it's with adults. You did something like that when you were interning for your master's, didn't you?"

"Yeah, I did although it was both adults and children. I was a reading specialist that volunteered at a homeless shelter. I was able to tutor some of the children and work with the adults that had reading difficulties."

"So, do you think you'll take it?"

"I'll find out more about it. It's only part-time, but depending on the number of hours, it might be too much." She sighed, propping her chin on her hand as she leaned her elbow onto the table. "But the extra money would be amazing. I talked to the realtor the other day, and he says he knows of a couple of houses that might be listed soon that would be great for me."

"Well, honey, you know your dad and I will help in any way we can."

She smiled, knowing she had their support. "I know, but I'm close to having enough for a down payment, so if this extra job will kick in a little more, I'll be good." After giving each other their love, she disconnected and went back to her laptop. She found the email for the warden and typed out a professional inquiry. *At least maybe I'll find out more about it soon.*

After another glass of wine and some mindless TV,

she made sure the house was secure then headed to her bedroom. She had several books on her e-reader but pulled up the latest romance that she'd downloaded. Thinking of Luke earlier had her in the mood for long looks, kissing, and sweaty sex, even if it was for the fictional characters on the page.

4

Luke parked his SUV in the municipal parking lot in Easton, a tiny town north of Baytown. Set back from the main highway that ran north to south of the Eastern Shore, most people would bypass Easton and never know what was there. But because it was the county seat for North Heron County, it held the courthouse, county offices, and the new, large regional jail.

As he walked down the sidewalk, he looked up and spied Hannah. He and the Easton police chief had shared an experience earlier in the year, one that he hoped to never repeat. She'd come into the jail clinic to check on an elderly inmate when another inmate took Hannah and Luke hostage. Luke had tried to get the inmate to let Hannah go but the inmate had instead insisted that she stay. When instructed to tie her up, Luke was careful to use knots that she could loosen. Since then, he, she, and her fiancé, Dylan, had formed a bond. And considering Hannah and Dylan worked in law enforcement and were also members of the American Legion, he saw them often.

As soon as Hannah's head lifted and her gaze hit him, she smiled and lifted her hand in greeting. "Luke, hello," she called out.

His lips curved as he offered a chin lift. "Good morning, Chief Freeman." Before either of them had a chance to say anything else, movement coming from behind Hannah caught his attention. The beautiful, dark-haired, bright-smiling woman that he'd been thinking about for the past week came running from the parking lot, her hair flying out behind her. *Allie.* He hadn't forgotten one second of their prior meeting and had hoped he would see her again. As she continued running toward them, his gaze devoured her.

Her makeup wasn't heavy but made her eyes appear larger and gave a rosy shine to her lips. She was wearing a modest green dress that fell below her knees in a full skirt and a thick sweater to ward off the early morning chill. Low-heeled ankle boots encased her feet, creating a rapid-fire tapping on the sidewalk as she ran toward them. A heavy bag slung over her shoulder slapped against her side as she came nearer.

"Hannah!" she called out, her hand lifted as she waved a small piece of paper. Hannah turned and smiled. Allie came to a stop, her chest heaving as she caught her breath. "I'm so sorry to catch you like this. I forgot to get my rent check to you yesterday, so I wanted to drop it off before I headed to work."

Hannah took the check from Allie and shook her

head. "Allie, you didn't have to rush. I know you're good for it."

Allie turned and looked toward Luke, her eyes now wide, and a blush splashed across her cheeks. He stared, unable to drag his eyes away from her face.

"Allie, I'd like you to meet Luke, the medic at the jail. Luke, this is Allie. She rents my former house and works as a local teacher."

Luke reached out and shook Allie's hand, barely listening as Hannah said goodbye to both and walked back down the sidewalk.

"Hey, Allie," he said, her hand clasped warmly in his. The same tingle that he'd felt on the pier hit him along with the reality that he'd never had that reaction to someone before... as though all his dreams and hopes could come true if he could just hold their hand and stare into their face.

Her lips curved, and her smile was blinding. *Christ, is she always so happy?*

"I'm glad I had a chance to see you again," she said, her fingers still resting in his. "I wanted to thank you for last week."

"You already did thank me for that evening," he reminded, not wanting her to feel indebted.

"Yes, but some things are worth repeating."

Her voice was soft, almost lilting. He wondered if she ever sang because he imagined the sound would be beautiful. Unable to think of what to say to keep her talking, he swallowed deeply. For the first time in his life, he wished he could think of something to say—small talk or witty. Instead, he blurted, "Well, you just need to be aware of your surroundings." Inwardly wincing at his words, he watched her smile falter. *Shit.* Flirting had never been something he'd tried to excel in... he'd left that to his brother when they were teenagers and then to his fellow soldiers in the military. "I mean, it's just that you're so beautiful. You'll always attract attention."

Her eyes lit again, and he sucked in a breath. Beautiful was too simple a word to describe her, especially with the way his chest seemed to squeeze. Desperate to think of something else to say, he opened his mouth when suddenly her eyes widened just before her nose scrunched adorably.

"Oh, shoot, Luke... I'm sorry, but I have to run. I've got to get to work!"

She pulled her hand from his, and he immediately felt the loss. Not sure if she was just looking for an escape, he glanced at the badge that was hanging from a lanyard around her neck. **Baytown Elementary School.** *A teacher. Hannah said she was a teacher.*

She took a step back and tilted her head to the side. "It was nice to see you again. I wish that we could... um, well, that I had more time to chat."

"It's okay, Allie. Maybe I'll see you around sometime."

Her gaze locked with his, and her smile returned. Tucking her hair behind one ear, she nodded. "I'd like that. I'd really like that." The alarm on her phone dinged, and she grimaced. "Phooey, I've got early bus duty. I'm so sorry!" She turned and flew back down the sidewalk, the staccato of her boot steps receding.

Reaching the small sedan he recognized as hers, she looked back and waved. "Bye! I hope you have a nice day!"

His hand lifted in a return wave, a smile on his face. He watched as she climbed into her vehicle, carefully backed out of her parking space, then pulled onto the road leading toward Baytown.

He stood, continuing to stare after her even when her car was no longer in sight. Their interaction had only lasted a moment, and yet he could still feel the touch of her palm next to his, the softness of her fingers, and the light floral scent that followed in her wake.

"Luke! You comin' to work or just going to stare at the parking lot?"

He jolted, turning to see one of the day-shift guards walking toward him from the side. Hoping his beard hid his blush, he silently lifted his chin in greeting. As they walked around to the side of the jail where the guard station for the employee entrance was located, he listened as Henry chattered away. Henry's wife just had baby number four, and Henry had a perpetual smile on his face, which Luke found curious. It had been his experience that the more kids someone had, the more exhausted they appeared. But Henry and his wife seemed to thrive on the busy life and chaos of a large family. Henry would tell anyone he was living the dream: a job he enjoyed, a wife he loved, and kids that made a whole family. In truth, Luke envied him. *Maybe one day.*

His job had just become full-time, so the pay was a

hell of a lot better, and so were the benefits, including health insurance. His tiny-ass apartment would do for now, but if he saved enough, he knew he could move into something larger eventually. *And family?* He snorted. *First, I'd have to meet a woman who'd be interested in me and hold my interest.* That thought usually brought nothing but blank to his mind, but the image of Allie and the sunset almost-kiss hit him. How the fuck an almost-kiss could make him think of things he wondered if he'd ever have, he didn't know. But, unable to keep her from his mind, his lips curved slightly as he moved through the metal detector at the guard station.

"Have a great day!" Henry called out as he headed toward the guard locker room. Dipping his chin, Luke headed in the other direction.

The North Heron Regional Jail was made up of several connecting brick buildings. Two wings made up the men's section. Another wing housed the women inmates. Each wing had its own laundry, small gymnasium, and outdoor area. Another smaller wing was for administrative offices. In the center were two cafeterias and a shared kitchen. One cafeteria was for men and the other was for women. One kitchen prepared food for both, but men and women inmates were not present at the same time. A library was also centrally located, but the times available were scheduled such that the men and women could not be there together.

When Luke had first started working at the jail, he'd been surprised at the modern facilities, including the clinic. In the military, he'd worked at stateside clinics, an American hospital in Kabul, and clinics set up in a tent in the Afghan mountains. The jail's medical clinic was well appointed, but carefully monitored scheduling kept the men and women prisoners separated just like the other facilities.

At first, he'd thought that would be difficult, but the clinic's placement was ideal. Like the library, it was centrally located and had two separate entrances—one from the men's side and one from the women's side. Prisoners had to request to come to the clinic and were only brought when escorted by a guard.

Each side was a mirror image of the other. Both had a nurse that completed the initial evaluation, and if the prisoner needed to see the doctor, they were taken to an exam room. In the very center were the small lab, medical supplies, and equipment. The clinic was able to handle illness, cuts and abrasions, routine medications, physicals, and basic lab tests. Everything else had to be sent to the county hospital with the inmate accompanied by a guard.

How effectively the jail worked was due to the warden, William Neely, and the local sheriff, Colt Hudson. Luke respected both men but had become friends with Colt through the American Legion, like most of his other friends.

Entering the clinic, he nodded toward Margaret Anderson, the longtime nurse. Her silver hair was cut short, framing her face, and her blue eyes twinkled as they landed on him.

"Good morning, Ms. Anderson."

"Same to you, Mr. Purdue."

Most of the jail employees referred to each other by

their first names when the inmates weren't around, but in the clinic, he preferred to maintain the professionalism. He smiled as they continued their daily ritual. "Is everything okay today?"

"The sun is shining, and God has granted me another day for his blessings. I couldn't be better."

Shaking his head, he had to admit he hoped she never retired. Moving into the small workroom, he looked at the schedule for the day, noting which inmates were coming in for appointments previously made. Several physicals. Two of the female inmates were pregnant and were coming in for OB checks. For those, he wasn't needed, allowing the female guards to be present along with Jerika, the full-time nurse on the female side, and the doctor. Three inmates were coming in for illness. One new inmate would need an intake physical coming in from the Seaside town jail. Of course, there would be the constant stream of inmates who decided today was the day to have an illness, whether real or imagined. All in all, not a bad day as long as no emergencies occurred.

"Good morning, Luke."

Looking over his shoulder, he watched as Bill Cisco walked in. Bill was the part-time doctor who worked mornings at the jail and afternoons at the local hospital. "Dr. Cisco," he greeted with another nod of his head. Martin Bailey, the full-time doctor, and Pete Sanders, the full-time drug counselor, moved into the room, and he greeted them, as well.

Bill walked over and peered at the board. "Looks like an easy morning." He moved to the computer and pulled up the log from the previous night. "Empty… just as I like it."

The jail's clinic was closed at night although Bill was on call in case a non-life-threatening emergency occurred. Martin had handled those calls for years, but with Bill on board, the duty fell to him.

Once Luke had logged onto the tablet he used during the day, he helped Margaret and Jerika set up the exam rooms for the first patients. As he completed the rote tasks, his mind rolled back to Allie. The way the early-morning light glistened off her dark brown hair, highlighting the auburn highlights. The way her smile always reached her eyes, letting him know she truly was happy. The way her dress showcased her figure while leaving a lot to the imagination. And when it came to Allie, he had a vivid imagination.

"You ready?" a voice called out from the doorway.

As the first guard arrived, he nodded, pushing thoughts of Allie to the back of his mind so he could concentrate on his job. At least, that's what he tried to do, but he was as unsuccessful in erasing her completely as he had been every day since he'd met her.

5

"Phooey, I've got early bus duty." Allie cringed. *A man called me beautiful, and that was all I could think to say?* She hung her head, shaking it slowly.

"What are you doing over there?" Shonna asked, walking up next to her.

The third graders were outside for recess, and the teachers were stationed around the playground, keeping an eye on the children. The former principal used to require the teachers to have formal recess complete with lesson plans. Allie appreciated the new principal's idea of recess—every child needed a break from structured learning, a chance to run freely, play a game, and be creative. As long as the teachers were keeping a close eye on the activities, the children had a chance to be children.

With her eyes pinned to the playground, she replied, "Sometimes I'm such a dork. It's embarrassing."

Shonna laughed and asked, "Oh, Lord. What did you do now?"

"I met a guy—"

"Do tell!"

Glancing toward Shonna's smiling face, she rolled her eyes. "He's gorgeous, and while I've only met him twice, I was a dork both times. The first time, he had to practically save me from a couple of drunk tourists on the beach when I was walking along, talking to my mom on the phone, and not paying attention to what was going on around me. Then, I saw him this morning when I was delivering my rent check, and instead of flirting when he said I was beautiful, I blurted out that I had to leave because of early bus duty."

Shonna lifted an eyebrow. "And you didn't get his number, did you?"

"I don't even know his last name!"

"Girl, you *are* a dork. But like he said, you're beautiful. And you don't need to change one thing about yourself. You're sweet and funny. You're loyal and nice. And if you tried to be anything but who you are, you'd never really know if this guy is truly interested in you."

Grinning, she looked over at Shonna, her heart lighter. "Thanks! And while I know you're right, sometimes I wish I could be smoother. You know, be able to flirt." Shrugging, she added, "Anyway, as nice as it is to dream, I doubt I'll have any time for anything other than work for a while."

"Did you find a part-time job?"

She hesitated, afraid to mention the possible job at the jail in case nothing came from it. "I'm checking into a few things, but nothing yet."

"Natalie! Don't you throw that!" Shonna yelled, her

attention diverted toward the playground, and she hustled over to a group of kids.

Allie walked in a different direction to make sure the boys were allowing everyone to join in their game who wanted to. She'd emailed the warden, and they'd already had a phone conversation. She was going in for an interview this afternoon after school. *I wonder if I'll see Luke again.* She had been so surprised when Hannah mentioned that he worked at the jail as a medic that she'd almost blurted that she was applying for a position there. *I'm glad I didn't. That would make me look even more dorky if I don't get the job.*

Hearing the whistle blow from one of the other teachers indicating recess was over, she gathered her students and walked them back into the building. Her class settled quickly, and she praised them as they got ready for their next lesson. Looking out over the group of eight-year-olds, her smile widened. At a time when so many people were getting out of education because of the poor pay and increased demands of the job, she loved what she did. For a moment, she wondered if she was crazy for considering working with adults. *"Life is all about challenges, sweetheart. Meeting them head-on. Overcoming them. Learning from them."* The words her father often quoted came back to her.

And at the end of the day, she said goodbye to her small charges, grabbed her bag, and as soon as she could, headed out the door. Parking once again in the lot near the jail, she looked up toward the large brick building. Sucking in a deep breath before letting it out slowly, she climbed from her car. "Okay… time to face a new challenge."

———

"Ms. Simpson, your qualifications are exceptional, and it will be my recommendation that you be submitted for the position."

She tried to hide the sigh of relief that left her while smiling at the warden. She'd had no idea what to expect when she met him but had been pleased to see that while he had a suit jacket hanging on the back of his chair, he'd opted for a more casual, shirt-sleeves-rolled-up outfit when meeting with her. His dark brown hair was sprinkled with a touch of silver, and while he was of indeterminate age, the photograph on his desk of his family with two teenage children made her think that he was aging well with his high-stress job. "Thank you, Warden Neely. I'm very excited about the position you've created and hope that I can not only meet your expectations but surpass them."

"I have every confidence that you will. As we talked about on the phone, the position would accommodate you being here two late afternoons per week and every other Saturday morning. While I certainly realize that our needs are greater than what you will be able to accomplish in that time, it's all the county can afford to pay for now. Considering that you're a full-time teacher, I hope that will be amenable to you."

"Yes, it will be. Right now, my schedule allows for Tuesday and Thursday afternoons after school. Those are two days that I don't have any school duties that go beyond my contracted hours. My Saturday mornings are free, so that won't be a problem."

"Excellent. What I think will make the most sense and utilize your time the best, the inmates you'll see will be those whose reading levels are below the national average. While we have some inmates that are high school and even college graduates and others who are working toward their GED, it's those who have the ability but have never learned to read even at a fourth-grade level that we would like to concentrate on. Those are the inmates that would have difficulty on a job application, filling out insurance or government forms, or being able to read the directions for any employment that they obtain once they leave our facility."

"I can imagine that they would be more likely to be your repeat offenders and come right back here," she said, understanding how difficult the outside world would be for an adult who was unable to read.

His expression was serious, but he nodded with enthusiasm. "Exactly. You hit the nail on the head, Ms. Simpson. Our idea is that you will work with the men on one day, the women on another, and then, on Saturdays, you would be able to see both groups, obviously at separate times."

"I wondered how that might work," she admitted.

"Our facility is a jail run by the two counties on the Eastern Shore. We are not a state or federal prison, and our inmates will usually be with us for a few days, a few months, or a few years. We house sentenced and pre-sentenced inmates as well as pre-trial inmates who are not yet found guilty or not guilty." He held her gaze. "While we house both men and women, they are never in the same area together. They have their own cafeteria, separate kitchen duties, their own laundry rooms, and even separate entrances and exam rooms with the clinic. You will be working in the library, which I'll show you in just a few minutes."

Tucking her hair behind her ear, she hesitated, then asked a question that she knew was pertinent but hoped it would not come out wrong. "Can you explain the security measures that I will need to adhere to as well for my... um... safety?"

He nodded, his smile gentle. "Never be hesitant to ask about security, Ms. Simpson. We take that very seriously. And we are very aware of the safety of all, inmates as well as employees. You would enter through the employee guard station at the administrative wing where you would display your badge and identification and pass through a metal detector. You would be escorted to the library by a guard. While in the library, you will be with the librarian, Everett Bennings, and in the presence of a guard, as well. At the end of your sessions, you would be escorted back to the guard station. You may certainly move freely around the areas that inmates are not able to independently access, such as the administration building, employee lounge, and clinic."

Allie nodded, relaxing at his explanation. "Thank you." She smiled. "I think that covers it, Warden Neely. Is there anything else you need from me?"

"You will have to have a background check by the

local sheriff's department, but since you had one for your employment with the school system, I don't anticipate that to take long. And then, I can offer you the position. You'll come in to meet with our HR director, and once your paperwork is complete, you can start."

He stood and extended his hand. Jumping to her feet, she shook his hand, then followed him into the hall. "This is, of course, our administrative wing. The library is just down the hall." She noticed a sign for the clinic and wondered if that was where Luke worked. Pressing her lips together, she inwardly chided herself for thinking of him when she was on a professional interview. Focusing her attention back to Warden Neely, she followed him into a well-appointed library. Several inmates in gray jumpsuits were around at the magazines, books, or computers and looked over with curiosity toward her. Swallowing her nerves, she kept her gaze averted, uncertain of what was the expected protocol at the jail. In the elementary school, as soon as she entered her classroom, she immediately made eye contact. It not only made the children feel special, but it also grabbed their attention. Now, grabbing the attention of the inmates was the last thing she wanted to do. *This is one more thing I'll need to check on before I start working!*

"Ms. Simpson, I'd like to introduce our full-time librarian, Everett Bennings. This is Allie Simpson, our new reading specialist. At least, I hope she'll be. We just have to do the background check, and she has to decide if this is the job she'd like to have."

She looked up toward Everett, smiling at the extraordinarily tall, wiry man with bright red hair. Thrusting out her hand, they shook as he smiled in return.

"Excited to have you aboard, Ms. Simpson. I do what I can to help those who have difficulty reading, but it's not my specialty."

"I'm happy to be considered for this position," she said. "I'm a full-time third-grade teacher at Baytown Elementary, also certified as a reading specialist. I've been hoping to find a part-time position, and I think this will suit me well."

"Wow, kids to adults. I admire your sense of adventure!"

Laughing, she shook her head. "Well, I'm not sure it's adventurous, but I'm excited to try a new challenge."

Saying goodbye, the warden walked back into the hall then called for one of the guards to escort her out of the building. Passing the clinic once again, she no longer tried to keep her mind from Luke. *He's a fantasy, that's all. But...* She grinned. *Nothing wrong with a little fantasy.*

Although, as she walked to her car, she wished she had more time to make her fantasy a reality.

A week later, Allie sat in the jail library at a table with three men. She'd been stunned when she'd received the call from Warden Neely letting her know that her background check had been fast-tracked and simplified since she was a county school employee. She'd finished with the HR admin, completed her paperwork, and received instructions on jail protocol, including how to dress, which was similar to what she already wore to work.

Now, she smiled at the three men, all eager to learn to read. They were working on a reading level assessment, giving her the opportunity to see where she would need to start with them.

"Are you finished, Jeff?" she asked the youngest man.

He nodded, his expression hopeful. He'd already told her that he had two little kids at home and wanted to be able to read to them when he got out in six months.

She determined that his reading level was about fourth grade and smiled at him as she pulled out several worksheets that they could begin with.

The next man, Corey, had eighteen months left to serve on his sentence and scored sixth-grade level. His goal had been to be able to read well enough to study for his GED.

And lastly was a man in his forties, his jaw tight with either embarrassment or anger, she wasn't sure which. His reading level was only at a third grade, but she smiled, hoping to put him at ease.

There were a few other men in the library, many curious but keeping their distance with Everett and a guard nearby. The two hours passed much faster than she thought they would, and soon her time was over. Congratulating the three on their early progress and interest, she accepted their gratitude, as well.

"You ready, Ms. Simpson?" Everett asked.

She smiled up at the friendly face and nodded.

"I'm leaving now, too, so I'll walk you out." He

turned toward the guard. "Officer Wells, we're ready to close up."

Officer Wells walked over as they walked out of the library and locked the door behind them. They walked past the now-dark clinic, and she glanced toward the door. "What hours is the clinic open?"

"The full-day staff is here from eight-thirty to five o'clock. There is a doctor on call for night emergencies that don't require a trip to the hospital."

"Hmm," she mumbled, realizing her path wouldn't cross with Luke. Her time at the jail was from four to six, so he'd be gone when she left. Frustrated that she couldn't seem to get him out of her mind, she lifted her head and continued to the guard station, where she said goodbye and walked to her car.

Driving back to her small rental, her stomach growled. *I need to take a snack on the days I work late.* Parking in front of the cottage, she blew out a long breath. As much as she loved her jobs, coming home to an empty house felt more lonely than independent right now.

6

"I'm telling you, she's gonna teach me how to read better."

Luke smiled at the man sitting on the exam room table being treated for a finger burn from kitchen duty. "Glad to hear it, Jeff."

"She's real smart and nice," Jeff continued.

"Not bad to look at either, is she, Jeff?" the guard at the door said, his smirk more of a leer. "Wouldn't mind a private tutoring session with that one, only I'd be the one teaching her a thing or two."

Luke glared over his shoulder toward Gary Perkins. He'd had a problem with the guard spending more time flirting with Hannah when she was at the jail than he was watching the inmates— a mistake that nearly cost Gary his life, but he didn't seem to have learned from his past mistakes.

Jeff continued, ignoring the pompous guard. "I told her I wanted to read to my kids when I get out, and she said that she loved my goal."

"That's a great goal, man," Luke agreed, finishing his treatment. "Now, focus on the hot stove the next time you've got kitchen duty."

Jeff grinned as he hopped down from the table. "Thanks, Mr. Purdue."

"Come on," Gary said. "Maybe we can walk slowly by the library to see if that hot piece is there."

"You're supposed to be modeling correct behavior, Officer Perkins. How about showing some respect?" Luke ground out.

Gary turned, his narrow-eyed glare shooting over his shoulder. He opened his mouth, but Margaret walked past.

"I agree. Don't make comments like that in my presence," she said. Holding his gaze until he grunted and turned toward the hall, she shook her head as he left the clinic. "That's one bad apple I would like to see gone."

Luke agreed silently. As he cleaned the exam room, prepping it for the next patient, he asked, "Who is this new person?"

"I heard that a reading specialist has been hired part-time. She works as a teacher and also tutors a few of the men and women to increase their reading level so that when they leave this facility, they have a better chance to succeed."

"Sounds good." He hoped whoever they hired had the constitution for working with inmates. Some of the population could be difficult at times, and others were very willing to improve. With the next patient coming in, he dropped all thoughts of the reading teacher and concentrated on the man with the cough.

Luke stood by third base, coaching the little boy bouncing on his toes as they waited for the next pitch. The AL baseball game was in the sixth inning, but Luke had spent more time glancing toward the stands where he'd spied Allie sitting than keeping up with the score. In truth, the score wasn't very important considering the AL youth teams were all about inclusivity, sportsmanship, team building, and just having fun. *But still, I should be paying attention—wait, where'd she go?*

After thirty minutes of making eye contact with her where she'd smile every time he offered a chin lift toward her, she was no longer sitting in the same place. Ever since he'd first laid eyes on her this morning, he couldn't believe their paths had not crossed before. She was surrounded by the wives of some of the other coaches and his friends. Colt's wife, Carrie. Hannah. The police chief of Baytown, Mitch Evans' wife, Tori. Baytown police officers Grant Wilder's wife, Jillian, and Lance Green's wife, Jade. There were a host of others, but he barely took any of them in as his eyes strayed only to Allie.

Now, there was an empty space where she'd been, but the crack of the bat caused him to jerk around, coaching his excited player on third base to run toward home.

Now that inning was over, he moved back toward the fence at the edge of the field where he now could clearly see Allie walking toward him. He grinned and leaned his forearms on the top of the chain-link fence as she approached. "Hey," he greeted.

She stopped in front of him, tucked a strand of hair behind her ear, and smiled. "Hey, yourself."

"I don't remember seeing you at the games before," he said.

"I've only come occasionally, but this year I have more of my students playing, and I promised them that I would stop by." She glanced over her shoulder toward the stands before turning back to him. "To be honest, I had no idea how popular the games were. I thought I'd be sitting by myself instead of surrounded by people I know."

"Most of them are friends of mine or married to friends of mine," he commented. "A lot of them head over to the pub after a game. Will you be going?"

Her smile widened, and he felt the punch in his gut like he did every time she beamed that expression toward him. "Yeah, that sounds good. I'm waiting on a phone call and might have an appointment this afternoon, but right now, I don't have any plans."

"Coach Purdue!" A little girl with pigtails came racing over and stood next to him, her hands on her hips and her freckled face turned up toward him. "You're supposed to be watching me bat!"

Allie laughed. "Looks like you're falling down on the job, Coach!"

He knelt to the little girl's level. "You're right. You ready to go show them how it's done?"

The little girl's arms shot into the air as she yelled,

"Yeah!" She grabbed his hand and started to pull him along.

Looking over his shoulder, he said, "I'll see you after the game?"

She nodded and waved. After the little girl swung and hit the ball, successfully making it to first base, he glanced over his shoulder and saw Allie back in the stands, her smile once again pinned on him. *Meeting her at the pub. Okay, not exactly a date, but close. And then I'll get her number.* The sun was shining. The kids were having fun. And the woman who'd filled his thoughts was finally going to be having an almost-date with him. Feeling positive about the way his Saturday morning was going, Luke turned back to the game, cheering the kids on.

An hour later, he looked toward the stands, but they were emptying and he didn't see Allie. Hoping she'd already left with some friends to head to the pub, he hurried through his goodbyes to the kids and their parents, helped pack the equipment, and checked to make sure the field was left ready for the next game.

"What's your hurry?" Joseph asked, coming up from behind and clapping him on the back. "You got a date?"

He grimaced at the group nearby whose attention was now squarely on him. "Just hungry. Thought I'd head to the pub."

"I saw you were talking to Allie," Jade said, her smile wide as she looped her arm through her husband's. "We work together at the elementary school. She's such a sweetheart!"

"Yeah."

The others shared looks and grins, and he hated every moment of being in their spotlight. Glad when they moved on toward the parking lot, he looked over at Joseph. "Christ, how do you stand everyone knowing your business?"

"Hell, I grew up here. Not a great place to keep a secret."

"The way you serial date, I'm surprised half the women in the stands aren't knocking each other over to get your attention."

Joseph laughed, shaking his head. "I'm not that bad. Anyway, how will I ever know if the right one comes along if I don't comparison shop a little first?"

Luke smiled but, anxious to get to the pub to see Allie, hustled to his SUV, already wondering how to have a private moment with her when the restaurant was going to be packed.

Arriving, he pushed his way through the crowd but couldn't find her. Turning around slowly with his hands on his hips, he scanned the entire area.

"Looking for someone?" Hannah asked, coming up from the side, a smile on her face.

For a second, he thought about denying what he was doing, then decided to be truthful. "I was supposed to meet Allie here after the game."

"She got called away."

Jerking his head down toward Hannah, he rushed, "Is everything okay?"

Hannah's lips curved slightly before she answered. "Yes, she's fine. She got a call from her realtor that pushed up their appointment to look at a house. She's had her eye on one, and it seems that it's just going on the market, and her realtor wanted her to see it before anyone else could."

Just hearing that she wasn't going to be there caused his stomach to drop. "Oh… okay. Thanks."

"The reason I came over was that she told me she didn't have your number and had no way to let you know that she wasn't going to be here. She wanted me to find you so that I could let you know."

Just as his shoulders had slumped when realizing he wasn't going to meet her, his spine snapped straight as renewed energy moved through him, knowing she cared enough to make sure he didn't think she'd flaked out on him. "Thanks, Hannah. I really appreciate you letting me know."

Hannah tilted her head to the side, her smile growing. "She wasn't sure if you'd be interested, but she gave me permission to share her phone number with you. I know she's busy now, but if you wanted—"

"Yes!" He'd barked out the word sharper than he'd meant, but Hannah only smiled wider. Clearing his throat, he repeated, "Yes, please." Pulling out his phone, he entered the number that Hannah gave to him. Thanking her again as Dylan walked over and pulled Hannah in for a hug, he hurried out of the pub without eating.

Sitting in his vehicle, he sat and stared at his phone, trying to decide what to say in a text. *Or maybe I shouldn't text. Maybe she was just being polite. No… women don't give out their number unless they want to hear from the guy, right?* His fingers hovered over the keys. Typing out a message then deleting it, he repeated the process four times.

The sound of laughter met his ears, and he looked up to see Grant and Jillian, Aiden and Lia, and Dylan and Hannah walking down the street. He knew no one's path to their soulmate was easy, but... *Damn, those guys probably never hesitated.* Blowing out a deep breath, he typed **Hope your house hunting appointment goes well. Luke**

He hit send. *There, that's done. Now she has my number, too, if she wants it.* Driving home, he tried to convince himself that it would be fine if she didn't but knew he was lying to himself. He really wanted to hear from her, too.

An hour later, his phone vibrated. Looking down, his heart leaped into his throat, and his phone almost fell to the floor as his fingers fumbled to open the messaging app.

Thanks. It did. I'll tell you about it when I see you again. Allie

He flopped back against the cushions of his sofa, his face relaxing into a stupid grin. *She texted back. And mentioned seeing me again.* Suddenly bolting straight, he quickly typed out another text. **Hope that will be soon. L**

He knew it might make him look overly anxious but didn't care. He'd never been a man who played games of the heart and wasn't about to start.

Me too! A

Now, sitting with a full-blown smile on his face, he knew he looked more like a fuckin' teenager who'd just got the cheerleader to notice him and wondered if he'd lost his damn mind. He was a man who was used to being alone. Preferred no one knowing his background. And yet, here he was, excited to have the chance to spend more time with a woman who looked like she could just smile and the world would be a little brighter. *Christ... maybe I have lost my damn mind!*

Allie stood outside the house with her realtor, tears brimming in her eyes. The house was one she'd heard was coming on the market and she was afraid she might miss being able to put in a bid. It was a two-story Victorian, painted a pale yellow with white trim. It was just to the south of Baytown, not on the beach but with a view of the bay in the distance and a path to the water just down the street.

Inside, she found a living room with a gas fireplace and a dining room separated from the modernly appointed kitchen by a granite-topped island. A laundry room was on the back and included a pantry, and next to it was a powder room. A breakfast room with a door leading to the patio was just off the kitchen. Upstairs were three bedrooms, a hall bathroom, and a master bathroom. There was even a partially finished attic room, but the realtor advised that it wouldn't take much to turn it into another bedroom. She didn't care... that could be a project she saved for and completed down the road.

But what intrigued her was the door from the

master bedroom that led to a small deck, just large enough for two chairs. It faced the west, and with the bay in the distance, she'd be able to enjoy views of the sunsets from there. Next to it was a trellis that extended from the ground, past the deck, and up to the window at the attic. Flowering vines bloomed along the trellis offering a gentle scent.

The wooden floors were in excellent condition. The walls were painted a soft cream, perfect for whatever furniture she wanted to use. When the realtor had stepped out into the backyard, she'd taken the opportunity to twirl in the kitchen, overjoyed at the prospect of owning the home.

She'd gotten a text from Luke, which made her already exciting day even more exciting. As much as she'd hated to leave the ballgame without talking to him again, just knowing he'd wanted to meet her at the pub had her thrilled at the idea of spending more time with him. She'd never had such a visceral reaction to a man before, and while part of her was nervous it might be all surface attraction, she was willing to take a chance. *At least find out if he felt the same tingles that I did.*

Hurrying out the back door to meet the realtor on the patio, she pushed thoughts of Luke to the side as she listened while the agent continued to point out various features of the house. Turning to him, she said, "I'm ready to put in an offer. I'll need an inspection, but since you said the owners were in a hurry to sell because their job is transferring them out of the state, I'll waive anything the inspector finds that's cosmetic only."

Nodding, the realtor rubbed his hands together and said, "Then let's get back to my office and get things in writing."

She spent the next several hours at the real estate office going over the paperwork and making sure everything was written to her satisfaction. She called her parents to send them pictures and ask a few questions, wanting to make sure she used all her resources for a good decision.

"All right," he said. "I'll get this scanned and emailed right now."

"And you'll call me as soon as you hear anything?"

"Absolutely."

Shaking hands, she headed out to the parking lot, butterfly nerves glittering in her stomach. *Or maybe that's hunger!* She'd missed lunch, and it was now early evening. Running into the local diner, she chatted with the cook while he fixed a hamburger and french fries. With the scent of her delicious food in a takeout bag, she drove back to the rental cottage.

Falling onto the food like a ravenous animal, she couldn't believe how fast she'd eaten. *Mom used to joke that I could eat a hamburger faster than anyone she'd ever seen, and I think I've just broken my record time!*

Finally leaning back in her chair, stomach full, she sipped her water as she sent Hannah a text letting her know that she'd put in a bid. Hannah had been gracious enough to offer to let her out of her lease any time she was able to buy her own home. And while her bid hadn't been accepted yet, she was hoping to let Hannah know as soon as possible.

Now, looking back at her messages, she grinned. Luke didn't strike her as a man who offered words he didn't mean, so saying he wanted to see her again soon must be true. Heaving a sigh, the sucky timing hit her. Working full-time at school, working part-time at the jail, and now a hopeful move and house to make her own left little time to start a new relationship. A snort slipped out. "A relationship! We've shared a couple of texts, a couple of very short conversations, and a sunset kiss. Hardly a relationship," she moaned out loud. Biting her lip, a little smile curved her lips. *But a girl can dream, right?*

7

"Did it ever occur to you that I might have something I wanted to do on a Sunday besides drive to Richmond to deal with your shit?"

Luke's growling question fell on deaf ears, but that wasn't unusual. His brother had only gotten worse with age, including the trouble he seemed to always manage to find.

"They got it all wrong, Luke," Larry argued. "They've got nothing on me. It's just the police profiling me."

Luke didn't attempt to hide the roll of his eyes. "Profiling, huh? Do you even know what the fuck that is?"

"Yeah. I'm not as dumb as you think I am. It means the police take one look at me and just think I'm trouble, so they arrest me for nothing."

"Sounds like they arrested you for driving without a license, drug paraphernalia in your car, and drugs in the trunk. Doesn't sound like profiling to me."

Larry waved his hand dismissively, shaking his head.

"All circumstantial. I'll get me a lawyer, and I'll be out of here in no time."

"Okay, Larry. It sounds like you've got all the answers, so why did I get an early morning phone call that said you needed to see me?"

"Because I tried calling Chelle, she's not picking up. She had the kids with her, and I don't know where she went. I need you to tell her I need bail money, and she'd better not be shacking up with someone while I'm sitting in jail."

Luke's plans of asking Allie out the day after the ballgame had fallen through when he'd received a phone call from his brother claiming Luke needed to come to Richmond as soon as possible. Larry's time spent in juvie had simply rolled into multiple stays in a variety of jails wherever he and his wife, Chelle, landed when they roamed from place to place, always looking for the next easy buck. Luke would've washed his hands of them years ago if it hadn't been for his niece and nephew. Jeremy was eight, and Jessica was five. Cute as hell, smart as could be, and sweet kids. He could never figure out how losers like Larry and Chelle managed to have such adorable kids, but he figured God must have sent guardian angels to watch over them.

Luke learned early on not to send Larry any money for the kids because it went straight to alcohol, cigarettes, or drugs. Whenever he visited, he made sure to take the kids out to buy them clothes, toys, and, more recently, school supplies. Chelle always complained that he spoiled them, but Luke had no problem shutting her up by reminding her that he knew what she did with her money.

"As soon as I get outta here, I'll call her and find out where she is, make sure the kids are okay," Luke promised. He'd do anything for Jeremy and Jessica, even if that meant putting up with his deadbeat brother and sister-in-law.

"Good, good," Larry said, nodding. A light sheen of sweat had broken out on his forehead, and Luke wondered if he was coming off whatever high he'd been on when arrested.

With his hands on the metal table, Luke pushed to a stand. "I'll let you know what I find out."

"Wait, Luke, that's not all."

Throwing a narrow-eyed glare down at Larry, he shook his head. "Why does that not surprise me?"

"Listen, man, for me to beat this, I'm going to need a good lawyer. I need you to—"

"No fuckin' way. I'm not forking over one dime for you to blow on a lawyer to try to beat a rap. Take the public defender, and take what's coming to you. Do your time. Get clean. And for fuck's sake, grow the fuck up." Leaning closer, he growled, "You've got two gorgeous, sweet kids. Be the kind of dad they deserve cause right now, you're just doing to them what Dad did to us."

Larry's face twisted into a grimace. "That's why I'm messed up, man. It's not my fault we had such a loser dad and a mom that gave up."

"No, it's not your fault he was a loser. But it *is* your fault you're turning out like him. You gotta rise above, bro. I'm here to help anytime you want help, but I'm not gonna let you pull me into your shit." He turned and walked to the door, then called over his shoulder, "I'll get hold of Chelle and let you know what the deal is." Not waiting for Larry to ask for anything else, he threw open the door and headed out into the hall. Scrubbing his hand over his face, he wished he could wipe the oft-repeated scene from his mind. Going through the protocols to exit the Richmond Jail, he climbed back into his vehicle and called Chelle. If the kids needed something, he wanted to be close by before heading back to Baytown.

"Luke?" Chelle answered after he let the call ring continuously. "You gonna help Larry?"

"No, I'm not. He got himself into this mess, and he can get himself out."

"That's not fair. The ones that are going to suffer are me and the kids. You gonna let that happen?"

"I'll get anything the kids need for them, but I'm not giving you money, and I'm sure as fuck not giving any money to Larry."

She remained quiet for a moment, and he had no doubt she was trying to figure out a way to get something out of him. Jumping in, he didn't give her a chance. "Are the kids home?"

"They're next door playing. I wasn't feeling too good this morning."

Luke recognized she was hungover and cursed under his breath. "I'm coming over to see them." Not giving her a chance to ask him to bring beer or cigarettes when he came, he disconnected.

Twenty minutes later, he pulled into the parking lot of the crappy apartment complex they lived in. The wooden shutters on the brick building were sagging and hanging at odd angles. Graffiti marred the side of the building. Rusty iron rails lined the breezeway. A crumbling concrete wall had a few people sitting on it, and he was glad they didn't look like the junkies he'd witnessed there before. Sighing, he climbed the outside stairs, making his way to their second-floor apartment.

He hadn't even knocked when the door was thrown open and two bright smiles greeted him. "Uncle Luke!" the kids shouted at the same time. Both with the same dark hair and blue eyes that he and Larry had, he was always struck with how adorable they were.

Bending, he threw open his arms, and they rushed in for hugs. Jeremy seemed like he'd grown an inch, but it didn't miss Luke's notice that the little boy's clothes no longer fit well. His fingers could feel Jessica's ribs, and he wondered if Chelle was drinking away the grocery money. He looked over their heads as she wandered into the room, glad to see that she wasn't stumbling drunk, but she looked like shit.

"Hey, Luke," Chelle said, her smile sloppy.

There had been a time when Chelle flirted shamelessly with him, whether to make Larry jealous or because she thought the brothers were interchangeable, Luke didn't know. He didn't care. But he sure as fuck shut it down as quickly as he could. Now, she just seemed glad when he came around and would take the kids off her hands for a break. "I'm gonna take them out for hamburgers. You want me to bring you one?"

"Um... do you think you could bring me—"

"No alcohol and no cigarettes, Chelle. If you want food, I'll get it."

She scrunched her nose, then shrugged. "I can go grocery shopping if you just want to give me some money."

"No, not doing that either. I'll take the kids grocery shopping and pick out some things they like." She shrugged, and he hoped she'd finally learned to stop asking for what he wasn't going to give her. Looking down, he grinned. "Grab your shoes, kids."

Jessica raced off and came back with her sneakers. Jumping around, she managed to get them on her feet then looked up. "I don't know how to tie them. Jeremy always does it before school."

With his hand on his nephew's shoulder, he gave a squeeze. "Good man, Jeremy." Bending to tie Jessica's shoes, he noticed the smile on Jeremy's face. Soon, he had the kids buckled in the backseat, hating that he didn't have booster seats for them. Driving with his precious cargo, they went to get hamburgers and fries. It might not be the healthiest food to start off with, but he wanted them to enjoy the special treat.

Jessica chattered nonstop about what she was doing in school, how much she liked her teacher, and the new words she was learning to read. Jeremy was much quieter but ate with a healthy appetite and kept an eye on his sister, making sure she stopped talking long enough to eat, as well. Luke's heart twisted at the sight, knowing Jeremy should be enjoying his childhood, not helping to raise his sister.

A trip to the grocery store made Luke's heart squeeze even more. The kids were excited to pick out food they wanted, spending more time with the fruits and vegetables than they did the snack aisle. "Where'd you learn to pick out such good food?" he asked.

"We learn about healthy food at school," Jeremy replied. "When we come with Mom, she says there's no money for fruit. But we get it with our school lunches."

Luke had found out two years ago when Jeremy was in kindergarten that Larry never put any money in his son's school lunch account and Chelle didn't pack lunch. Since then, Luke paid the school directly to make sure the kids had enough money for whatever they wanted to eat for lunch. He wished he could do more but couldn't trust their fuckin' parents to do right by them.

By the time they got home and put the food in the refrigerator, he needed to get back on the road. Chelle was lying in her bed, so he just told her goodbye from the door then kneeled in the living room to say goodbye to the kids.

"When will we see you again?" Jessica asked, placing her little hands on either side of Luke's face, squishing his cheeks.

"I'll make sure I come again soon, darlin'." She giggled as he kissed her, then he turned to Jeremy.

"If you need me, I'm only a phone call away. You've got my number, right? And you've got my email."

Jeremy nodded, his face more serious than any eight-year-old should be. Hugging them both goodbye again, he waited as they locked the door behind them, and he climbed into his vehicle.

During the two-hour drive from Richmond to the Eastern Shore, Luke's mind was unsettled as thoughts of Larry's fucked up decisions, Jeremy and Jessica, and even Allie filled every thought. He hated that his niece and nephew's childhood was tarnished by their parents' weaknesses. He had no doubt that Larry would be convicted of what the officer had told him he was charged with, and while that would take his dysfunction out of their lives, it would only give Chelle more of an excuse to give in to her weak and selfish decisions. *Christ almighty.*

And then thoughts of Allie moved through him, but instead of feeling warmth, he felt the cold dread of reality. *Yeah, sunshine-Allie would probably run for the hills at my fucked-up family.*

"Luke, you can go ahead and leave early since you got here so early this morning and worked late yesterday."

"Are you sure, Doctor Bailey?"

"Absolutely. You got the clinic prepped for the state visitors we had this morning, which I greatly appreciated. I'll see you tomorrow."

Not one to turn down the opportunity to leave early, especially since the clinic was not busy and he had worked extra hours in preparation for the visitors, he said his goodbyes and headed out. Walking past the library door, he glanced through the small window and saw a woman sitting at one of the tables with several men. Her dark hair was pulled back into a ponytail. *Must be the reading specialist.* He continued down the hall for a few steps, but a strange niggling moved through his mind, and he halted. Backtracking, he glanced through the small window again.

The woman turned to speak to the man facing away from the door, giving Luke a clear view of her face. The air rushed from his lungs at the sight of Allie sitting in the jail library. Throwing open the door, he stalked inside, offering a chin lift to the guard nearby and the librarian behind the desk. His movements caught her attention, and her head swiveled to see who was walking in. Her eyes widened in recognition, and so did her smile, and once again, the air rushed from his lungs.

"Luke! How nice to see you!"

With his hands on his hips, his chin dipped as he looked down at her still seated at the table, and her smile faltered ever so slightly. Hating that he was the cause of it, he tried to bring his surprise and irrational irritation under control. Clearing his throat, he said, "Allie. I never expected to see you here."

"I've been hired part-time as the reading specialist."

His gaze raked over the three men, all with curiosity on their faces, but quickly turned their attention back to the books in front of them. "I can see that."

"I remembered Hannah mentioning that you worked here, but I arrive before you get off and leave after you do." She shrugged, still smiling. "But I'm glad I got to see you today." She glanced toward the table before looking back at him. "Well, um... I need to get back to the lessons."

"Yeah, sure. I'll... we'll talk soon." He wasn't sure what else to say with others around, but once again, her face shone as she grinned.

"That'd be great," she enthused.

Walking out of the library, he caught the chin lift in acknowledgment from the guard but noted Everett's tight smile. He had no doubt the librarian had his sights set on Allie. *What man wouldn't?* But just the thought of them together set Luke's teeth on edge.

As he moved to the guard gate and out into the parking lot, he sucked in a deep breath of fresh air and let it out slowly. Approaching his vehicle, he wondered if she wouldn't be better off with someone like Everett. Someone with a college degree. Someone whose parents probably more closely matched what he imagined hers were like. Someone who didn't have a brother in jail.

Leaning his back against the driver's door, he dropped his chin and stared at his boots, sighing heavily. An hour later, he was still standing in the same place and looked up as Allie and Everett walked out of the jail together.

8

Allie had been thrilled to see Luke. She'd hoped he would text or call sometime since the game on Saturday, but she hadn't heard from him. To look up and see him walking toward her, she'd had the same reaction she always had when he was around: heart pounding, stomach fluttering, the desire to smile until her face hurt from her cheeks being pulled tight.

When she walked into the parking lot, she was barely aware of Everett next to her when she looked up and spied Luke leaning against an SUV. His chin was down, but at her approach, he lifted his head, and their gazes locked onto each other. Everett's presence disappeared completely, and all she could see was Luke. His dark, almost military-trimmed hair and dark beard. He had taken off his scrub top, wearing just a T-shirt even though there was a chill in the evening air. His arms were crossed over his chest, the muscles stretching the material of his shirt. In fact, she could see the delineation of his abs through the thin material. His thighs filled out his khaki pants, and when he'd walked away from her in the library, she hadn't been able to pull her gaze away from his ass.

A touch on her arm surprised her, and she jerked her head around to see that Everett was still there. He was pleasant, but right then, she wanted him gone. "I'll see you on Thursday, Everett," she said, offering a slight smile before walking directly toward Luke.

"Oh, okay, Allie. Have a nice evening," Everett called out.

Not stopping until her feet were directly in front of Luke's boots, she looked up at him. "Why are you still here?"

His blue-eyed gaze held hers. "I was waiting on you."

She cocked her head to the side but said nothing. His words made her happy, but there was something in his tone that gave her pause.

His gaze moved past her shoulder before returning to her. "I think Everett would have liked to ask you to dinner."

"He's a nice man, but I'm not interested in having dinner with him."

She watched as Luke's eyes widened slightly. "You're not?"

"No. But I'm not sure if the man I'm interested in having dinner with has any interest in having dinner with me."

This time, she watched as his lips barely twitched upward. They remained quiet as the seconds ticked by, the world disappearing, leaving just the two of them in the middle of their swirling emotions.

"Why do you think any man would not want to have dinner with you?"

"Because he hasn't asked me yet," she answered softly. She felt as though she was playing a game but didn't understand the rules, and she hated the feeling. "Luke, I'm terrible at flirting. I have no idea how to be coy and don't really want to learn. So, here's the truth... you're the man I'm interested in having dinner with." Blowing out a breath, she added, "There... it's out there. If you're not interested, just let me know—"

He pushed off the side of his vehicle and stood closer, reaching out to take her hands in his. "Allie, would you do me the honor of having dinner with me?"

His strong fingers wrapped around hers, and she felt lightheaded as though the oxygen wasn't quite reaching her head. She nodded, her head moving in jerks before she smiled widely. "Yes, I would."

As soon as those three words left her mouth, she watched the most amazing transformation take place. The stoic, serious, but oh, so gorgeous Luke smiled, and she felt that joy right down to her very bones.

"There's a quiet restaurant right around the corner, near the historic courthouse block," he said.

"That sounds perfect."

He turned, and they began to walk side-by-side, but he'd only let go of one of her hands, his fingers still linked with the other.

The walk was short, and soon they were ensconced at a corner table in a little Italian restaurant. They'd barely placed their orders when he said, "I can't tell you how shocked I was to see you at the jail today."

"I'd planned on telling you the next time I talked to you, but, well…"

"I didn't text or call," he said, finishing her sentence for her.

She felt her cheeks blush at the realization she sounded like a four-alarm clinger. "I just figured we'd meet up sometime."

"I was actually going to call you on Sunday and ask you out, but I got stuck with a family situation. And then yesterday, I had to work extra to get ready for some state visitors coming by the clinic."

The server brought their wine and appetizers, and she tried to eat delicately, chewing slowly and only putting a tiny portion on her plate.

His gaze moved from her plate up to her face, and he tilted his head to the side. "Do you not like the appetizers?"

Blushing even more, she sighed. "Usually, I eat with a very healthy appetite, but no woman wants to be caught snarfing food in front of a man she's trying to impress."

Luke barked out laughter, and she realized she'd been wrong earlier. If she thought he was gorgeous when he smiled, it was nothing like the thunderbolt that hit her heart at the sight of him laughing. So entranced with his expression, she forgot to be embarrassed about her confession.

"Allie, eat what you want, as much as you want, as fast as you want. I'd rather know that you were enjoying

your food and happy than trying to mee
sible standard that you think a man wants.

Lifting a brow, she picked up a mozzare
popped half of it into her mouth, chewing v
loving that he was still smiling.

As their meal came and they continued to enjoy their food, he said, "So, tell me about your part-time job."

"I love being a teacher, and I love my third graders. The salary is okay, but not great for teachers. And while Hannah has been an amazing landlord, it's been my dream to own my own house. A place that I picked out, bought, decorated, and is all mine. I know homeownership has a downside. If something breaks or tears up, then I have to have it fixed. But there's just something about putting my money into my own home that appeals to me. I don't just want a house… I want to make a home."

As soon as the words left her mouth, she watched Luke's expression change, a strange gentleness that passed through his eyes while at the same time his jaw seemed to harden. But it quickly passed, and he simply nodded.

"And your dream is about to come true?"

"I've been saving for several years, but I knew a part-time job would help cover a few of those early expenses that always seem to crop up. I saw the advertisement for a reading specialist at the jail in the teacher's lounge. I talked to Warden Neely, then came in and interviewed. The background check was easy since I'd already had one for the school system, and I got the job!"

So, how many inmates do you work with?"

"On Tuesday afternoons, I have three of the men, and on Thursday afternoons, I have four women. I work every other Saturday morning, where I spend two hours with the men and two hours with the women. It's not a lot of hours, but the pay was much more than what I'd get working retail." It was hard to read Luke's unsmiling expression, so she asked, "What are you thinking?"

"Honestly?" He shifted slightly in his seat. "It's a little strange to know that you're working there. It sounds like an obvious thing to say, but jails aren't a nice place to be, even for visitors. Necessary... can be made as good as possible... but not nice."

She sucked in her lips for a few seconds, pondering his statement. "And yet," she said softly, her hand reaching out to land on his arm, "you work there."

He shrugged, his jaw tight again. "I'm... it's what I'm used to now."

By then, they'd finished the meal, and she reached for her purse as the server came with the check.

"No way, Allie. I asked you to dinner." He handed his credit card to the server, but his gaze never wavered from Allie.

She scrunched her nose. "So, if I ask you to dinner, then I get to pay?"

"No," he chuckled, the sound rumbling deep in his chest.

"Then I'll just have to fix you a home-cooked meal," she said, knowing that she'd like to see him again but wondering if he felt the same. His eyes flashed, and his lips curved upward, giving her hope.

"I'd like that," he said, his voice gentle. He stood and held out his hand toward her.

She eagerly acquiesced and once again loved the feel of his fingers wrapped around hers.

As they made their way outside, the sun had already set, and she shivered. His hand left hers, but before she had a chance to feel the loss, his arm curved over her shoulders, and the warmth was immediately felt along with the tingle that always seemed to occur when they touched. He walked her to her car, and they stood in the glow of the well-lit municipal parking lot.

"I had a good time, Allie," he said, his gaze holding her eyes as he stood close but not crowding.

Her smile widened. "I did, too."

"When do you work again? Thursday?"

She nodded.

"Then I'll wait for you out here."

"Luke, you don't have to do that—"

"Don't *have* to, but I *want* to." He leaned a little closer.

Her hands landed on his chest, one flat over his heart, feeling the steady beat underneath her fingertips. "Okay," she whispered.

He bent slightly and placed his lips on the corner of her mouth, leaving a gentle kiss like the one she'd gifted him with. As he stood straighter, she so wanted the kiss to last longer, but with everything about Luke, she realized he moved slowly, cautiously. And that was fine with her. Her lips tingled just as they had with their first almost-kiss, and she wondered what it would be like when they finally gave in to the urge to kiss fully.

"See you Thursday, Allie," he said, stepping to the side so that she could open her car door.

"See you, Luke." Climbing into her car, she smiled as she waved, then backed out of the parking spot and headed toward the rental cottage, her mind filled with him. He was so unlike any man she'd ever spent time with... calm, quiet, always in control of himself. Not hesitant and unsure of himself but cautious as though he wanted to make sure each step with her was right. She had a feeling he never made a hasty decision.

Her phone vibrated with a message as soon as she stepped into her house. Anxious to see if he was already sending a text, she spied her realtor's number instead. Quickly reading, she squealed.

Owner accepted offer. They need quick closing. I'll schedule inspection for tomorrow. If all goes well, you can close by the end of the month.

Dancing around the room, she threw her hands into the air. Falling onto the sofa, she dialed her parents. "Mom? I got it! I got the house!!"

"Oh, Allie, how exciting! Your dad and I were just talking about coming this weekend for a visit. We'd love to see it with you."

"Yes, as long as dad promises not to walk around finding everything wrong with it!" she warned jokingly.

"No, no, he promises! We're just as excited as you are," her mom laughed. "How about we come Friday evening, and then we'll have to come back home on Saturday."

"Perfect," she agreed. As she tossed her phone onto the coffee table, she leaned back, her heart light. *Dinner with Luke and hopefully the start of something with him. I'm getting my own house. And my parents are coming.* "Yep, just perfect!"

9

Luke walked into the exam room, his attention focused on the man sitting on the examination table. Blood ran down the side of his head from a cut just above his eyebrow. From the scars on the man's arms, this wasn't the first fight he'd been in.

He was never one for small talk outside of work, but at least in here, he tried to put the inmates at ease. If they were comfortable, the work of the medical staff was usually easier and faster, making it better for the inmate, as well.

One look at this man, though, and he knew there was no need to try to have a conversation. This inmate had a tough look and cold expression that came from someone who'd been in and out of the system and didn't give a fuck what anyone thought of him. Sometimes, he wondered if Larry would end up like this man: tough, scarred, angry, and trying to be king of the dung heap.

He worked in silence, cleaning the man's wound,

treating it against infection, then securing it with butterfly bandages. The inmate appeared to appreciate the silence, grunting his thanks as Luke finished.

Hearing Officer Perkins at the doorway always set Luke's teeth on edge. An unbidden grimace crossed his face before he realized the inmate could see him. Wiping his expression clean, he didn't miss the slight lip quirk from the inmate, indicating he felt the same way about Gary. As the inmate walked past the guard, Gary puffed out his chest, glancing toward Luke.

"You ever see that hot piece reading teacher? I think she's here again today. Why she wastes her time on the shitheads, I'll never know. I guess the paycheck is good for something, though."

It took all of Luke's self-control to keep from ramming his fist down Gary's throat. Trying to get the man to have any respect for women was pointless, but Luke hoped that if he was lucky enough to become involved with Allie, he sure as hell would shut Gary up, even if he got fired doing it.

By the time he got to the end of his day, he couldn't wait to see her. Changing clothes in the clinic restroom so he wouldn't still be in his scrub top, he shoved everything into a backpack. He tried to walk past the library door without looking in but was unsuccessful. Just seeing her genuine smile as she talked to the women at the table made him hope for things he'd never allowed himself to hope for.

Tossing his bag into his truck, he hurried down the street to a little sandwich shop. Uncertain what she might like, he ordered several sandwiches and chips and grabbed water bottles. By the time he made it back to the parking lot, he didn't have long to wait before she walked out of the building, Everett right on her heels. Standing straighter, he kept his gaze on her but observed the instant Everett clocked him waiting. The other man waved, a rueful grin on his face as he said goodbye to Allie. It didn't pass Luke's notice that her smile only beamed toward him as she hurried down the sidewalk.

"Hey," she said, her eyes bright. "I was hoping you'd be able to be here but hated that you had to wait."

Humbled by her simple expression of faith in him, he smiled and stepped closer. "Hey, yourself. And I'm right where I want to be." If it was possible for her smile to widen more, he couldn't imagine it and loved that he was able to place that expression on her face. Suddenly unsure of his dinner idea, he blurted, "I bought some sandwiches and water, thinking we can walk around historic Easton, but maybe that's not a good plan—"

"It's perfect! Sandwiches sound wonderful, and that gives us more time to ourselves."

He loved that's what she wanted and nodded. Grabbing the sacks from his SUV, they walked past the courthouse toward the green courtyard surrounded by small, old brick buildings with historical signs outside.

"The new courthouse was actually built in eighteen ninety-nine," he said. Inclining his head toward one of the older buildings, he continued, "The old courthouse and clerk's office over there were built in the early 1700s. That building on the far side is an old prison and was built in the early 1800s. Obviously, they're closed now, but the clerk's office contains records from back in the 1600s."

"Wow, you really know your history of the area," she said, looking around at the buildings surrounding the courthouse green.

Shrugging, he admitted, "Always liked history. I did well in math and science, and so that's why I made it into medic training with the Army, but history was just a fun subject to learn."

"You and my father would have so much to talk about. He loves local history."

Luke didn't reply but doubted that he and her father would have much common ground. Not that he didn't wish they would, but he had a feeling that he wasn't the kind of man her father would approve of. Leading her over to a bench still warm from the afternoon sun, they unwrapped the sandwiches and dove in.

"Tell me about being in the Army," she prodded, twisting her body so that she was facing him.

Glad that she hadn't asked about his family, he swallowed before wiping his mouth. "Not a lot to tell. I was a decent student in high school and did well on the ASVAB, the test you take to show what jobs might be offered to you in the military. My scoring on math and science was high, so there were a number of career paths I could have chosen. I can't say I ever thought of being in the medical field, but when medic school was offered to me along with a signing bonus, I couldn't imagine turning it down."

"Did you serve overseas?" Her voice was soft, almost hesitant, as though she were afraid of the answer.

"Yeah," he nodded. "I did three tours in Afghanistan."

"Wow," she said, sighing. Holding his gaze, she added, "I never know what to say, Luke. I want to thank you for your service, but some people don't like that. I want to let you know that I admire you, but I have no idea if you like hearing that, either."

He chuckled, touched that she cared about his reactions. "Anything you want to say to me, Allie, I'd love. I'm a man who knows where I've been, knows what I've done, don't look for praise but won't turn it down."

Her head dropped back as she laughed, and her beauty struck him in the gut as it always did. As her mirth slowed, she asked, "Did you ever consider making a career out of the Army and staying in until retirement?"

Knowing they were approaching dangerous territory, he simply shrugged. "Wasn't quite sure what I wanted to do. When I got out, it just seemed to be the right time." Breathing a sigh of relief when she accepted that answer without asking for more, they finished their sandwiches and water, tossing the refuse. He reached down and linked fingers with her, the gesture so natural he did it before realizing he'd done so. "You're easy to talk to," he blurted.

She turned her face up toward him and smiled. "I'm glad you think so. I like learning more about you."

He squeezed her fingers but wondered if she'd feel the same way knowing everything about his family. The more he was with her, the more he wanted her in his life. And the more frightening it was to think that she wouldn't continue to feel the same way.

The sun had passed beyond the trees and buildings, the sunset casting a glow of bright orange and yellow throughout the sky. And just like the first night on the pier when he'd seen her, the ethereal illumination on her face caused his breath to halt. Lifting his hand, he cupped her cheek, drawing her nearer with their clasped fingers. She lifted her chin, her upturned face bringing her mouth closer to his. They'd only shared two almost-kisses, but now he wanted everything she was willing to offer. He bent, stopping a whisper away, handing control over to her, already feeling every synapse fire throughout his body at just the idea of truly kissing her.

Without hesitation, she lifted on her toes, her free hand grasping his shoulder, and sealed her mouth over his. Their lips moved slowly with extreme gentleness. The delicate touch sent shock waves of vibrations to his chest, then down to his cock. She moaned slightly, and he angled his head to swallow the sound, pulling her body flush against his.

The kiss flamed, stealing the oxygen from his lungs, but all he cared about was the woman in his arms. Their mouths moved, both exploring, growing almost desperate as their bodies ground together. He didn't even realize when their fingers unlinked, only knowing that his arms banded around her back, pulling her close as her hands clutched the material of his shirt.

Angling the kiss, he plunged his tongue into her warmth as she opened her mouth, yielding to him. She tasted just as he knew she would—sweet with a touch of spice. So like Allie.

He wasn't sure the kiss would ever end until the sound of footsteps on the sidewalk in the distance managed to force its way through the rushing waves of lust filling his ears. Regretfully lifting his head, he could see two of the guards in the distance. His arms loosened, and looking down at her face, he spied the confused and disappointed expression. "I don't want to stop, Allie, but some people are walking into the parking lot. I don't want to do anything to draw untoward attention to you."

She opened her mouth, and he wondered if she was going to refute what he said, then she snapped it shut. Pressing her lips together, she finally said, "Thank you. While I don't care who sees me kissing you, I suppose it doesn't look very professional for us to be making out in the municipal parking lot, does it?"

Grinning, he shook his head. "Probably not." Her lips were kiss-swollen, and her hair was no longer neatly pulled back into a ponytail. Glancing around, he could see that the two guards had made it to their vehicles without spying them. Giving his attention back to her, he said, "I'd like to see you again if you're interested."

"Absolutely," she smiled.

"Tomorrow?"

She nodded, then her head jerked to a stop. "Oh, phooey. I completely forgot to tell you that my bid on the house came through. My parents are coming in tomorrow to take a look at it. They'll be leaving on Saturday. Maybe I can show it to you sometime."

"Then I'll call you on Saturday." He wished it could be earlier but was glad she had parents interested in what she was doing. "Be safe going home and enjoy your family tomorrow."

Smiling again, she climbed into her car and, just like the other evening, tossed him a wave. He watched as she left the parking lot, rubbing the spot over his heart that twinged every time he thought of her. This was now the third sunset kiss they'd shared, and he was addicted and couldn't wait until he saw her again.

Saturday came and went, but Luke didn't call. He'd managed to send a text, but it was vague. Hating himself, he knew it was for the best. And it was all because of Friday night. Fucking Friday night.

He'd driven to the Seafood Shack in Baytown after work for takeout before heading to his apartment. Standing at the end of the bar, he'd heard laughter and looked over, already recognizing Allie's laugh. He'd smiled, thinking she was the most beautiful woman in the crowded restaurant. Shifting slightly, he could see the couple sitting with her. The woman, her dark hair attractively streaked with touches of silver, was laughing, as well. She looked so much like Allie, he would have known they were related even if she hadn't told him her parents were visiting. The man with salt-and-pepper hair appeared lean and fit, his smile aimed toward his daughter. Luke had unabashedly watched the trio as they chatted and laughed. Then a slow niggling of unease moved through him. The realization that he'd never had that in his life.

No one at his high school graduation. He'd stood in formation when he graduated from boot camp, the stands filled with excited and smiling faces from the family members of his platoon. There was no one there for him, but it had always been that way. He assumed you couldn't miss what you'd never had.

And since living in Baytown, especially at the American Legion meetings, he'd been faced with multigenerational families filled with love and pride. Mitch Evans and Grant Wilder's fathers nearly burst with smiles every time they were at a meeting with their law enforcement sons. The same could be said for Aiden and Brogan's dad, as well. In fact, standing at the takeout end of the restaurant, he'd realized how many of his friends had supportive families in the area.

While those thoughts pushed into his joy at seeing Allie, he'd startled at the sight of Everett approaching their table. Hot jealousy jolted through him, and he'd watched as the affable jail librarian walked over. Leaning further so he could keep an eye on the proceedings, it appeared that Everett was simply saying hello. It didn't escape Luke's notice that while Allie's smile was polite, she didn't beam toward Everett the way she did toward him.

But it was apparent that Allie's father warmly shook Everett's hand. *Would he do that so eagerly with me if he knew my background?* Everett had walked away, and Luke had battled the desire to head directly to Allie, claiming her with a kiss. Scoffing at that idea, he'd felt relieved when he looked up to see Joseph walking toward him.

89

"Hey, man. Got time for a beer?" Joseph asked, thrusting his hand out to shake.

"Thanks, but I've got my dinner coming, then heading home." He'd glanced to see a pretty server walking toward him with a bag in her hand.

"Here you go," she said, her voice soft. She glanced to the side of him, and her eyes widened, her shy smile dropping.

"Hey, darlin'," Joseph said, tossing out his trademark smile. "I wondered if you were working tonight."

She nodded, but then turned quickly and disappeared into the crowd.

"Looks like you're losing your touch."

"Nah… she's just playing hard to get." Joseph's lips pressed together for a few seconds then he sighed. "Maybe… or maybe she thinks I'm a dick."

Not in the mood to try to convince Joseph that his luck would be better with the pretty server if he'd stop flirting with other women in the restaurant, he'd lifted his bag and said, "Well, I'm out of here."

Joseph's gaze was assessing, then moved to the windows of the brightly lit restaurant. "Any reason you're hightailing it out of here when I can plainly see Allie inside?"

Luke wished Joseph would shut up but forced his feet to stay in place. Shrugging, he replied, "She's with her folks. Didn't want to interrupt."

Joseph continued his narrow-eyed gaze, then finally sighed. "Okay." That was all he'd said, but Luke read a whole lot of meaning behind the one word. Joseph may have been raised completely differently than Luke, but he seemed to understand the battles Luke fought from his upbringing.

With a chin lift, he passed his friend but halted as Joseph called his name. Turning, he looked over his shoulder.

"Don't fuck this up, Luke. Let go of whatever shit is in your mind and don't fuck up something this good."

He'd held Joseph's gaze with another chin lift, then said, "I hear you, but you might want to take your own advice."

Joseph's eyes widened and he threw his head back and laughed. "You're probably right, man."

Turing, Luke headed to his car. After he'd eaten, his fingers hovered over his phone, desperate to send a message and yet not convinced it was the right thing to do. Before he could decide, his phone rang, and he looked at the caller ID, sighing heavily. Connecting only because he knew it was hard to get phone privileges, he answered, "Yeah, Larry?"

"Bro, I need Chelle to bring me some stuff."

"And you can't ask her yourself?"

"She won't do it. She says there's no money. But I know you were over there last weekend, so maybe instead of buying the kids some shit they don't need, you'll get some things for me."

"Maybe it's time you started worrying about what your kids do need instead of yourself. How about that for a change?" he growled.

"Don't start in with me, Luke," Larry whined.

"I'll see if I get hold of Chelle, but what I do give, I give to your kids." Not in the mood to listen to Larry's litany of complaints, he'd disconnected. The desire to text Allie was gone.

He'd moped through Saturday, convincing himself that she was better off without the shit swirling in his life.

By Sunday, his mood was low. Desperate to get out of his tiny apartment, he drove to the Baytown beach, parking near the pier. With just a few fishermen at the far end, he reveled in the peace, sucking in deep breaths of fresh air as the salty breeze blew in from the bay.

He lost track of time but realized as the sun was setting he'd probably wasted enough time feeling sorry for himself and trying to get Allie out of his mind. He hadn't been successful. Scrubbing his hand over his face, he shoved his fingers into his jeans pockets and stalked back down the pier. Part of him hoped she might appear, but as he climbed into his vehicle to drive back home, he was still very much alone.

10

A week had gone by with very little from Luke. Allie sighed. She'd sent a few texts only to have him reply hours later with short, somewhat vague replies. And both days she'd been at the jail tutoring, he'd had an excuse as to why he wasn't able to meet her afterward. She scrolled through her texts.

Hope you're having a great day! Allie

You, too. Luke

I had such a great time last week with you. Allie

Same. Luke

I had a good visit with my parents. Allie

Good. Luke

Sighing, Allie stared at the screen during her lunch break. She thought of trying again, but even though she sometimes felt clueless when it came to men and dating, she could read the writing on the wall. Or rather, the phone. Luke had decided that she wasn't what he was interested in after all.

Great... just when I find someone that sparks all my

interests, he goes cold. The desire to bang her head on the table was strong, but her forehead was spared when the door opened, and Shonna and Jade walked in.

Shonna plopped down next to Allie and said, "I just heard that Terry is going to have minor surgery next week, and the principal has already decided that the three of us will have to do planning with the subs they bring in. Terry thinks he'll just be out for two weeks, and he'll have lesson plans, but you know the bulk will fall to us."

Allie wasn't surprised considering all teachers filled in and supported each other, but suddenly, she felt ill at how much was on her plate.

"Are you okay?" Jade asked.

"Yeah… it's just that I'm getting ready to move in about two weeks to my new house, and the part-time job at the jail will take up the next Saturday, as well." Shrugging, she plastered a smile onto her face. "But it'll be okay. Nothing new."

"Why don't you have a moving party?" Jade suggested.

Allie's brow scrunched. "A what?"

"A moving party. It's what we did when Lance and I moved into our house. We got some of our strong-armed friends to help move, and then we supplied them with food and beer. Katelyn organized it, and Jillian jumped in to help. We had a ton of manpower to move the furniture and boxes. Then others brought food, and it was great. At the end of the day, our friends had a good time, and we were moved in."

"Well, I—"

"Leave the details to me. I'll get Lance to announce it to his buddies, and then you know the rest of us will pitch in."

Smiling, Allie blew out a breath of relief. "That just might work!" As the trio of third-grade teachers headed back to their classrooms, she wondered if Luke would be waiting for her when she left the jail. *Probably not.* While that thought was depressing, she squared her shoulders and greeted her returning class with a huge smile. *I've got more to focus on than a man who doesn't want to spend time with me.* Clapping her hands, she called her class to attention. "Time for math, guys. Let's see what we're going to learn today!"

It had now been almost two weeks since she'd seen Luke. She'd barely settled into the library for her reading lessons when Everett walked over to her. "I just got a call from the guard who normally brings the women over. There's a stomach bug going through that cell block, and they don't want you exposed."

Sorry the women were ill, she couldn't help but be pleased to have more time to pack at the cottage. Chatting for a few minutes with Everett, she waved goodbye after packing up her materials. She waited as he called for a guard to escort her out. Once outside, she hustled to her car, her mind filled with what needed to be done before her moving party the next weekend.

Rounding the back of her vehicle, she was surprised to see Luke at the driver's door of his SUV parked near hers. Unable to duck out of sight, she forced a smile onto her face when he turned, his own surprise evident in his wide eyes.

"Hello, Luke," she said politely, making sure to keep her smile in place as she unlocked her door.

"Allie," he greeted, his intense gaze staring straight at her.

Turning from him, she mumbled, "Well, have a nice evening."

"How are you?" he asked, his voice holding a touch of uncertainty.

Looking over her shoulder, she replied, "I'm fine." She hesitated, then added, "And you?"

"Fine, also."

She turned back to her door, her hand on the handle, hating the way her heart pounded and stomach clenched. His hand landed on her shoulder, and she jumped, twisting her head around in surprise.

"Allie," he said again, and this time her name seemed dragged from the very depths of him.

"Yes?" she barely whispered, now knowing the uncertainty was in her voice.

"I'm sorry that I've been... that I didn't..." A grimace twisted his handsome features.

She battled the urge to reach up and smooth the lines from his forehead. Clutching her keys tighter in her hand, she resisted. *He doesn't want that from me.*

His expression settled on hers as his spine straightened and he squared his shoulders. "I'm sorry that I was such a dick and didn't call or text when I said I would."

She gently shook her head, his apology crude and

yet effective. She sighed heavily. "Luke, you were under no obligation to me, therefore you weren't a dick."

"I backed away without any explanation, and that was a dick move," he proclaimed, his hands jammed into his front pockets. "The truth is, I pussied—um... chickened out. I wanted to call. I wanted to text. I wanted to see you again. But..." He dropped his head back and stared into the sky for a moment while she waited patiently. Lowering his chin, he speared her with his clear, blue eyes. "I convinced myself that I shouldn't continue building a relationship with you. That I'm not the kind of man you should be with."

Blinking, her head jerked back. "Huh? You're not the kind of man... what the heck does that mean?" Irritation was building, but another tortured grimace crossed his face, and this time she lost the battle to keep her distance. Lifting her hand, she cupped his jaw and soothed her thumb over the lines emanating from the sides of his eyes. "Please talk to me, Luke," she begged softly. "Please help me understand."

He stayed perfectly still for a moment, and she thought he was going to refuse. Then he closed his eyes and leaned his head against her palm, his features relaxing. He opened his eyes, and she breathed a sigh of relief.

"Okay," he agreed. Looking around as though surprised at where they were standing, he added, "But not here."

"I'd invite you back to the cottage, but it's filled with boxes. We can probably push them to the side—"

"No, my place. If you're okay with leaving your car

here for a little while, I'll take you back to my apartment. We'll talk there. And I think once you see it, you'll understand."

Her interest was piqued, and she nodded. "Okay," she agreed. Turning, she locked her car before climbing into his SUV as he held the door open for her.

The drive to Baytown only took a little over ten minutes, but neither spoke. She couldn't say the silence was awkward, but it certainly wasn't comfortable. It was obvious Luke had a lot on his mind, and she was determined to let him say whatever he needed to say in his own time.

He parked on one of the streets that turned off Main, and she waited as he walked around and assisted her down. The nondescript brick building was old, and he pulled out a key, letting them into a door straight off the sidewalk. Stairs to the next floor were directly in front of them, and she followed him as he led them up two flights.

He unlocked a door on the third floor and looked over his shoulder. "This is where I live."

The way he said it made her feel as though he was almost daring her to see it. Curious, she followed him inside as he flipped on a light. A cozy, L-shaped kitchen greeted them on the right as they walked in. A small living room that held a sofa, end table with a lamp, and TV on a stand filled the space. There was only one door, and since it was open, she could see a bedroom.

He stepped forward, turned toward her, and threw his arms out to the side.

She glanced around, uncertain what he wanted her

to say. "O… kay." Looking back at him, she sucked in her lips, pressing them together as she waited.

"This is the best place I've lived, Allie."

She walked forward, took his hand in hers, and led him over to the sofa, dropping her purse onto the floor. Pulling him down next to her, she shifted to face him, tucking one leg under her butt. "Okay, Luke. Here's the deal. You obviously want to make a point with me, but I'm not getting it. You feel something strongly, but I can't read your mind. And you seem to be struggling with something, but I'm totally lost. And you know I don't play games, so I'm going to ask that you don't either."

He jerked back, his chin lowering. "You think I'm playing a game with you?"

"If you don't speak plainly so that we can either move forward as just friends or something more, then yes, I do. Probably not on purpose, but they're still games I don't understand."

His jaw clenched, and she watched in fascination as the muscle ticked. He looked away for a moment, then blew out a long breath before turning his gaze back to her. "From the first moment I saw you wandering on the pier, a smile on your beautiful face, and heard you were talking to your mom, I knew you were someone that I'd like to know better while also knowing that you were out of my league."

Not expecting that, it was now her turn to jerk. She swallowed deeply, determined not to interrupt.

"And every time we've been together, you've done nothing but prove that you're exactly what I thought you were that first night. Beautiful. Kind. Special." He glanced around his living room again and sighed. "This is the nicest place I've ever lived, Allie. And it's tiny, furnished with secondhand crap, and has no view. But after years in the military where I shared a bunk with at least five other guys, I like having my own space. And before that, my childhood home was shit."

Definitely not expecting that, her heart squeezed, and her hand darted out to grab onto his, wanting to anchor both of them together.

"I never planned on using my Army medic skills in a jail, but I'm no stranger to them. It's not the first time. My dad left us when I was a kid, and I grew up fast, having to be the man of the house. He was a deadbeat, always looking for an easy buck. Mom always said he just ran out on us, and she fell apart. She didn't hold down a job, money was nonexistent, and I was going to school and taking care of her and my little brother. I was almost out of high school before I found out that my dad ended up in prison for stabbing someone during a robbery gone wrong. I visited him one time before leaving for the Army. I had no idea what I expected. Remorse? Regret? 'Gee, Son, I'm proud of you?' All I got was a bitter diatribe from a man who only thought about himself."

If she thought her heart had squeezed earlier, it was nothing like what she felt as he gave her more of himself. Wanting him to unburden, she remained quiet, her hands still holding onto his.

"I worked hard in school, kept my grades up, and worked part-time in a grocery store for a good man who'd give me extra food to take home, knowing my mom was about as worthless as my dad was. I tried to do the best I could for my brother, but he spent more time in trouble and in juvie. As bad as this sounds, sometimes I was relieved when he was in juvie and I had a break. Mom railed at me when I joined the Army right after high school, but I had to get out." He squeezed his eyes tightly shut for a few seconds, shaking his head as though to dislodge the memories. "Christ almighty, Allie. I had to get out."

"So, what happened that made you suddenly back away from me?" she whispered, still not understanding.

"I saw you and your parents. That night at the Seafood Shack. You looked so happy, and they looked like they were bursting with pride over you."

"You were there?"

"Picking up takeout."

Her brow crinkled in confusion. "Why didn't you come over? I would have loved to introduce you to my parents. I mean, I know we're not… or rather, we're just friends, but… oh, you know what I mean. I would have loved for them to meet you."

His hand jerked underneath hers, but she held tight.

"Don't you see what I'm trying to tell you?"

Shaking her head, she huffed. "No, I don't. You've told me about your family, and that breaks my heart, Luke. I ache for the little boy who had to become a man too early. I ache for you that your dad was such a horrible dad, and your mom couldn't get her act together, and your brother followed in their footsteps. But don't you see? That just makes you so amazing.

That you rose above your background to serve in the military, become a medic, and have a full-time job in a place that isn't easy to work in, but you do it so well. To have an apartment that's your own. You're not defined by your family. You're defined by who you are and what you've done for yourself and for others. That's the man I'm interested in. That's the man I want to get to know even better."

He stared, his gaze never wavering from hers. Ensnared by their blue depths, she jolted when he lurched forward, loosening his hand from hers so that he could clutch her cheeks with his palms, his thumbs sweeping across her skin. "I want to kiss you," he groaned.

"Good," she declared, and the word had barely left her lips when his mouth sealed over hers. As their tongues danced, she felt her world righten once again.

11

"You're not defined by your family. You're defined by who you are and what you've done for yourself and for others. That's the man I'm interested in. That's the man I want to get to know even better." With Allie's words ringing in his ears and reverberating through his entire being, Luke dove into the kiss like a man starved and she was the only way to feed his soul.

He'd meant for the kiss to be a gentle affirmation, but one touch of her lips, her tongue darting out to meet his, and he was swept over the cliff. He held her face in his hands, clutching almost desperately, afraid she would disappear like a mirage, too good to be true. But with every swipe of her tongue, he grew bolder, knowing she was real.

Wanting more, needing more, he slid his arms to her shoulders, then around her back, pulling her tightly against him. Her soft breasts crushed against his chest, her body tucked perfectly against the tight planes of his. His cock reacted, aching as it swelled, filling the confines of his jeans. But he ignored the desire to set it free and plunge deep into her warm body, instead devoting his focus to Allie. The soft gasps of air as she breathed between their sealed lips. The little moans that escaped every time his tongue dragged over hers. Her short fingernails digging in as her fingers clutched his T-shirt.

He slid one hand up, wrapping his fingers around the silken strands of hair captured in her ponytail. He'd wondered if it was as soft as it looked and discovered that indeed, it was. His jean-clad knee was pressed between her thighs, and he wasn't sure she realized she was rubbing her core, seeking friction. That little maneuver nearly sent him over the edge that he was so precariously clinging to.

He had thought he'd made tough decisions in his life before her, but lifting his head to separate their mouths was harder than he ever could have imagined. He immediately felt the loss but kept his arms banded tightly around her as they stared into each other's eyes, chests heaving. Her lips were parted, her eyes dark with lust, and she looked adorably confused. Uncertain what to say, he waited for her reaction, and she didn't disappoint.

"Wow," she whispered on an exhale.

A chuckle rumbled from deep in his chest before erupting, and he pulled her tighter. "Yeah, babe, wow."

With her head tilted back, her lips curved upward, she said, "I'm having a moving party."

He blinked slowly, his chin jerking slightly. Those

words were even more unexpected, and he wasn't sure he'd heard her correctly. "You're having a what?"

"A moving party. Will you come?"

"Allie, babe, I don't have a clue what a moving party is, but if you're inviting, I'm accepting."

Her top teeth landed on her bottom lip as though to keep from smiling wider. "Jade Greene told me about it and is making the arrangements. It's a way for me to get a bunch of friends together to help me move from Hannah's rental into my new house. The men can provide the muscle, and the women will provide the food." Her nose scrunched. "Actually, that sounds rather sexist, doesn't it?"

"I get the drift and would be honored to come to the moving party. I'm just sorry I haven't been around to help celebrate this new chapter in your life during the last couple of weeks. It was stupid on my part, and I promise to make it up to you."

Her arms banded around his middle, squeezing his waist. "But you're here now."

He bent and kissed her lightly, forcing his head to lift again so that he wouldn't fall into the honey sweetness of her kiss and not be able to stop. "Yeah, I am."

"It's going to be this Sunday because I have to work, and I know most of you all have a ball game to coach on Saturday. Everybody is supposed to get to the rental about ten o'clock."

"Then I'll be there by nine," he said, knowing it was the right thing to say when her smile widened. A heavy sigh left his lungs. "I need to get you back to your car so you can get home. Not that I want to, but I know you've got to get up early for school tomorrow."

He led her to the front door, bending to snag her purse from the floor. Handing it to her, he locked the door behind them and led her to his vehicle. It struck him how different their trip from his place was versus their arrival. At that time, he'd assumed she would be turned off by his simplistic way of living. He had money in the bank but didn't spend it on his place to live when he figured he might need it for a rainy day. He'd assumed she would be horrified to be associated with a man whose dad had been in prison and whose brother was currently sitting in jail. Instead, she'd praised him for who he'd become and admitted she was interested. His lungs stung as his chest swelled with pride.

This trip was just as quiet as the previous one, only their hands remained linked as they rested on his thigh. Pulling into the still-empty parking space next to her car, he looked over to see her smiling. "Whatcha thinking?"

She shrugged. "Just happy, that's all."

Surprised, her answer sent warmth through him, and he pressed, "Why?"

Squeezing his hand, she replied, "Because when you backed away from me, I tried to tell myself it was okay. That I had a full life and was fine. But the reality is that I missed the idea of getting to spend more time with you. Even though we were just starting to know each other, I already missed you."

His heart clenched. "Christ, Allie, I want to kiss you again. And this time, I'm not sure I can stop."

She threw her head back and laughed, but he was already moving forward, capturing her lips in a laughing-kiss, one that shot straight through him. She quickly reciprocated, and the kiss flamed hot once more. Noise from the sidewalk caused them to jump apart, and while he cursed under his breath, he knew it was for the best. The last thing he wanted was a public show of affection right outside the jail.

Dragging in a ragged breath, he tried to still the pounding of his heartbeat as well as the ache in his cock again. "Text me the address of your rental, and I'll be there early on Sunday."

She nodded, and as she pulled out her phone, he climbed down and walked around the hood to her door. His phone vibrated in his pocket as she climbed down, and he knew she'd sent the information to him. It was on the tip of his tongue to ask if he could see her earlier, but with an AL meeting the next night and both of them busy on Saturday, he knew Sunday would have to do.

She unlocked her car, then stood in the opened doorway as he lightly kissed her again. "Drive safe and text me when you get to your home."

Her smile was her answer, and he forced his body backward so that she could settle behind the wheel and close the door. Watching until she was out of sight, he blew out a long breath, his heart light as he thought of her acceptance as well as interest. Sunday morning couldn't come soon enough.

Luke lifted the back of his packed SUV, glancing over his shoulder at the gathering. He'd arrived early this morning, unable to stay away from Allie. He'd caught her just out of the shower and tried not to drool over her short robe that had wet spots near her breasts where her hair dripped water down the front. She'd greeted him with a smile, gifted him with a quick kiss, then whirled and ran back to her bedroom. Adjusting his crotch, he'd blown out a long breath, now doubting his sanity for showing up so early. But a few minutes later, they'd shared breakfast, and as they'd stood casually in the kitchen sipping coffee, he wouldn't have traded the simple experience for anything—even an aching cock.

Boxes were packed, and she'd gathered the last of her toiletries and clothes. He'd begun loading his SUV with everything he could cram into it, and soon the others began to arrive. He hadn't asked her who was coming but wasn't surprised at the gathering, pleased that he knew everyone, many of them first responders.

Mitch and Grant had pickup trucks large enough for her sofa and mattresses. Colt and Liam wrangled her bed frame into another truck along with some boxes. Lance and Zac handled her dresser and chest of drawers. Dylan and Wyatt were able to get her dining room table and chairs. Other friends loaded boxes and the rest of the smaller furniture. He followed directly behind Allie's car as she led the caravan to her new house after the women convinced her to leave the last cleaning to them. She'd visibly struggled with the idea of someone else cleaning until Hannah jokingly threatened to kick her former tenant off the property.

As soon as he parked behind her, she leaped from her car and raced to him. "Isn't it adorable? Don't you just love it!"

It was hard for him to even notice the house when all his attention was focused on her. Her face glowed, and her smile beamed. She grabbed his hand, dragging him forward, and he finally allowed himself a moment to admire the house she'd purchased. Two-story, with a picket fence around the yard. The house was painted a pale yellow with white trim. It was exactly the type of home he could imagine her in. The kind of home where love would abound and family would grow.

To keep her from running herself ragged, he asked where she wanted certain pieces of furniture so that he could help as the men brought them in. It didn't take long for the large pieces to find their new place in her home.

She fretted as loads of boxes were coming in, and again, Luke suggested she direct the box placements for the bedrooms and he'd handle the kitchen and dining room. By the time everything was in, the women had returned, exclaiming that Allie had already completed so much of the cleaning there was very little to do.

He watched as she stood in the middle of her living room, her hair falling from her ponytail, a smudge of dirt on her cheek, and her smile wide. He lifted his hand and rubbed his chest over his heart. Her eyes met him across the room, and he felt the punch to his gut. For a few seconds, everyone faded away, and it was just the two of them.

"Time to start the party!" one of the women called out.

He watched as Allie blinked, like him suddenly aware that they weren't alone. A blush graced her cheeks, and he laughed. Everyone moved outside to begin setting up, giving them a moment alone, and he wasn't about to squander a second of that time. He stalked over to her and wrapped his arms around her, staring down at her upturned face. "Happy?"

Her arms banded around his waist, and she nodded. "I can't believe it. It's a dream come true." She looked around at her furniture already in place. "I also can't believe that I'm already moved in. I thought I'd have to spend a lot on a mover, but with everyone's help, it went so fast!"

"Good friends never mind helping out," he said. "Especially for someone as wonderful as you."

She remained silent for a moment, pulling in her lips as her eyes cut to the side. He gave her a moment to work through whatever she seemed to be pondering, then finally asked, "Are you okay?"

She glanced around as though checking to see who might be listening, then lifted on her toes and whispered, "I'm so grateful for everyone, but is it bad that I'll be glad when they leave and it's just you and me?"

His arms tightened, and he grinned. "Hell no. In fact, say the word and I'll kick them all out!"

A giggle slipped out. "Well, let's enjoy the party with everyone, and then we can have some time for ourselves." She blinked and sobered. "I guess that was very presumptuous. I'd love it if you could stay after everyone leaves, but I—"

"Nowhere else I'd rather be. You want me here? I'll be here."

Grinning, they kept their arms around each other as they walked side-by-side out onto the back patio. If their friends were surprised that they were together, no one commented. Soon, the gathering had grown into a housewarming party filled with about twenty couples, some singles, and kids running through the yard. At one point, Luke looked around at the gathering, hearing the laughter and observing the camaraderie. He might not have been raised in one, but he sure as hell knew what one should be. *This is what a home should look like.*

The party lasted for hours, and each time Allie sidled over to him to take his hand, look up and smile at him, or slide her arm around his waist, he felt like a king. He didn't miss the grins from the others, and their silent approval moved through him. Most of the law enforcement leaders knew of his family situation when he'd applied for the position of jail medic. Being informed that he would be judged on his own merits had given him hope. Participating in the American Legion as a member and coach had given him purpose. But being seen as worthy of someone like Allie sent chills through him.

Finally, the parents gathered their tired children and toddlers, and the babies were bundled up. Goodbye hugs and handshakes made the rounds. With his arm around her shoulders, he led her back into her living room.

"Babe, you look dead on your feet."

She didn't bother to argue but simply nodded even though she still had a smile on her face as she looked around her house. "Do you like it?" she asked.

"The more important question is do you like it?" he countered.

She laughed. "Yeah, I do. I can see this being a place I live for a long time." She looked up and said, "I'm stuffed, but how would you like something to drink? Can we sit in the living room and take it easy?"

"Are you sure you don't want me to help unload more boxes?"

"Nah. The girls got most of my clothes and kitchen put away. I have no idea where to hang pictures yet, and I'll go through my books later. Now, I just want to sit and enjoy being with you."

They walked toward the sofa when his phone vibrated. Checking the caller ID, he winced. "Allie, I'm sorry, but I need to take this."

"Of course," she readily agreed.

He walked out onto her front porch but left the screen door open. "Chelle? What's going on? Are the kids okay?"

"That's all you care about," she whined. "Yes, they're fine, but I'm going to need some money to make it to the end of the month."

"What do you need the money for? I ordered groceries online to be delivered."

"Yeah, I know, but bills are piling up, and I don't know when Larry's getting out."

"Look, Chelle, you callin' me on a Sunday night isn't good timing. I've got work this week. Where are the kids?"

"They're in the other room watching TV," she huffed. "So, are you going to send money or not?"

"Not until I can get there and see what needs to be taken care of. I'll come on Saturday." He hated that he was giving up a day with Allie but was torn because he wanted to check on Jessica and Jeremy.

"Fine, fine," Chelle groused just before she disconnected.

"Fuck." Dropping his chin, he stared at his boots, then felt the gentle caress of Allie's arms reaching from behind and wrapping around his middle as she pressed her front to his back.

"You okay, Luke?"

"No… but it's part of who I am."

"Tell me," she whispered.

"Babe, you need to focus on you, your beautiful house, and the first night you get to sleep here. You don't need to hear more of my life."

She circled his body, keeping her arms around his waist until she was now pressed to his front. "I wouldn't ask if I didn't want to know. Please."

Sucking in a deep breath, he let it out slowly as he pulled her in tight. "Okay. Let's go in and get comfortable, and I'll give it all to you. I wanted us to have more time together before I laid more on you, but you might as well have it all now."

With their arms wrapped around each other, they walked back into her house, but this time, his heart was heavy. It didn't seem right to lay his burdens on her. But maybe it was better now at the beginning of the relationship. If it was more than she could take, he'd rather know now.

12

Allie and Luke settled on her sofa, and once again, she shifted around so that she could face him, her knee bent on the cushion, touching his leg. She steeled herself, having easily overheard his side of the conversation through the open screen door. *Chelle. The kids. Grocery money.* If Luke had kids and an ex-wife, she wanted to know. Not that it would make a difference in how she felt about him, but it would certainly add complexity to a new relationship she hadn't considered. Pushing those thoughts aside, her gaze roved over his face, the lines extending from his eyes deepening. She reached out and placed her hand on his, and he jerked, quickly linking his fingers with hers.

Lifting his gaze, he said, "When we were talking the other day, I told you about my upbringing. What I didn't add was what's going on now with my family."

Her fingers flexed involuntarily, and she simply nodded for him to continue.

"I got out of the Army when I found out my mom was going into hospice for cancer. I was ready to get out anyway and figured I could use my medic training to help her. So, I came back, moved into the old house filled with old memories I'd left behind, and took care of her until she died about four months later."

"I'm so sorry, Luke," she said softly, aching for the child whose mom had never been in his corner and for the man who'd set that aside to care for her.

"I hadn't heard from my brother, Larry, in years. About the only time he'd try to get hold of me when I was in the Army was when he needed money. It was always the same story. I'd had it lucky. He'd gotten the short end of the stick. I owed him. Sometimes even told me the money was for Mom." Luke sighed heavily. "I'd send him some until I got out after ten years in and found out he wasted it, smoked it, drank it, and even started dealing drugs with it. I told him that was the last time he was ever getting any from me."

She gently rubbed her thumb over his knuckles, hoping to infuse some warmth into his strong hands—and maybe help him to feel less alone.

His gaze moved from their hands up to her face. "Then he dropped his bombshell on me. Turns out while I'd been gone, he'd gotten a girl pregnant and, to my great surprise, actually married her. That was who was on the phone. Chelle. And then he introduced me to his two kids. Jeremy was about five, and Jessica was just two at the time. Christ, cute and sweet and so fucking precious. Their apartment wasn't very clean, and Chelle was quickly losing whatever looks she must have had at one time with cigarettes, alcohol, and hard living. But I fell in love with Jeremy and Jessica and vowed that I'd do anything I could to make their life better. God knows, having Larry and Chelle for parents was a tough way to start out life."

"I wasn't trying to eavesdrop, but I overheard you mention groceries," Allie said.

"I learned early on that I couldn't give Larry or Chelle money. So, when I visited, I'd take the kids out and let them buy what they wanted at the grocery store, making sure to get healthy food, and I'd buy them clothes and school supplies. I made it clear to their parents that I was doing this for the kids only."

"Why do I get the feeling that things are getting worse?" She shifted on the sofa so that she was closer, wanting to erase the distance between them.

He snorted and nodded. "Let's just say that when I applied for the job at the jail a year ago, I had to come clean to Colt and Warden Neely. I explained that my father had been in prison but was now deceased and that my brother had been in and out of jail. They did the background check and discovered that I had nothing to do with any of their activities. They were impressed with my military career. I remember Colt looking me square in the eye and telling me that I was my own man, not responsible for the actions of others, including my brother. You can't imagine how good that felt." He shifted to face her more fully, also. "Almost as good as what you said to me the other night. That I'm not defined by my family." Lifting his free hand, he tucked a strand of hair behind her ear, his forefinger tracing over the soft skin.

She shivered at the gentle contact, battling the urge to lean forward, clutch his face, and kiss him until the worry was erased. Blinking, she pushed that desire down, wanting him to keep unburdening himself.

Luke grimaced, the expression of disgust on his face deepening. "Found out recently that Larry was back in jail, only this time, he'd really fucked up. He's got a number of charges against him, not the least of which is having enough drugs to sell. I'm not giving him a dime, but I know that Chelle is worthless as a provider, so I'm trying to make sure the kids have what they need. I've worked out a deal with the local grocer. They deliver food that I pay for, and they're not allowed to change the order or let her deny it so that she can get money back. The kids qualify for reduced meals, so I put money in their school account so that they get breakfast and lunch at school. Although, with Larry in jail, I need to check because they might qualify for free meals. Anyway," he sighed, "that was her on the phone saying she needed money. I don't know why she bothered because she knows I'm not going to give money straight to her."

With her career in early childhood education, Allie had seen the effects of drug and alcohol use by parents on their children. Her heart squeezed at the thought of Luke's niece and nephew, his concern for them evident in his voice. "And the kids? Are they safe?"

If she'd thought his earlier grimace was heart-wrenching, the worry that slashed through his eyes made her heart clench again. Grabbing his hands with both of hers, she sent up a prayer for strength.

"It's not a great situation, but they seem safe. Chelle drinks and smokes pot, but I don't know that she does anything harder. When I check on them, the kids are usually clean but their clothes are often too small and need washing. Because they get fed at school and Jeremy tells me they have peanut butter sandwiches for dinner, I at least know they're eating something. Neither Larry nor Chelle are physically abusive, just mostly neglectful. They're both so into their own shit, and the kids aren't first and foremost on their minds." A heavy sigh resounded from deep within his lungs. "Jeremy takes too much on himself, always making sure that Jessica is cared for. But that's too fuckin' much for an eight-year-old boy to do."

"It sounds like he's a lot like you," she stated.

At that, his gaze jumped to hers, surprise written in the way his eyes widened. "Never really thought about it that way. But I sure as hell hate that he has to do that."

"Is there anything I can do to help?"

The muscles in his face relaxed, and for the first time since they'd started their conversation, his lips curved slightly. "No, babe, but just your offer means the world to me." He heaved another sigh, then continued to hold her gaze with intensity. "So, there it is, Allie. You now know my past, and you know what I'm now faced with. It's fucked up, no doubt about it."

She cocked her head to the side, not flinching under his scrutiny. "I'm glad you told me, Luke. But I get the feeling that you think I'm supposed to scream and run away."

"Not sure I'd blame you if you did. Being with me means that you'd have to deal with my fucked-up brother and his fucked-up wife, but also their two children that mean the world to me."

Shifting even closer so that her legs were draped over his thigh, she let go of his hands so that she could clasp his face and hold him close. "I told you that I was interested in you. Interested in getting to know you more. And that hasn't changed. Everything I learn about you simply makes me want to spend more time with you. I work with a lot of children like Jeremy and Jessica. It's not their fault who their parents are any more than it was your fault who yours were. But they're so lucky to have you in their lives. You'll make all the difference to them. So, if you're expecting me to be frightened away by your honesty, I'll be happy to prove you wrong."

His hands moved to clasp her face also, and for a long moment, they simply held each other's gazes. "Christ," he breathed. "You're so fucking beautiful. Inside and out."

Closing the scant distance, they met in a fiery kiss that had both of them gasping for air, their tongues sweeping together in a dance of dominance. Allie felt each stroke of his tongue like a velvet caress, the electric waves moving straight to her core. She wanted him in every way. Wanted to discover his thoughts, feelings, needs, desires. His favorite foods. His favorite book. His favorite music.

He angled her head, and she yielded to his ministrations, knowing whichever way he led their kiss, she was going to love it. Lifting on her knees, she straddled his lap, now facing him fully with the thick bulge of his erection pressing against her needy sex. With his tongue gliding and exploring her mouth, she wrapped her arms around his neck and pressed her breasts to his wide chest. Now, she wanted to discover what that chest looked like with no shirt on. She wanted to feel the thick muscles and smooth skin. Rocking against his crotch, she really wanted to have both of them strip and throw out the last barriers to their coming together.

She was ready to insist that they move into the bedroom once she remembered the girls had found her sheets and made her bed, but he pulled back, his breath ragged. A moan slipped from her lips at the loss, but she anticipated he would plan for the naked continuation of what they'd started.

"I should leave," he said, the rough words pulled from the depths of his lungs.

"Wh... what? Leave?" she gasped, her fingers digging into his shoulders with shameless desperation.

His lips lifted in a quirk. "Not because I want to. But you've had a long day. Said goodbye to Hannah's cottage, moved into your new house which you haven't even had a chance to enjoy for a moment by yourself. You hosted a party, and then dealt with all my shit." He smoothed her hair back from her face, his hands still warm upon her cheeks. "I want to be with you, Allie, but I want to do this right. I want to take care of you. And right now, you need rest more than anything else. You've got to get up and go to work tomorrow—"

"Stay with me tonight." The words rushed out, but she had no desire to take them back.

His brows lifted. He opened his mouth, but she was on a roll and spoke first.

"It doesn't have to be sex. Just… just… sleep. Rest. Being together." She winced, then sighed. "Maybe that's not fair to ask you to sleep with me and not have sex. Oh, Jesus, I'm so messing this up." Sucking in a deep breath, she let it out and let his blue-eyed gaze ground her. "Luke, if you want to leave or need to leave, I get that. It's been a long day for you, too. And I know you have a lot on your mind with your family—"

"Do you want me to stay?" he interrupted.

She nodded, her chin bobbing rapidly.

His smile widened, but he continued to keep his eyes on her. "Sleeping with you would be an honor."

Although his words didn't displease her, they did surprise her. Tilting her head to the side, she scrunched her brow. "An honor to sleep with me?"

"Allie, I've never spent the night with any woman."

She blinked in surprise. Over the years, she'd had a few relationships that had lasted for months, the longest one lasting half a year, and those included many nights spent together although she'd never lived full-time with anyone. Once she'd determined they had no real future, she'd broken things off, or, occasionally, it was a mutual decision. And since moving to the Eastern Shore, she'd rarely dated. But hearing that Luke had never spent the night with a woman took her by surprise. "Never?"

He shook his head. "When it was just physical, there was never a need for intimacy. The few relationships I've had that have lasted longer were still not with anyone I felt the need to spend the whole night with."

Realizing he was trying to let her down easy, she nodded, trying not to let her disappointment show, but he moved his hands gently, giving her a little shake. Her eyes jumped back up to his.

"I'm telling you this because I want to spend the night with *you*. And it's fine that it's not about sex. In fact, I think it's a helluva lot better that tonight isn't about sex. When we're ready, that will come. You're the kind of woman I want to treat right. You're the kind of woman that deserves to be treated right. And what I feel about you is way more than sex. So, if you're asking me to spend the night curled around you, I consider that an honor."

"Wow," she whispered, finding it hard to breathe. "I think that's one of the nicest things anyone has ever said to me."

He shook his head slowly. "If that's the nicest thing you've ever heard, babe, get ready to hear a whole lot more. And you'd deserve every word."

Leaning forward, she kissed him lightly. As the kiss ended, she slid off his lap and stood, extending her hand toward him. Latching fingers, he lifted from the sofa. Ignoring the boxes scattered about the room, they walked up the stairs to her bedroom.

After separate showers, she dressed in a T-shirt and sleep shorts, and he stripped to his boxers. Seeing him almost naked, silky skin over steel muscles, she felt the oxygen rush from the room and doubted her sanity for offering to let him stay. But as soon as they crawled underneath the covers and he'd wrapped his arms around her, she relaxed into his warmth. She'd been sure that she'd never find sleep, but the fatigue and emotions of the day won out, and she grew sleepy. *First night in my new house. My very own house. And with Luke here, it's perfect.*

13

Luke had fallen asleep with Allie's weight resting against his side and his arms wrapped around her. Soft, silky hair nestled under his chin, and her legs tangled with his. Sure, the urge was strong to wake her with kisses and strip them both before plunging his cock deep inside, but last night hadn't been about sex. It was about comfort. Care. Intimacy.

He'd drifted to sleep much easier than he'd imagined, slept much deeper than usual, and when he woke, couldn't believe how rested he felt. What he could believe was how horny he was. *Damn... her ass is pressed against my cock, and if I just slid her shorts to the side... nope!* As hard as it was to shut down that line of thinking, he managed to roll to his back and count backward to control his dick.

She started to stir, her eyes fluttering open. For a few seconds, her gaze shot around the room as though uncertain where she was before landing on him. Then her smile took his breath away.

"Happy first morning in your new house," he said, his fingers tracing over her cheek.

"It is with you here, that's for sure."

Her alarm sounded, and she scrunched her nose. "Shoot, I have to get ready for work. I really should have taken today off."

"I've got to get ready, also."

"Any chance you can stay for a quick breakfast? I might not have time for much, but I can offer you a bowl of cereal."

"I've got a clean scrub top in my vehicle," he replied, earning another smile.

"Well, all right." She leaned over and kissed him before tossing the cover off and darting into her bathroom. Calling over her shoulder, she said, "If you're wondering why I'm in such a hurry, I know if I stay in bed with you and your half-naked glory, I'll have to take a sick day because I won't let you out of my bed!"

She closed the door, and he fell back against the pillows, her words striking him in the heart as well as his cock. "Damn," he breathed out, then sucked in a deep breath before climbing from the bed, as well. He hadn't taken much time to really look at her house yesterday but now noticed the small deck and smiled at the two chairs she already had placed there. He wished they had more time to enjoy a leisurely cup of coffee sitting out there. *Maybe next time.* The idea of a next time had a smile curve his lips.

Once showered and dressed, he met her downstairs, where she'd found a couple of bowls and a box of sugary cereal. Lifting a brow as he raised the box, he grinned. "Seriously?"

She winced and nodded. "I know, I know. I tell my students they need to eat a good breakfast but never confess that I eat cereal that's so high in sugar. I swear, sometimes I do eat bagels or English muffins, occasionally a scrambled egg and bacon. Of course, that's usually on the weekends." Scrunching her nose, she added, "Sorry."

He leaned over the counter and kissed the end of her nose. "Hey, you opened your new home to me and offered me breakfast. I'm not gonna balk at what you have!"

They ate quickly, both needing to get to work, but compared weekly schedules. Rinsing out his bowl, he said, "I'm on call this week with the rescue squad, so any plans we make might change at the last minute. But I want to take you to dinner. Just figure out the best day for you."

She lifted her bowl, drained the last of her sweet milk, and nodded. "Other than the hours on Tuesday and Thursday afternoons at the jail, my after-school time is going to be spent here, unpacking and starting to make this place my own."

"I'll come help when I don't have a call-out," he offered, glad when she smiled easily and nodded. He didn't want to pressure her or come on too strong, but the desire to spend as much time with her as possible was hard to resist.

They walked out together, and even though her workday started before his, he figured he could get to the clinic early to make sure the exam rooms were ready.

All day at work, Luke felt as though the weight of the world was off his shoulders. He'd checked with Jeremy and Jessica's school to make sure they had money in their accounts for breakfast and lunch. He'd checked to make sure the older lady next door to them could still keep an eye on the kids when possible. He'd given Allie his whole story, past and present, and she hadn't bolted for the hills but instead had offered support and, in her special, sweet way, offered words of kindness.

Looking up as the next inmate walked in, just spying Gary was enough to knock Luke's good mood away. The pompous guard always liked to throw his weight around, and with this prisoner, he was no different. But as Luke looked toward the newcomer, he felt sure this man was not going to be cowed by the likes of Officer Perkins. He didn't need to see the records to recognize this middle-aged man had spent many years behind bars. Cold eyes. Bulked muscles. Skin covered in prison tattoos. Gary always made the mistake of threats and bluster, which might work on a younger, less hardened inmate. But for the likes of Ivan Stepanov, he looked like he could chew up and spit out a dozen guards like Gary.

It had never been Luke's dream job to work in a jail, but he wasn't afraid of the workplace. He figured it was better to have a big man like himself to deal with the inmates, in part to protect the female medical staff. Plus, he knew some inmates would only respond to another strong male, especially one who wasn't a guard. So, when the opportunity presented itself, and with the pay and benefits, he'd taken the job and hadn't regretted it.

And now, he instinctively knew how to handle Ivan. Calm. Quiet. Few words. Simple instructions. Not threatening. "I need to get your weight and height, Ivan. Then we'll do blood pressure, and I'll go over the check-list with you."

Ivan nodded and stepped onto the scale. Continuing the routine medical information gathering, he and Ivan spoke little, but there was no problem. He wished Gary would shut the fuck up, but the guard was determined to run his mouth.

"Too bad Ivan doesn't need help reading, 'eh? He could meet the pretty little teacher we got."

Ivan never lifted his eyes, appearing to completely blank out the mouthy guard. Luke prayed he could do the same. Focusing on the inmate, he recognized a few of the prison tattoos but gave no outward indication.

"Although, he might have forgotten how to—" Gary's words halted as his radio went off. He called out to Luke, "You okay here? I gotta get to the cafeteria."

Lifting his gaze to Ivan, he held the inmate's gaze before answering the guard. "Yeah."

As Gary hustled out, Ivan mumbled, "Man's a dick."

He didn't say anything, but then, he didn't need to. His silence could be interpreted by Ivan however he wanted, but in truth, Luke agreed.

As he finished with Ivan, he looked up and saw the man's gaze pinned on his nametag, which simply had his position and last name. North Heron Regional Jail

Medic, Purdue. The inmate's expression remained impassive as his gaze moved from the tag to Luke's face, but Luke wondered what the fuck the man was thinking.

Just then, Margaret walked out of the exam room with another inmate and guard. With that guard taking both men back to their cell blocks, Luke washed his hands.

"Other than having our favorite guard in here, you've seemed very happy today," she observed. Lifting a brow, she cocked her hip to the side. "Any particular reason? Such as maybe the sweet reading specialist?"

Normally stoic and in control, his head swung around so fast he almost felt dizzy. "What?"

"I happened to see the two of you in the parking lot the other evening," she said, her smile gentle.

His jaw tightened. Before he had a chance to come up with something to say, she walked over and placed her hand on his arm.

"You're a good man, Luke Purdue. And from what I hear, she's a good woman. Some people at my church have kids at the elementary school, and they sing her praises. If I could have picked out a woman that I think deserves you, it would be her."

He swallowed audibly, still uncertain what to say.

She smiled widely and patted his arm. "And don't let anyone like Officer Perkins get to you. He could only have a woman like her in his dreams."

She walked back into the lab, leaving him staring after her. And slowly, another smile crept over his face.

Between Allie's tutoring and his AL coaching schedule, it was Friday night before they finally had an evening all to themselves again. He'd wanted to take her out, but she'd insisted on cooking dinner. He wasn't sure if he'd be spending the night, but just in case, he tossed a backpack with a few toiletries and some clothes into his SUV.

Pulling into her drive, he could already see her stamp on the house. Two rockers sat on the porch, and he could already imagine them sharing a cup of coffee in the mornings out there. Curtains hung in the windows, and with the sheers closed, the soft glow from inside the house cast an inviting appeal.

He parked, and by the time he made it to the front door, she'd flung it open, greeting him with her bright smile. *Beautiful.* Her dark hair was pulled back with a headband, the gentle waves hanging around her shoulders. Her pink, long-sleeved T-shirt and jeans showed off her figure to perfection. And with pink fuzzy socks on her feet, she looked adorable. Bending, he placed his hand on her waist and kissed her lightly.

"Come in! Come in! I can't wait to show you what I've done!" she cried, grabbing his hand and pulling him forward.

He laughed and followed, then blinked as he took in the room. The boxes were gone, and the room looked much more spacious. The bookcases that flanked the fireplace were filled with groups of paperbacks and hardbacks, and he found himself curious as to her favorite genres to read. The sofa was placed against the front wall facing the fireplace and was now graced with a few comfy pillows and a warm blanket draped over the back. He could easily imagine her reading there then taking a nap. Two comfortable-looking, over-stuffed chairs were against the far wall, and a coffee table sat in the middle on a large rug.

Besides the curtains and sheers covering the windows, he could now see that the mantle contained framed photographs as well as several jars of sea glass, and the walls were decorated with an eclectic mix of paintings of the Chesapeake Bay as well as seafowl.

Turning in the other direction, it was easy to see the dining room was also larger than he'd originally thought. The room was centered with a table and four chairs, a wooden chest with a hutch that held dishes, photographs, and more sea glass.

"What do you think?"

He turned to see her standing next to him, uncertainty written over her face, and he wanted to erase all doubt. "Allie, babe, it's beautiful. It's a great house, and I can't believe you've gotten all this done this week along with everything else you had to do. I love it, but I wish you'd waited to let me help."

His words must have had the desired effect because she blew out a deep breath and her shoulders relaxed.

"Don't worry. There's still lots to do. I wanted to get this area done first so that if anyone came by, it would look nice. I've had a few friends stop by with house-warming gifts of casseroles which have almost filled up my freezer. I took care of the living room first and just finished the dining room yesterday when I got home from the jail. This table seats four easily, but there are two leaves that can be added to the middle. So, if I have a larger group, we'll have room for everybody as long as I can get some folding chairs."

Her brow furrowed, and he lifted his hand and smoothed her forehead. "Don't worry about that now. If you have people that come by, they can sit anywhere they need to."

She laughed and nodded. "You're right. I get so impatient that I want it all done now, but there's really no rush." She led him through the dining room and into the kitchen, saying, "I also got this room organized so that I could find what I needed to cook. The upstairs is pretty much a mess, but I've got time."

He stepped into the kitchen and sniffed appreciatively. He had no idea what she was cooking, but it smelled great.

She opened the oven door, pulled out a casserole dish, and set it on a trivet on the counter. Popping in some rolls, she closed the door. "I'm not a gourmet cook by any stretch of the imagination, but I love experimenting. This is chicken, vegetables, and ranch dressing all mixed together. Sounds weird, but I think you'll like it."

"Babe, other than the Army, I've never had anyone cook for me, and their food is hardly worth bragging about. So, this is amazing."

She beamed again, and it hit him how readily her smiles came. His mother taught him early that her smiles came with a price of him giving her what she wanted. And it had been his experience with the few women he'd dated that their smiles often were not much different from his mother's. He'd seen his friends' women laugh and smile from the heart but had never had that directed toward him. And he fucking loved it.

Glancing over her shoulder toward the back door, he linked fingers with her and said, "Come here."

She followed, and they stepped onto her patio. He turned her gently so that the sunset was shining over the bay beyond the trees in her backyard. She lifted her head, still smiling. "What are we doing out here?"

Bending, he kissed her in the middle of a smile with the sunset's light shining on them. Her lips were soft, and she immediately molded her body to his. His arms encircled her, holding her tight. He kept the kiss gentle and reverent, pouring emotion into every movement. He didn't want to end the kiss but neither did he want to ruin the dinner she'd fixed. Lifting his head regretfully, he smiled down at her. "We shared our first kiss at sunset. I wanted to share another one."

Her smile rivaled the brilliance of the sky, and with one last tug, he led her back into the kitchen.

After dinner, they reclined on the sofa, the TV on a music channel with a soft melody creating a calm atmosphere. They'd covered the basics of favorite colors, books, and music, and now she sat with her head on his shoulder, her hand resting on his chest, right over his heartbeat.

"Why the jail?" she asked softly.

"Hmm?" he mumbled, comfortable in his position,

his stomach full of the delicious dinner, and loving her in his arms.

She lifted her head. "I was just curious why you applied for the position in the jail." As soon as the words left her mouth, a wrinkle formed across her forehead, and she quickly said, "You don't have to answer. I'm sure it's private—"

He lifted her chin with his knuckle so that he could hold her gaze. "Babe, it's not private. And even if it was, I have no more secrets from you." He watched her face relax, then cupped her cheek, his thumb smoothing over her soft skin. "I spent part of my medic career at Fort Leavenworth in Kansas."

She blinked, her eyes widening slightly. "That's the Army's prison, isn't it?"

"In layman's terms, yes. It's the U.S. Disciplinary Barracks. I served there for one tour before going to Afghanistan. Vastly different experiences, both teaching me a lot. I know you might make the assumption that it was because of finding out my dad was in prison, but it wasn't. They needed medics, and I'd heard good things about the master sergeant there. I'm no bleeding heart, but it was my job to make sure the soldiers imprisoned there received quality healthcare. When I got out of the Army and my mom passed, I was looking for another job, but the career of medic doesn't immediately translate into a civilian job. I'd visited the Eastern Shore before, and when the jail position was advertised, I was interested. Mostly because it was Monday through Friday daytime hours, good pay, good benefits, and I knew I could handle the job."

She cocked her head to the side. "Handle the job?"

"There's a certain element of being with an inmate where being a physically big guy carries certain respect. They take one look at me and know that I can handle myself when needed. I'm quiet, don't get in their faces, and don't try to prove my dick is bigger. Believe me, with that population, all that works in my favor. My job isn't to shove it down their throats that I'm free and they're not. My job is to see them as individuals and take care of their medical needs to the best of my ability."

"Luke, I don't think you realize how amazing that sounds," she said, staring at him as though he'd hung the moon and stars.

He snorted. "Babe, think about your job. Hell, first of all, you work with a bunch of eight-year-olds all day long. Plus, the school system throws a bunch of duties on you that cut into your evenings and weekends. On top of that, the pay is shit for someone with your education! Then, you take on a part-time job working with men and women in jail, and you do it in a way that lets them know you're trying to help them without making them feel stupid. To me, that's pretty fuckin' amazing."

She smiled, and a little giggle slipped out.

Unable to resist, he kissed her smiling lips. This time, there was no reason to hold back, and the kiss flamed with their bodies pressed tightly together. Noses bumped as they twisted their faces, both attempting to obtain the best angle and erase any space between them at all.

His tongue swept through her mouth, and she

groaned, her fingers digging into his shoulders. Putting enough pressure with the flat of her hands, she pushed back, her breath ragged. "Take me to bed, please, Luke. And I'm not talking about sleeping."

Her words dove straight into him, his body vibrating with need. He clutched her face, holding her so that he had her full attention. "Babe, you are no fuck. We're not casual. What I feel for you is no friends with benefits, no fuck buddies. I'm all in, Allie, and I need to know if you are, too."

Her fingers clenched into his shoulders again, and she nodded. "I'm all yours, Luke."

"The beginning of us, right? Us as a couple?" he continued, wanting to make sure they were on the same page because he wasn't certain his heart could stand having her and then losing her.

Her smile widened, and she nodded slowly, her gaze never leaving his. "The beginning of us as a couple. Absolutely."

14

With linked fingers, Allie led Luke up the stairs. Their actions were so similar to the last time they'd climbed the stairs together, but this time, everything was different. Oh, the end result would be the same, with them wrapped around each other sleeping. But what would happen before that was going to change everything between them.

She knew sex didn't have to mean everything, but for her, it needed to mean something. She'd tried casual sex a couple of times in college and when she'd first been teaching in Virginia Beach but quickly learned that after the physical satisfaction, she was left feeling empty. She'd even envied her friends who walked away after a few hours of pleasure with smiles on their faces. For her, she'd always looked at her reflection in the mirror afterward and, while not feeling guilt, just felt nothing. Finally realizing that for her, sex needed an emotional connection, she'd been much more selective.

Even though she'd had a couple of boyfriends, they were nothing like what she felt when she was with Luke.

"What are you thinking about so hard?"

She jumped, realizing they were now at the top of the stairs and her mind had been a million miles away. Looking up, she smiled. "I guess I should warn you that for me, sex means something. So, if that scares you away, you should know it now."

He grinned as they reached her bedroom door and pulled her to a stop. With fingers still linked, he lifted his free hand and cupped her jaw. "There's a lot of things to love about you, Allie, but one of them is your honesty. I never have to figure out what you're thinking, where your mind is, or over-analyze something you say or do. You can't imagine how much I appreciate that. So, I'll be straight with you, too. Meaningless sex for me is just that: meaningless. Fun when I was younger, confusing when I was a little older, and not worth it now. So, just like you, sex means something. And what we're getting ready to do, with *you*, means everything."

The air left her lungs in a rush. "You're not a man who talks a lot, but when you do, I love what you have to say."

He bent slightly, his arms banding about her middle and lifting her easily. She wrapped her legs around his waist and held on as he stalked into her bedroom. Once he was next to her bed, he set her gently onto the edge of the mattress. Her hands toyed with the bottom of his T-shirt, slowly lifting it to expose the delectable ridge of muscles of his abs. He stood very still, his gaze pinned on hers, allowing her to appreciate the beauty of this man in front of her. When her arms had pushed the material as high as she could reach from her position, he snatched the material over his head, dropping it at his feet. Reaching into his pocket, he pulled out a condom packet and tossed it onto the nightstand.

Her gaze followed his movements before lifting back to his face. Smiling, she said, "Prepared?"

"And hopeful. As well as grateful to be with you," he replied, his voice rough with need.

She sucked in a quick breath. "Good answer. Really good answer."

Their clothes didn't come flying off in a flurry of arms and hands but rather a slow progression as though they both savored every tiny bit of exposed skin. Their movements weren't a tease but rather a small taste of what was to come. There were no words extolling the virtues of each other's bodies but rather a reverent appreciation. And to Allie, it was the most erotic experience she'd ever had, and they'd barely touched.

She lay back, her weight resting on her forearms, her legs dangling over the side of the bed, completely naked. He stood in front of her, his body on full display, and she dragged in oxygen with difficulty, wondering if it were possible to pass out from gorgeous overload. He was large but with muscles that bunched and moved underneath smooth skin. It wasn't that he looked like a bulging bodybuilder who'd just spent time in the gym but a man who valued his body and worked to stay in shape. A smattering of dark hair covered his chest, trailing down to where his erect cock jutted forward, a drop of pre-cum on the tip. She pulled in another breath as her gaze moved back up his body to where his eyes held hers.

"I think you're the most beautiful man I've ever seen," she whispered, unable to hold back the thoughts crowding in her mind.

His lips curved upward slightly, and he dropped to his knees in front of her, his hands resting on her knees. "I've never known such beauty existed until I knew you."

Her breath once again caught in her throat. She opened her mouth but slowly closed it, feeling too overwhelmed for words. As though he must have felt the same, he lowered his head and kissed both of her legs, his lips moving gently over the skin. She felt a tingling from the trail he left and felt sparks from such a simple touch.

As he moved forward, her legs opened wider to allow his shoulders to have enough room. Continuing to kiss along her inner thighs now, he moved toward the apex, his lips burning a path. Just when she thought the anticipation would drive her insane, his mouth settled over her sex, and she fell back onto the mattress, her arms no longer pretending to be able to hold her up. As he slowly licked and sucked, she was sure that flames would descend and didn't care if she ended up a pile of embers.

Her hand reached down to clutch his hair, glad it

was long enough on top for her to feel the silky strands as her fingernails lightly dragged over his scalp. His talented ministrations continued to send not just tingles but true electric jolts through her body, the synapses connecting from her sex to her nipples and outward in all directions.

Closing her eyes, she gave over to the physical sensations. She felt his tongue lick up her folds, and then a finger inserted as his mouth closed over her clit. Unable to control her movements, she writhed, lifting her hips in an involuntary desire to be closer to the source of the magic he was weaving. She was barely aware that her thighs rested over his shoulders, but she crossed her ankles behind his neck, pulling him closer, clutching him tightly. His free hand moved up her body, palming her breasts and rolling her nipples. Every inch of her was on fire, but it was deep inside her core that began to tighten, a yearning building.

"I need... I need..." she moaned, opening her eyes.

"I'll give you what you need, babe," he mumbled, and she felt his words vibrate against her sex.

The onslaught on her senses finally reached a peak, and she squeezed her eyes as her orgasm sent fireworks sparking through her body. Her fingers clutched the bedspread as he continued to lick and suck, and slowly, the sensations ebbed, and her legs fell limp. Uncertain she could move, she was barely aware of him crawling over her body, holding his weight off her as he kissed each breast and then moved to the ticklish side of her neck. A giggle erupted just before he slid his lips over to hers for a light kiss before he lifted again. She blinked her eyes open and stared at the blue eyes holding her captive.

Somehow finding the energy to wrap her arms around his neck, she pulled him down, kissing him deeply, tasting her essence on his lips.

She wrapped her legs around his waist, this time with her heels digging into his ass, urging him to take their bond to the next level, desperate to feel his thick cock inside and wanting to give him as much pleasure as she'd just felt.

His eyes cut to the side, and he rolled, flipping their positions. Surprised, she'd still managed to jerk her legs apart and now straddled his hips as he reached for the condom packet. Grinning, she took it from his fingers and ripped it open, then rolled it down his impressive erection. With his fingers clutching her waist, she lifted, positioning herself over him.

For a second, she considered plunging down, then decided to draw out the pleasure. Slowly easing, allowing his girth to fill her, her fingers were once again digging into the muscles of his shoulders. When she was halfway seated, she dropped her chin and stared at his face, witnessing the exquisite agony etched in his expression. Bending forward, she gently placed her lips on his as she settled fully. A groan rose from his chest, and she swallowed the sound. His fingers clenched tighter against her ass, and she felt certain she would have possessive marks the next day.

Lifting and plunging, she soon found her rhythm,

her body stretching to accommodate all of him. Her long hair fell around them, cocooning them from the world. His cock dragged along her inner core, the tingling once again increasing with each movement. She'd never felt this connected to any man. Sharing bodies... sharing souls. He completed her.

He slid one hand around to her tummy, then up, his palm stopping between her bouncing breasts before moving over to caress one, his thumb teasing her nipple. Once again, she was overtaken with sensations firing between her sex, deep inside her core, and her breasts. Her movements slowed, and with his grip, he lifted her slightly so he had room to piston his hips upward, taking over their rocking motion.

Feeling her body shake, she knew she wasn't going to last long. "I'm going to..."

"Let go, Allie. Give it all to me," he ordered, the words guttural.

As though all she needed was his permission, her body tightened, and she shuddered as another orgasm flung her over the precipice she'd clung to. As the coils inside her finally loosened, he seemed to swell, and then he groaned loudly, his face red and muscles taut as his own release had him plunging as far as he could go. She knew before their bodies joined that Luke was much more endowed than any man she'd been with. Now, she'd never felt so full, so complete.

Her arms gave out, unable to hold her up anymore, and she flopped on top of his chest. With his cock still buried deep inside, she pressed her face into his neck and breathed deeply. The scent of their coupling filled the air, mingling with the woodsy musk from him. Uncertain if she was crushing him, she was very certain she was incapable of moving. The ability to speak coherently seemed to have left her as she grunted, "Too heavy?"

He chuckled, and her whole body felt it through his chest.

"Hardly," he replied. His one-word answer seemed to prove that he had also lost the ability to speak.

She giggled, and at the sound, he rolled them again, this time so that they were side-by-side facing each other. Her head rested on his bicep as his arms were still banded around her. Their legs were tangled, and their bodies were pressed flush together. She was still smiling when he dipped his head and kissed her, his tongue sweeping inside.

Pulling back, he grinned. "I love kissing your smile."

She bit her lip, blinking at the sting in her eyes. Swallowing deeply, she said, "Every time I think you've said the sweetest thing, you say something even sweeter."

This time he had no reply, but his arms flexed and somehow managed to pull her closer. Her body sated, she started to close her eyes when he sighed heavily. Popping them open as his arms loosened, she hated the idea that he was leaving. "Do you have to go?" She hoped her voice didn't sound whiny but had no problem with begging.

He chuckled again. "Gotta take care of the condom, Allie."

"Oh," she grunted, scrunching her nose. "I never thought about that."

"But if you're inviting, I'm staying—'"

"You're invited!" she rushed, grinning. She loosened her grip, and he slid from the bed, stalking into her bathroom. She took the opportunity to also climb out before pulling the covers down. She heard the toilet flush, and he walked out, looking every inch as gorgeous as when she first laid eyes on him. "Wow," she breathed. "I don't think I would ever get tired of staring at you."

He pulled her tight, kissing her forehead as her cheek rested over his heartbeat. "I know I'd never get tired of looking at you, babe."

She jerked her head toward the bed and said, "Go ahead and get settled. I'll be right back." Scooting into the bathroom, she quickly took care of her business, brushed her teeth, took off her makeup, and moisturized, then flipped off the light before she hurried back to the bed. He was lying in the middle, propped up with his elbow bent and his head in his hand.

"In case I didn't make myself clear earlier, I also would never get tired of seeing you in my bed," she admitted, her smile wide.

He patted the mattress. "Don't keep me waiting while you stand over there."

For just a second, she considered taking a sultry walk toward the bed, giving him a teasing show, then almost immediately dismissed it as she raced forward and jumped into the bed, landing next to him. Rolling quickly, their bodies slammed together, eliciting an 'umph' from him. Laughing, she mumbled 'sorry' as they kissed again. She'd thought she was ready to go to sleep but found that he had stamina, and she had renewed energy. And it didn't take long for her to be glad for both.

15

A buzzing from the floor slowly pulled Luke from his deep sleep. Still wrapped around Allie, he rolled to his back and discerned where the sound was coming from. He wanted to ignore his phone still buried in his jeans pocket but grew concerned when the buzzing began again. Wondering if something had happened at the jail, he carefully slid his arm from underneath her neck and shifted to the side of the bed, making sure to tuck the covers warmly around her.

Allie kept a small nightlight on in the bathroom, and with the slight illumination, he found his jeans and pulled his phone out. Blinking, he stared at the unknown number. The buzzing continued, so he connected the call. "Luke Purdue."

"Mr. Purdue, this is Evelyn Harper. I'm a neighbor of Chelle Purdue—"

"What's wrong? Are the kids okay?" He knew who she was since he'd asked her to keep an eye out for the kids.

"Yes, they're fine. There's been activity next door, and the police and rescue people have been in and out. I brought the kids over here with me until I knew what to do. But they're upset, and I don't know how to get hold of their daddy—"

"Keep them with you. Don't let them out of your sight. I have no idea what's happening, but I'll get there as soon as I can."

"Now, don't you worry, Mr. Purdue. You be safe, and the kids will be fine with me until you can figure out what's going on." She lowered her voice to a whisper. "They're upset, but they're fine. But you need to know..." she lowered her voice even more, "the rescue people left with their mom on a stretcher. I heard one of them say something about an overdose."

"Oh, Christ. Jesus Christ," he groaned, barely able to catch his breath. "I'll... I'll get there as soon as I can." He disconnected but stared at his phone shaking in his hands, trying to sift through what Mrs. Harper had told him.

"Honey, what's wrong?" Allie dropped from the bed to his side as he knelt on the floor, wrapping her arms around him.

He looked toward her, seeing anguish on her face as she stared at him. Swallowing, he sucked in a deep breath. "That was Chelle's neighbor... she's got the kids."

"What did she say? What's happened?"

"She said the police and the rescue squad had been over there. She didn't know what was going on, but the kids were upset so she took them back to her place.

They know her. She babysits when Chelle can't handle things or is partying or too drunk to look after them. Whatever. Anyway, they must be nearby because then she lowered her voice and said…"

He halted, and she tightened her grip on him. "What did she say, Luke?"

He stared at her, his mind filled with so many different scenarios, barely able to focus. "She warned me that Chelle was taken out on a stretcher. She may have overdosed."

"Oh, no!"

She leaped to her feet and rushed toward the bathroom, still as naked as when they'd gone to bed. Calling over her shoulder, she said, "I'll get dressed, and we can go together!"

Suddenly coming unstuck, he jumped up from the floor. Jerking on his boxers and jeans, he'd barely gotten them zipped when she came bolting from the bathroom wearing panties and bra, pulling her hair into a pony-tail. Stalking over to her, he stopped her forward movement with his hands on her shoulders. "No, babe. Allie, I don't want you to go with me."

"Why? I can help! I can help with the kids!"

With the fog of surprise now lifted, he went into planning mode. "Listen, sweetheart, I'm not keeping you out of anything, but I don't know what I'm walking into." She opened her mouth to speak, but he shook his head, grateful when she waited. "The kids are safe with Mrs. Harper, and they know her. I'm going to be making calls while on the road, trying to find out what happened and seeing if I can get hold of Larry.

Normally during the night, I couldn't, but if there's been an emergency, then I think I can get through."

"Luke, are you sure you don't want company?"

He dropped his head back and stared at the ceiling for a few seconds and sighed. "I don't know." Lowering his chin, he held her gaze. "No, I need to figure out what to do and it may take a while. I'm family and the kids will want me to be with them. And if something has happened to Chelle, I want them to be with me." She was nodding, but as soon as those words left his mouth, he thought about his apartment. "I hate to ask you to do anything but—"

"Ask, please ask. I can't just stay here and not do something."

"I won't be back for a while. It will take me a couple of hours to get there. I might have to go to the jail to see Larry, I'll have to find out from the police or hospital what's going on with Chelle, and then I've got to get the kids. So there's no rush, but if I give you keys to my apartment and some money, can you at least get some food that the kids will eat? I'll—"

She stopped his words with her fingers against his lips. "Give me your keys, and I'll take care of everything here. I desperately want to go with you, but I understand that you've got a lot to do, and I don't want to be in your way. So, at least if I'm here, I'll make sure everything is ready for you and the kids when you get back."

He pulled her in close, his arms holding her close. As her hands snaked around his waist and pulled him tight, he felt the shaking in his body ebb. "Can't thank you enough, Allie. If I was doing this alone…"

She leaned back and held his gaze, her lips curving, but he could see it was forced under the circumstances. "Luke, we decided last night that we were a couple. Together. Us. You and me. And there's never a good time for a crisis, but we're going to face this one as a couple together. It doesn't matter that we've just started, we've got this."

Her words left him breathless as his heart clenched. He'd never had anyone in his life that was offering so much. He'd had fellow soldiers who'd given friendship and support. And since he'd been in Baytown, he'd found that same kind of rapport with new friends. But he'd never had anyone look at him with such trust and adoration, giving him everything they had in return. If he had the time to stand and revel in her embrace and words, he would have. But now, with a clear mind, he had to get to Jeremy and Jessica.

He dressed quickly as she raced downstairs, still in her underwear, but his focus was now firmly on what he needed to do. *Chelle taken out. Stretcher. Overdose. Christ almighty... what did the kids see?* He couldn't summon any emotions about Chelle at the moment, not having enough information, but just knowing Jeremy and Jessica might have witnessed something traumatic had his chest ache.

By the time he got downstairs, Allie was already pouring a travel mug of coffee. She also had an insulated bag that she handed to him. "Here. This is cheese crackers, granola bars, my diet-buster stash of candy, and some water bottles. Don't forget to give me your keys."

"Oh, yeah," he mumbled, the sight of her in her underwear rushing around the kitchen seared into his brain. He jerked out his keys and worked off one. "This is the apartment. Now, don't do much, but if you can get some food for the kids, that'd be great."

She hurried around the counter and pressed close, her palms flat on his chest as she looked up. "Don't worry about a thing. I'll take care of everything here. But please, Luke, be safe, and if you get a chance to shoot me a text or call so I know how you're doing, I'd love it."

Wrapping her in his arms, he kissed her, fast but heavy, full of emotion. "Last night was fuckin' fantastic, Allie. Best night I've ever had in my life. I hate like hell it had to end this way."

Still holding his gaze, she reached up and cupped his jaw. "Luke, honey, last night was just the beginning. We can have a lot of nights like that. Now, go so you can bring those precious children back."

With one last kiss, he headed out to his SUV and ten minutes later was already on the Bay Bridge heading west. Trying to decide who to call first, his phone rang. Grateful it was tied into his vehicle, he touched his steering wheel to connect. "Luke Purdue."

"Mr. Purdue, this is Mrs. Harper again. The kids have gone to sleep, so I thought I'd give you a call since I was trying to be careful of what I said earlier. When I ran over to see what was happening, one of the detectives let me take the kids since I was a neighbor and had babysat the kids before. I told the detective that I was going to call their uncle and that their dad was in jail.

He told me that social services would come by if there was no one in the family to take the kids, but I told him that I felt sure you'd come to get them."

"Absolutely. I can't thank you enough, Mrs. Harper."

"Chelle talks about you, so I knew you were a good man. Not that she would say that, but she always talked about how you would buy things for the kids and not her. I read between the lines and knew you were just taking care of those kids and not letting her waste any money. But Mr. Purdue... you need to know." She sighed heavily. "Chelle wasn't moving when they took her out. I was busy making sure the kids didn't see anything, but I don't know what they saw before someone called 9-1-1."

"Who made the call?" he asked.

"I don't know, but the kids were asleep."

His chest depressed as the air rushed from his lungs. He wasn't surprised to know that Chelle was using drugs, but... *Fuckin' hell... an overdose... using with the kids there?* At that moment, he didn't care what kind of man it made him. If he'd had any idea it was that bad, he would have fought to take the kids from her and Larry.

"Mr. Purdue? Are you still there?"

Sucking in a deep breath and trying to settle his mind but failing miserably, he replied, "Yes, ma'am, I'm here. I'm afraid I'm still trying to wrap my mind around everything. But the most important thing is that the kids are safe. If anyone comes by, make sure you tell them that their uncle is on his way. I might have to stop by the jail first, but I'll be there as soon as I can."

"You take care of what you need to," she advised.

"The kids are fast asleep in my second bedroom. It's not the first time they spent the night here, so they're fine."

Wincing at whatever reason Chelle would have left the kids overnight with an elderly neighbor, he forced that from his mind. Getting pissed at Chelle right now wasn't going to do anyone any good. "Mrs. Harper, do you have the name of that detective you spoke to?"

"Yes, he gave me his card and told me that if I can get in touch with you to have you call him."

"Can you text me his name and number? I'm driving, but I can call him from my vehicle."

"Oh, yes. My grandson showed me how to do that. I'll send it right now."

Thanking her again, he disconnected the call and waited anxiously until her message came through with the phone number and the name of Detective Matt Dixon. With another push of a button, he called the number.

"Detective Dixon? This is Luke Purdue. It's my understanding that you were the attending detective for Chelle Purdue earlier this evening."

"Yes, I was."

"I'm her brother-in-law. I've heard from the neighbor who has my niece and nephew. I'm on my way to Richmond now to pick them up. I was hoping you could give me some information so I have a few more facts before I do that."

"I take it you're Larry Purdue's brother?"

"Yes, sir, I am. But if you're wondering if my brother and I are anything alike, then no, sir, we're not. You can check me out before I get to Richmond so you'll know who you're dealing with. I work for the North Heron Regional Jail as a medic after having spent ten years as a medic for the U.S. Army. Warden Neely and Sheriffs Colt Hudson and Liam Sullivan can vouch for me."

"That's an impressive list of character references, Mr. Purdue."

"I'll be frank with you, Detective Dixon. There's no love lost between me and my brother and sister-in-law. But I'll do anything for my niece and nephew. They're just children who are innocent victims in this. I've been assured by Mrs. Harper, the neighbor that has them, that they didn't see anything. But I'm hoping you can give me some information so that I'll know what I'm walking into when I pick them up."

"A 9-1-1 call came in from a woman who claimed to be a friend of your sister-in-law. She said they'd been out partying, and when they got back to Chelle's apartment, her friend passed out and wouldn't wake up. The call came in from your sister-in-law's phone, so we don't know who made the call, but by the time the rescue squad got there, this *friend* was gone, assumedly because she'd been taking whatever Mrs. Purdue had taken."

"She was out partying and the kids were alone?" His voice rose with each word, his blood boiling.

"As far as we can tell, yes."

Choking back the rage that coursed through him, he asked, "Do you know if Mrs. Harper is right and they didn't see anything?"

"The paramedics worked on her. One of the police officers noticed a bedroom door opening and discovered two children inside. A female officer stayed with them in the bedroom until Mrs. Purdue was taken outside. She was transported to the hospital. Once the paramedics left with her, Mrs. Harper hurried in and took charge of the children. They appeared to know her and trust her, and the female officer went next door to make sure everything was okay. She said she was calling you, and to be honest, you were on my list to call. I just got off the phone with the warden at the Richmond jail, and they are letting Larry know his wife is hospitalized and the children will need to be cared for."

"Christ!" Luke bit out, fury at Chelle renewed. Forcing his voice to calm so that the detective didn't think he was a hothead who couldn't be controlled, he sucked in a ragged breath and let it out slowly.

"Mr. Purdue, you'll need to talk to the hospital tomorrow for an update on her condition. She was unresponsive when they took her in."

His mind racing, he tried to think of all the questions he needed to ask. "Detective Dixon, do I need to go to the jail? Do I need to get written permission from my brother to take the children? Can I get the kids and get them back to Baytown so that they're with me and safe first and then deal with my brother?"

"Legally, of course, your brother is their father and would have a say over where they go. If you're the only relative who can take care of them, then the state would much prefer a relative to handle everything. To be on the safe side, it might not be a bad idea to go by the jail, talk to your brother, and get him to sign any kind of paper that says he agrees for you to be the guardian of the children until he's able to take care of them himself."

"Okay, that's what I'll do." Luke hated to take the time to do that, but if the kids were still asleep, it was better to go ahead and get that done. "One last question, Detective Dixon. I don't want the kids to go into a foster situation. I have a full-time job. I'll make sure they get into school, and I can take care of them. Is there anything I should prepare for?"

"I can't say for sure, Mr. Purdue, but be prepared for a state social worker to come by sometime to check on the children. I don't know when that will happen or how it will happen. And to be honest, they're so backed up with cases it might not even happen. What I will need you to do is leave your contact information with me."

Readily agreeing, Luke rattled off his phone number and address before thanking the detective and disconnecting the call. Scrubbing his hand over his face, he sipped the coffee that Allie had made as he drove west through the Hampton Roads area on Highway 64 toward Richmond.

With nothing else to do for the moment other than drive, he allowed his thoughts to focus on her. His beautiful Allie. The night they'd spent making love. The acknowledgment of what they wanted to share and what they wanted to become. The future he hoped they had. *And now... who knows what will happen?* Blocking out the fear that clawed its way up his throat, he focused on the road as the sky barely began to lighten as a new day was dawning.

16

A couple of hours later, Luke sat in a stark, painted cinder block room at a metal table bolted to the floor, in a hard plastic chair, staring at his piece-of-shit brother. After arriving at the jail, he had to wait as his special request to see Larry was approved by the warden due to a family emergency since it wasn't regular visiting hours. When they brought Larry into the visitor's room, Luke had no idea what he'd expected, but some show of emotion over Chelle's condition or concern over the kids would have been fitting.

Instead, Larry had been twitchy. He constantly looked around as though he expected a detective to burst in and accuse him of Chelle's drug use.

"I don't know, bro," Larry said, shaking his head. "I can't believe she fuckin' OD'd. I mean, Christ, she should have been smarter. She was never smart, though. Shit!" He grimaced, looking around again. "I mean, who knows who she was involved with? They can't pin this on me. I didn't know what she was taking. I didn't know she had anything. They better not try to come after me for this!"

After ten minutes of listening to Larry say the same thing over and over, Luke lost his patience. "Look, man, this isn't getting us anywhere. All I want to do is make sure Jeremy and Jessica are taken care of. So, for once, will you stop thinking of yourself and think of them?"

Larry blinked, his gaze jerking back to Luke's. Nodding, he said, "Yeah, yeah. Jessica and Jeremy. Sure, you can have 'em."

Luke's brows lifted to his hairline, a growl erupting. "Have? Like you're giving away an old piece of furniture? What about when you get out here?"

"Come on, Luke, you know what I mean. Once Chelle gets her stomach pumped, she can have 'em back. Or if she's fucked up, then I'll find someone else."

"Someone else?"

Larry's hands twitched on top of the table. "Yeah. Like some chick who'll make sure they get fed and stuff. I know you'll always help out, too. But I can't be playing daddy and take care of myself, too."

Playing daddy. A strange mixture of icy cold and hot fury combined as it ran through Luke's veins. He'd never made excuses for Larry's weaknesses but often ignored them. But now, it didn't matter how much he was used to those weak traits in his brother, there was no coming back from the anger he felt at hearing Larry's easy dismissal of his children. It took every ounce of self-control to keep from planting his fist in the middle of Larry's face.

162

Instead, he pulled out a form the warden had provided as he explained that often, parents in jail had to make provisions for their minor children. Glad to have it, he'd thanked the warden and now pushed it across the table toward Larry. "Sign this."

Larry leaned back as though Luke was handing him a snake. "What's that? Is this a trick? Is that some kind of confession?"

"No, asshole. Read the top line. This form gives me temporary guardianship over Jessica and Jeremy." He knew Larry didn't care about the kids but also knew Larry would be quick to look for a way to make money out of any situation. Deciding to hit Larry where he would care, Luke said, "This means that I'll pay for their care while they're with me and you won't have to."

At that, Larry gave the expected wide-eyed jolt. "I don't have any money to take care of the kids!"

"Then it will be good for you to sign so that I'm the one who takes care of them. They can be covered under my health insurance, and I'll pay for their food and clothes and school supplies." It was on the tip of his tongue to add that other than health insurance, he'd been paying for them anyway, but he kept his mouth shut.

At the idea that someone would expect him to take care of his kids financially, Larry grabbed the pen that Luke held out to him. Signing at the bottom, he said, "This is good, Luke. They're a lot better with you. And with Chelle gone and you being their uncle, it'll be good for you to have them."

Breathing easier now that Larry had signed, he

pushed his chair back and stood. "The warden will be talking to you later today—"

"About what?" Larry squeaked, eyes wide again.

Sighing, Luke shook his head. "I expect it'll be about Chelle. Her in the hospital… maybe facing charges… who knows." Seeing Larry opening his mouth, he threw his hand up. "No, man. That's on you. My deal is to care for the kids. They'll be with me." At that, he turned and walked out, noting the chin lift of approval from the guard at the door. He acknowledged it but didn't need it. It was not only the right thing to do for Jeremy and Jessica, but it was also what he wanted. *I just wish I'd known how bad it had gotten, and I would have done this sooner!*

By then, it was almost lunchtime, and he hurried to the apartment complex to get the kids. He'd called Mrs. Harper to let her know he was on his way. Pulling into the parking lot, he ignored the pang he felt in his chest when his gaze moved to Larry's apartment. There was no yellow tape across the door, but then, if it wasn't a crime scene, there wouldn't be. He needed to get in to pack the kids' clothes and hoped Mrs. Harper would have a key.

Climbing from his SUV, he clicked the doors locked, then hurried up the concrete steps. The kids must have been watching for him because the door next to theirs flew open and they rushed out together. He squatted, throwing his arms open wide, bracing as their slight weights hit him full force. Gathering them to his chest, he squeezed his eyes tightly shut for a moment as they burrowed closer to him. Then, needing to check them over himself, he opened his eyes and moved his head from side to side, but they were so tucked into him all he could see was the tops of their hair.

"Hey, guys. You need to loosen your grip a little bit so I can make sure you really are Jessica and Jeremy."

Jessica's head popped back first, her smile beautiful. "Silly Uncle Luke! Of course, we're Jessica and Jeremy!"

Jeremy's grip loosened also, but when he leaned back, there was uncertainty in his gaze. "Uncle Luke, we came out to make sure you knew we were at Mrs. Harper's."

"Yeah, she called me and said you guys are having a sleepover."

Jessica grinned. "I like having a sleepover at Mrs. Harper's. The bed is soft, and her place smells nice. And she makes cookies!"

"That's great, sweetheart." Glancing at Jeremy, he got the feeling that his nephew wanted to say something, but Jeremy's eyes kept cutting toward Jessica. "Hey, Jessica, why don't you go tell Mrs. Harper that I'm here? I'll be right in."

"Okay!" she agreed and turned to skip back to Mrs. Harper's apartment. Disappearing inside, they could hear her call out, "Mrs. Harper! Uncle Luke is here!"

Still kneeling to stay on his nephew's level, Luke put his hand on Jeremy's shoulder. "I know we've only got a moment, but is there something you want to tell me?"

Jeremy winced. "Mom got sick last night, Uncle Luke. I don't know what happened, but when I woke up, there were police and an ambulance there. I guess they took Mom to the hospital. But Mrs. Harper came and got us, and we spent the night with her. She said you were coming, and we were going to go with you but..."

He shrugged, wincing again. He turned his eyes up toward Luke, and this time hope was shining out of them. "I don't like the people that come to visit Mom. And she was always taking the stuff that you gave us and selling it. And lately, she's been drinking a lot, sometimes not waking up for hours. Can we come home with you? Please?"

Feeling as though his heart was being ripped from his chest, he pulled Jeremy in for a hug, understanding this eight-year-old boy knew a lot more about what was going on than Luke realized. *And Jeremy was handling a fuck-of-a-lot more than any eight-year-old boy should have on his shoulders.* "Jeremy, I'm here to take you and Jessica home with me. There are a lot of things we'll talk about, but the time that you stop worrying about anything other than just being a little boy is now. I'm gonna take care of you."

He felt Jeremy's body shudder and then relax, and it was all he could do to keep from squeezing him even tighter.

Just then, Jessica popped out of Mrs. Harper's doorway again, calling, "Come on, sillies!"

Standing, he kept his hand on Jeremy's shoulder as they moved into Mrs. Harper's apartment. Luke was more than pleased to see that while the apartment complex was crappy, her apartment was clean, warm, and inviting.

Thanking her profusely, she waved her hand. "I was just being neighborly, and to be honest, these two darlings are always wonderful to have around."

"We come over here all the time!" Jessica announced. "Mrs. Harper makes cookies. Mama never makes cookies."

Luke smiled, sharing a look with Mrs. Harper over Jessica's head. Then, smiling down at her, he said, "Sweetheart, why don't you and Jeremy gather all of your things that are in Mrs. Harper's house, and I'm going to talk to her for a moment."

Jessica, happy as always, skipped toward the back bedroom. Jeremy, appearing to sense that the adults needed to talk, held Luke's gaze, then nodded before following his sister.

He lifted his hand and rubbed it over his chest, shaking his head. "Christ, that eight-year-old looks like he's got the eyes of an adult." Turning back to Mrs. Harper, he said, "I know we need to talk fast, but I promise to fill you in more as I can. Chelle overdosed on God knows what drugs. I knew Larry did drugs, but I had no idea Chelle was a user. If I had, I'd have stepped in earlier. I have a signed form from Larry that gives me guardianship, and the warden and Detective Dixon know I'm taking the kids back to the Eastern Shore with me. I'll get them in school and take care of them. My girlfriend is a teacher, and I've got friends who are in law enforcement. In fact, one of my close friends is the fire chief, and his wife is a counselor. I'm going to make sure the kids have everything they need."

She reached out and grasped his hands, tears shining

in her eyes. "Mr. Purdue, I've done what I can, but I've prayed for those children so much. You are the answer to my prayers."

"Well, you've got to know you have my undying gratitude, as well. I'd like to get everything out of their apartment that belongs to them. Do you happen to have a key? And do you know what it looks like over there?"

Her head bobbed up and down as she reached over to pull a key out of the small tray on her kitchen counter. "When the police left, I took a quick look, and there's nothing to see. It just looks like their apartment. Here's a key. Chelle gave it to me last year when she often wasn't home when the kids got out of school. Jessica's preschool would bus her to Jeremy's school, and they'd come home together."

Sucking in a deep breath through his nose, he let it out slowly, once again trying to tamp down his anger against Chelle. Barely managing to stay in control, he nodded as the kids bounded back into the room. Telling the kids to hug Mrs. Harper and thank her, he watched as they clung to her with promises to call, come back and visit, and have her come to see them. He picked up their backpacks then moved them to their apartment.

"Okay, kids, here's the deal. Right now, you know your dad isn't around, and neither is your mom. So, you two are going to come live with me."

Jeremy sighed in relief, and Jessica jumped up and down.

"I don't know when we'll be back, so we're going to pack everything you have and take it with us. I need to get the car seat and booster out of your mom's car—"

"We don't have one," Jeremy said.

Lifting his brows, he stared. "Never?"

Jeremy shook his head. "I remember she had a baby thing that was buckled in for Jessica, and I guess I had one when I was a baby. But we haven't had anything since then."

"Okay, then as we're driving back to my place today, I need you all to stay buckled in. And first thing tomorrow, I'll get the right kind of seats for you two. So, let's get everything packed." It didn't take him long to realize there was no suitcase, but he found garbage bags under the kitchen sink. Helping Jessica first, he filled the bags with her clothes and what few toys and books he could find. Angry that so much of what he had bought them wasn't there, he tamped down those feelings as well, but his stomach churned. Wondering if he was going to get an ulcer from burying so much frustration, he focused on the kids.

By the time he finished helping Jessica, Jeremy had most of his things stuffed in garbage bags, as well. The kids had shared a room but were to the age where that needed to stop. *Christ, they're going to be sharing a room at my place, too.* He'd be sleeping on the sofa but didn't care about that. *As soon as I can, I gotta find something better for them.*

He and the kids made a couple of trips to his SUV, filling the back with the few bags. They made one last visit to the apartment, and he opened the refrigerator to toss out any food that might go bad, finding it almost empty. Dropping his chin to his chest, he closed his eyes and counted to ten. Feeling a presence near him, he opened his eyes to see Jeremy looking up at him.

"She'd sell the food that you would have the grocery store deliver. Jessica and I learned to hide some in our room."

Swallowing deeply, he placed his hand on Jeremy's shoulder and squeezed. "I'm sorry, buddy."

Jeremy shrugged. "It's not your fault, Uncle Luke."

He nodded but silently disagreed with his nephew, feeling the weight of not having checked on them more often. "You and your sister take a look around the living room, your room, and the bathroom to make sure there's nothing else you need. I'm going to check your mom's room."

Opening the door to Chelle and Larry's bedroom, he grimaced at the mess. Clothes lay scattered around. The carpet appeared as though it had never seen a vacuum cleaner. The nightstand held an ashtray filled with cigarette butts. Beer cans and liquor bottles were scattered about. Opening the closet, it only held a few clothes and shoes. Moving into the connecting bathroom, he noticed the medicine cabinet open but no pill bottles. Figuring the police officers took anything they found as possible evidence of what she might have been taking, he walked out.

Meeting the kids in the living room, he faced them with a smile. Clapping his hands and rubbing them together, he said, "Who's ready to go to Uncle Luke's place?"

"Me! Me!" the kids yelled.

"I'll warn you, it's not very big. But it'll do for now."

Jessica was twirling, and Jeremy walked straight to him, looking up. "Don't worry about it, Uncle Luke. Anything is better than this. And just being with you will be the best of all."

Feeling those words in his heart as well as his gut, Luke dipped his chin. "Well, okay, then. Let's get going."

17

Allie paced the floor of Luke's apartment, alternating between checking her phone for the latest message, looking at the time, and going back through the space to make sure it was perfect. As soon as he'd left, she'd dressed and driven to his apartment. It didn't matter that it was before daylight. She knew she wouldn't be able to go back to sleep and wanted to make sure she had plenty of time to get it ready.

Once there, she'd scrubbed the entire apartment even though it was already clean. Luke was very neat, but she'd felt the urge to make sure it was spotless. Plus, it gave her a way to burn off the extra energy she'd felt coursing through her. She had no idea what his niece and nephew had gone through but had worked with enough children over the years to know that they would need extra love and protection.

Once the apartment was thoroughly scrubbed, she'd checked his refrigerator and pantry, making a list of what she would need to buy. Glad he had a stackable washer and dryer in his apartment, she'd stripped the bed and threw in the linens. Once that was accomplished, she took her list and drove to the closest grocery store as soon as they opened. Seeing the dollar store next to the grocery, she hit it first.

An extra set of sheets, new towels and bath cloths, new pillows, kid's shampoo, toothpaste and toothbrushes, and soap went into the cart. She had no idea what size they were but grabbed some crayons and coloring books, a few reading books, a board game, and ponytail holders, as well. Just before she made it to the checkout line, she spied a soft, purple stuffed cat. Tossing that in as well, she paid for the items and shoved them into the backseat of her small car.

Once inside the grocery store, she'd walked up and down the aisles, filling the cart with everything that the kids would need and want. Fresh fruit and vegetables, whole-grain bread, fish and chicken, milk, juice, and several tasty pre-made meals from the grocery's deli. Knowing it would only take a call to their friends to have meals and desserts brought over, she'd decided to wait and talk that over with Luke first. Not knowing what he wanted to tell people, she knew that was a boundary she didn't want to step over.

In the bakery section, she'd added fresh rolls, cookies, and an apple pie before heading to the frozen foods. There, chicken nuggets, pizza bites, frozen veggies, and, of course, ice cream finished her shopping.

The cashier glanced at the cart piled high and lifted her eyebrows. "Are you buying for an army?"

Laughing, she'd shaken her head. "A friend has some

relatives visiting, so I wanted to help them out." Using her credit card, she'd quickly paid and rolled all the bags out to her car. She'd filled the rest of the space, including the passenger seat, and drove back to his apartment. After several trips up and down the stairs, she was gasping by the time she'd unloaded her car. Standing in his living room, she'd looked around at the mess she'd made.

Checking her messages, she'd spied that he was just leaving the jail after having met with Larry and was heading to the kids' place. Relieved she had plenty of time, she put away all the food in the pantry and refrigerator, washed the new sheets and linens, unfolded the sleeper sofa in the living room, and put Luke's clean sheets onto that bed before pushing and tugging the squeaky spring frame into a sofa. After making his bed for the kids, she'd placed the crayons, books, game, and stuffed cat on the coffee table to greet them when they arrived. Finally, she'd gathered all the bags, making sure the apartment was neat once again.

She'd typed out a quick message. **Apartment ready. I'm fixing kid-friendly food for your arrival.**

It only took a moment for Luke to send a message in return. **Don't go to any trouble. I'm grateful for anything you've done. See you soon.**

She'd looked around, pleased with her work, but nerves still made their way through her veins. Heading into his small kitchen, she'd decided that chicken nuggets, carrot sticks, apple slices, and french fries would be the perfect welcome meal for two tired kids and a probably very-tired uncle.

Making sure everything was ready to pop into the oven, she'd sat on the sofa and channel surfed until her eyelids grew heavy.

When her phone buzzed, she jumped and looked at the time, seeing she'd slept for an hour. Grabbing her phone off the coffee table, she blinked through blurry eyes to see Luke's message telling her they were about thirty minutes away. Hopping up, she popped the chicken nuggets and french fries into the oven and set plates on the small table. Then she began to pace. Again.

A noise from outside had her rush to the window and looked down to see Luke's SUV parking outside. Hurrying to the door, she threw it open as the sound of his heavy footsteps could be heard on the stairs along with much lighter steps. Around the bend in the stairs, her gaze landed on him, and her heart leaped at the sight. In his arms, he carried a blue-eyed, dark-haired little girl, and a young, blue-eyed, dark-haired boy was trailing right behind him.

Luke lifted his tired gaze to her, and his smile nearly brought her to her knees. "Hey," she said, her voice soft.

"Hey, you," Luke replied, reaching the landing.

She stepped back in haste and smiled down at the little boy who was looking up at her with wide eyes. "Hello. You must be Jeremy. I'm Allie."

Jeremy's gaze jerked from his uncle to her before he smiled. "Allie. Cool name."

She laughed. "It's short for Allison."

"I'm Jessica!" the little girl said, lifting her head from Luke's shoulder. "You're pretty!"

"Well, I was just going to say the same thing about you, beautiful."

Jessica smiled again, her whole face bright. "Are you Uncle Luke's girlfriend?"

Allie's gaze jerked toward Luke, uncertain what he wanted her to say. He jiggled Jessica in his arms and said, "Yes, she is. Allie's my beautiful girlfriend, and she gets to be your friend, also." He placed Jessica down and looked around, his gaze sweeping the room. "Jesus, Allie, what did you do?"

"Um... I just wanted to make them feel at home."

"Jeremy! Look!" Jessica cried out, running to the coffee table laden with books and toys. Jeremy's eyes lit, but he hesitated.

"It's okay," Allie encouraged. "It's all for you two."

He nodded and followed his sister, eagerness in his steps. She looked up as Luke stepped over to her, uncertain how to greet him. He immediately wrapped his arms around her, kissing her lightly. "Is it okay? What I did here?"

"Babe, this is a helluva lot more than just making them feel at home. You didn't have to do all this."

"I just wanted to do whatever I could for all of you." She smoothed her fingers over his forehead. "You look tired." Her gaze slid to the side, watching the kids play. "How... is there anything you can tell me?"

"Yeah, but later. When they go to bed, I'll call. That is, unless you want to stay for a while with us—"

"I want," she rushed.

He smiled. "Okay, tonight, after they go to bed, we can talk."

"Uncle Luke? I gotta go to the bathroom," Jessica said, clutching her stuffed cat.

"I'll take her," Allie said, sliding from Luke's embrace and reaching out her hand. Jessica took it easily as though she'd never met a stranger and skipped alongside as Allie led her to the bathroom.

Once inside, she busied herself while Jessica took care of her business and then helped her wash her hands. "I bought you a pink toothbrush," she said, much to Jessica's delight.

"Oh, I only get new toothbrushes when Uncle Luke buys them. I like this one!"

"And you have shampoo, new soap, and bubble bath, too," Allie said, loving the little girl's happiness over such simple items.

With Jessica skipping beside her again, they emerged back into the living room, and she caught Luke peering into the oven. He stood and lifted his brow. Laughing, she said, "Who wants chicken nuggets?"

Jessica clapped her hands, and Jeremy, more subdued, looked over with a shy eagerness. Glad to have made the right choice, she blew out a sigh of relief and headed into the small kitchen.

After she'd helped Jessica with a bubble bath, Luke watched over Jeremy's shower, and they'd read books and colored pictures, the kids finally fell asleep in Luke's large bed on new, clean sheets. Tiptoeing into the living room, she bent to pick up the crayons on the floor, but Luke snagged her around the waist.

"Come, sit with me," he said, pulling her down to the sofa with him.

They cuddled, her legs draped over his and his arms around her. Kissing his cheek, she pressed her forehead to his for a moment. Finally, leaning back, she whispered, "I know you're tired, honey, but what can you tell me?"

"You're right, babe, I'm wiped." He sighed, his chest heaving. "Chelle overdosed. On what drugs, I don't know. She was taken to the hospital, and while I haven't talked to the doctor yet, I have a feeling she won't be in any shape to take care of the kids. I'm in contact with the lead detective, and I have no doubt Larry is in for some questioning that he'd rather not have to face. I have a signed guardianship form from him, so I can act as the kids' guardian, and they can stay with me. I know I'll need your help to find out how to enroll them into school here."

"That won't be a problem, sweetie. We can take care of it on Monday."

"Good. One problem down." He sighed again. "The kids didn't see anything other than what Jeremy said. The neighbor got them out quickly. How much they know about their mom and dad's drug use, I don't know. But that will have to be dealt with at some point. I know Zac's wife is a counselor. I thought we might have them talk to her."

"And when we get them enrolled in school, there's a counselor there, as well."

"I don't know how they'll be with the transition. As you've seen, Jessica is just happy to have attention and soaks it up with a smile. Jeremy's older. He's a watcher. He's cautious."

"And he takes care of his sister," she finished.

Luke lifted her brow. "Caught that, did you?"

"Hard to miss, honey." They were silent for a moment, and then she plunged ahead. "I got the feeling that your visit with Larry didn't go so well."

"My asshole brother proved that he is more of an asshole than I ever imagined, and believe me, I knew he was an asshole."

"Whoa…" she breathed.

"He didn't give a shit about the kids. Couldn't care less. Just expected me to take them and didn't want to be bothered about them at all." A grimace crossed his face.

She sucked in her lips, hating that he had to endure that. "Luke, maybe… I mean, in the end, maybe it's best. If he can't be a good father, then it's better that he's not in their lives."

He nodded slowly. "I thought about my old man while I was driving here. He was an asshole, too. And while I resented him, and my mom was worthless without him, at least he wasn't around to spread his asshole-ness for my whole upbringing."

"That's a lot of a-holes you're saying. You might need to get them all out of your system before the kids wake up."

He chuckled again, his arms squeezing. "You're right. There's a lot of things I need to work on."

Shaking her head vigorously, she said, "No, there's not. It's obvious the kids love you just the way you are."

"Christ, you're good for my ego." He kissed her lightly and shifted slightly, his gaze lifting from her face to around the room before coming back to her. "I know I'm neat, but you must have spent all day getting this place ready."

"I had a lot of nervous energy, Luke. It was clean, but I just needed to do something. My mom used to always say she did her best thinking when she was scrubbing floors, so I decided to see if she was right."

Another chuckle rumbled up. "And was she?"

"I can't say that I did my best thinking, but it was really good to have something to do besides let my imagination wander down dark paths. So, your place is practically sanitized. I wanted to make sure you didn't have anything to worry about when you got here with them so that you could just spend time with them. Refrigerator full of good food and snacks. Pantry is full, as well."

"They won't know what to do with all that food," he said, his voice taking on a strange tone. Sighing heavily, he said, "Jeremy told me that his mom was selling some of the food that I was having delivered."

"You're kidding?" Not hiding the incredulity, she shook her head. "I don't know why I'm surprised. If she was using, especially addicted, her behavior was probably normal for her."

"I know I should be worried about her in the hospital, but she was a worthless, deadbeat mom. A drug user who stole from her kids to support her habit. And that only scratches the surface. I'm sure there's a lot more Detective Dixon will be able to tell me once they do more investigating."

"You know, honey, we have to be careful what we say in front of the kids. No matter what she was, she was their mom."

He nodded slowly. "Yeah, I know. But I have a feeling there's a lot of resentment that's built up in Jeremy toward his parents."

"More reason to make sure he talks to a counselor."

He nodded, then his eyes fluttered, and he tried to stifle a yawn.

"I need to get out of here so that you can go to bed. I'll come over tomorrow morning, but in case you all get up first, there's eggs, bacon, and bread for toast, oatmeal and cereal, milk, and juice."

"I wish you could stay," he said, his blue eyes warm as they roved over her face.

"I do, too, but with all the changes, there's no need to shove your girlfriend into their faces."

"I'm not going to hide you, Allie. And to be honest, those kids need to be around a normal, healthy relationship. But I also know the sleeper sofa is crap, and I want you to have a good night's sleep."

They stood, and he walked her to the door, his arm wrapped around her shoulders. Kissing again, he finally pulled back and groaned. "The timing of all this sucks. We were just discovering ourselves as a couple. I wanted to spend more nights alone in your bed. And now I have to watch you walk away and know that you're driving to your house in the dark."

"There's never a good time for some things. But what's important is that the kids are safe, they're with you, and you and I are fine. And tomorrow, we'll make sure that the kids are still good, and you and I can come up with a game plan for them."

His eyes blazed with intensity, but he remained silent. Kissing her again, she melted against him for a moment, then pushed back, knowing if she didn't leave, she'd end up on that sleeper sofa with him.

"Text me when you get home and get locked down, babe."

Smiling, she nodded, then jogged down the stairs. On the road, she thought about the changes that had hit in the last twenty-four hours. And as crazy as it had been, with those beautiful children tucked in safe with Luke and knowing he wanted her, she smiled.

18

Luke felt someone staring before he even opened his eyes. The hard spring poking him in the back sent pain as he rolled over, his gaze landing on a bright-eyed, ruby-cheeked, cherubic face just a few inches from his.

The cherub grinned widely and giggled. "Are you awake, Uncle Luke?"

He knew a grunt was not acceptable, but "Uh-huh," was the only thing he could manage at the moment. Then he heard another giggle, and his heart squeezed. "Come here," he play-growled, grabbing her and pulling Jessica on top of him, tickling her tummy.

"No! Jeremy, come save me!" she shouted between giggles.

Jeremy stayed by the side of the sofa bed but smiled as well. Luke peered over Jessica's head and held his nephew's gaze. "Sleep well?"

"Yeah, Uncle Luke." A wince crossed his thin face. "Thank you."

Sitting up, he kept his arms around Jessica as she

snuggled against his chest. There was something in Jeremy's expression and words that stabbed Luke. Reaching one long arm out, he wrapped his hand around the back of Jeremy's neck and guided him to sit on the edge of the bed. "You don't have to thank me for anything, Jeremy. Just knowing you're safe and with me is all I need."

Jeremy nodded, another slight wince marring his face as he looked down at the sofa bed. "It's just with us being here, and you're having to sleep here… it's a lot…" His voice drifted off as he glanced toward Jessica.

Luke could easily tell that Jeremy understood the situation and felt deeply about it. Wanting to curse Chelle and Larry for the millionth time in the past twenty-four hours, he just shook his head. "Not a lot. It means the world to me having you with me. So, if this little rugrat here will let me up, you guys can help me turn my bed back into a sofa."

Jessica squealed. "I can't get up because you're holding me!"

"Then you better give me a kiss so I can let you go."

She grabbed his cheeks with both of her hands and gave him a smacking kiss right on his mouth. "There!" She bounded off the bed and grabbed her stuffed cat from the floor.

Standing, he bent and straightened the sheets from one side as the kids mimicked his behavior from the other. Ordering them to watch their fingers so no one got pinched, he showed them how the bed folded back into a sofa. Amazement filled their faces as they put the cushions back on. The kids were still in their pajamas, and it dawned on him that he had no idea what their typical routine was. Glad it was Sunday and they had another day to figure things out before school the next day, he asked, "So, you guys are going to have to help me out. I know you got clean last night, but is there anything special you do in the mornings? Or do you just get dressed and have breakfast?"

"Sometimes we don't get dressed when Mama's still sleeping," Jessica said, then cut her eyes toward Jeremy. "But on those days, Jeremy helps me."

Swallowing down the thoughts about Chelle, he said, "Well, I guess there will be some fun days when you can stay in your jammies extra-long, but most days, you'll need to get dressed. Jeremy, I know you don't need me for that, and I can help Jessica. One thing we need to do today, besides just resting and enjoying the good food Allie brought over, is for me to go through your clothes and figure out what we need to buy."

"New clothes?" Jessica asked, her eyes wide at the prospect. "Can we keep them?"

Shooting his gaze over to Jeremy, he watched another grimace pass over the young boy's face. Jeremy shrugged. "Mom would sell some of the clothes you bought."

"Well, no more. What I buy, you keep." Thinking of how small his space was and now needing privacy, he added, "I'll get changed in the bathroom, and you two can play out here for a few minutes till I'm back." He walked to the bedroom then looked over his shoulder. "Make sure you don't open the door to anyone."

"What if it's Allie?" Jeremy asked.

"Allie would be okay, but I think she's going to send me a message before she comes over. Once I get out of the shower, we'll have breakfast."

With the kids grinning, he turned and headed into the bathroom after grabbing his clothes. But the instant the door shut, he gripped the counter until his knuckles were white, rage pouring through his veins. He'd had no idea what Chelle did with the money when she sold the food and the kids' clothes, but he knew it wasn't to take care of them. And now that he knew she did drugs, he had a damn good idea where the money went. Finally, sucking in a ragged breath, he let it out slowly. The anger ebbed as he thought about the kids in the next room, and not wanting to waste any more time on the past he couldn't change, he jumped into the shower.

Ten minutes later, he walked out of the bathroom and discovered a text from Allie telling him she was on her way. By the time he'd overseen the kids getting dressed, there was a knock on his door. Jessica was already racing toward the door since he'd told them she was coming. With his hand on her shoulder, he held her back. "Never open the door unless you know who's there, sweetheart." He peeked through the security hole and spied Allie grinning and waving at him.

"But I'm not tall enough to see through your peekie-pie hole," Jessica pointed out. He lifted her up, and she giggled, pressing her face against the hole. "I see her! She's waving at me!"

Opening the door, he didn't get a chance to greet Allie properly before Jessica had rushed into her arms, hugging her tightly. Then she grabbed Allie's hand and dragged her into the apartment.

"Uncle Luke slept on the sofa, but he turned it into a bed, like magic. He showed us how to do it. I can show you, too!"

Laughing, Allie hugged Jessica, told her she was beautiful, then stood and smiled toward Jeremy, greeting him softly. Finally, turning toward Luke, she beamed, but her gaze was assessing. He stepped forward and, placing his hand on her waist, kissed her lightly. "You can stop worrying, babe. I'm fine," he whispered.

"Have you had breakfast?" she asked, just as softly.

"Nope."

"Good." Turning toward the kids, she called out, "So, who's hungry?"

With shouts of 'me' ringing out, she laughed and walked to his tiny kitchen. He was amazed at how quickly Allie had plated scrambled eggs, pancakes, and bacon. Handing him the syrup, she inclined her head toward Jessica. "You'd better take charge of this."

Bowing to her experience with kids, he quickly discovered she was right as Jessica still managed to get syrup over most of her plate. Grateful it wasn't in her hair yet, he watched as Allie stepped behind Jessica and pulled her hair back and secured it with a ponytail holder. He looked down at his plate, and worry washed through him, knowing there was so much about kids he didn't know. As though she could read his mind, Allie moved closer as she grabbed her plate and whispered, "You'll be fine, honey. Remember… they're in a much better place."

Her words were just what he needed to help ease his mind. Nodding, he met her smile with one of his own and then shoveled in the delicious breakfast.

―――――――

By late afternoon, Luke was wiped. He cast his gaze around the living room and spied the board game now abandoned, little pieces scattered over the coffee table mixed in with the crayons and paper. Jeremy was in the corner of the sofa, a book in his hands, but his eyelids kept closing. Jessica had already lost the battle to stay awake and was now curled in Allie's arms as she sat on the other end of the sofa. Luke glanced toward the kitchen counter now piled with a few plates that hadn't made it into the sink, one last apple slice that hadn't been eaten although the rest of their fruit dish had been decimated, two drained glasses with remnants of milk in the bottom, and a jar of peanut butter with the lid not screwed on.

After breakfast, he and Allie had taken the kids to the Baytown Park to run around outside, and they came up with a list of things that needed to be taken care of. Allie had called her principal even though it was a Sunday to let him know what was happening and how they would bring the kids in the next morning to register.

Luke called Colt and Warden Neely to let them know of the situation, both of whom had received a call from Detective Dixon checking Luke's references. He'd called Zac to let him know he'd be off the volunteer rescue rotation for a while and then talked to Zac's wife, Maddie, setting up a counseling appointment for the kids later in the week.

At Allie's suggestion, he called Ryan Coates, a fellow American Legionnaire and captain of the Baytown Virginia Marine Police. His wife, Judith, was a family doctor, and he wanted to get her opinion on what the kids might need. Agreeing to bring them into the clinic in a couple of days, he felt better as he finished the calls.

With his blessing, Allie had initiated a phone tree of their friends to let them know about the kids. All were supportive and ready to lend assistance as needed. Several offered playdates, which Allie accepted for the future but said that right now, they wanted to take things slowly with the kids. She had also made notes of what clothing items and sizes the kids would need. She got online and ordered a few things to come before they would have a chance to get to the closest BigMart.

He'd taken another call from Detective Dixon, who'd informed him that Chelle's toxicology report had shown cocaine in her system as well as fentanyl. Luke closed his eyes, his jaw tight.

"The doctor might not talk to you, but as the lead detective, I can get information. Right now, she's in intensive care. They think she'll make a recovery but have no idea what shape she'll be in for a while." Detective Dixon continued to tell him that they were interviewing Larry about his wife's drug use and possible dealing, and they might need to talk to the kids as well.

At that, Luke's eyes snapped open, and he growled, "Not happening."

The kids were in the other room playing, but Allie heard. She walked over and placed her hand on his. Her gentle touch gave him a modicum of peace in a swirling shitstorm. Finally, he agreed that if an interview with the kids was necessary, it would only happen with him and possibly a counselor present. Detective Dixon agreed, and they soon disconnected.

Now, twisting his head, he settled his gaze back on Jeremy and Jessica. The kids were safe, fed, clean, and happy. Allie had a beautiful smile on her face, and his chest tightened at the view. If he had to sleep on the lumpy sleeper sofa for years just to see them at peace, it would be worth it.

Wanting to get the kids out of the small apartment as often as possible, they were soon walking to the Pub. Once there, Jeremy and Jessica's eyes grew large at the fun decorations and the lively music playing in the background. Aiden waved as he walked over. Introduced to the kids, he grinned. "I've got a little girl. Emily. She's eight years old and in third grade."

Jeremy grinned. "I'm eight, too."

"Hey, you might be in her class. I'll tell her to look for you. In fact, let me see if my wife can bring her over now."

Luke noticed Jeremy's smile stayed as Aiden walked off, his phone to his ear. As the server brought their nachos, the kids' smiles grew wide at the sight of the huge plate of food. Soon, Aiden and his wife, Lia, walked over with a little girl skipping along with them. Once the kids were introduced, Emily settled into the booth between Jeremy and Jessica, all three talking at once.

"What's that in your ear?" Jessica asked, her brow scrunched.

"I have trouble hearing, so this helps me," Emily answered matter-of-factly.

"Oh... does it hurt?" Jessica asked, her eyes wide with worry.

Laughing, Emily shook her head. "No, but some-times I still have trouble hearing. So, if I don't answer you, just get my attention so I'll know to look at you."

Luke watched the conversation play out, noting that Lia and Aiden never stopped smiling. He assumed they were used to the curious questions from others. Lia stayed and chatted, but Aiden went back to work behind the bar. His brother, Brogan, stopped by the table to meet the kids, as well.

Later, as they said goodbye, Emily hugged Jessica and turned to Jeremy. "I hope you're in my class!"

Both kids were grinning ear to ear as they walked back to the apartment.

Allie oversaw Jessica's bath again and then brushed her hair while Jeremy took a shower. She told them all about the school they would go to the next morning, and it didn't pass Luke's notice that they were both visibly relieved to hear that Allie worked in the same building. To be honest, he felt the same.

By the time the kids were tucked in, the kitchen cleaned, and the toys put away, Luke flopped down onto the sofa, pulling Allie down with him. With her in his lap, his arms wrapped around her, and his nose nuzzling her neck, he inhaled her delicate scent deeply, recognizing that it was more Jessica's sudsy bubbles than perfume.

"I can't thank you enough for all you're doing, Allie," he said, lifting his head to peer into her eyes. "I feel like I'm taking advantage. You never signed up for any of this and we haven't had much of a chance to focus on us."

She pressed her soft fingertips against his lips. "You didn't sign up for this either, Luke. And while our relationship isn't exactly following some nebulous ideal of normal, it's life. And you know that life happens, and you've got to roll with the punches."

He nodded slowly, then confessed, "I can't help but worry about them. What they may have witnessed. What they've had to deal with. How that's going to affect them."

"Kids are very resilient, and just in the day that I've spent with them, they seem very well-adjusted. Jessica is a bloom-where-she's-planted kind of girl. She's happy to be around people she cares about. Mostly, that's her brother and Uncle Luke. I don't know what kind of mom-memories she'll have about Chelle, but she wasn't afraid around her mom. Maybe that's because Jeremy shielded her from Chelle and Larry's negligence? I don't know, but she's thrilled to be here with you."

"And Jeremy? What are your gut instincts about him?"

"He loves his sister and you. He's watched out for her, and I don't think that's a bad thing because it's taught him to be caring. He was much more aware of what his parents were doing, and he's cautious because he's not sure what's gonna happen next."

Gut-punched, Luke knew she was right. "Somehow, I've got to get him to understand that they're with me and I'm not going to betray them as their parents did."

Allie lifted her hands and placed them on either side of Luke's face, holding his attention. "You just keep being you, and the rest will take care of itself."

He kissed her lightly, wanting to take it deeper but having another question he needed to voice. Lifting his head away, he rested his forehead against hers. "I need to look for a bigger place before I get a surprise visit from the social worker."

"Let's take care of one thing at a time. Tomorrow, school registration, and then you can buy car seats and a booster seat. This week, a doctor's visit. Next weekend, a chance to take them shopping for more clothes. Then, when they have their basic needs met, you can look for a larger place."

The air rushed from his lungs as he stared at the beautiful woman, so in-control, helping him with the swirling changes thrown into their lives. "Is there anything you can't figure out?"

Grinning, she said, "Right now, I just want to figure out how to get you to kiss me again."

His arms tightened around her, and he grinned. Angling his head, he murmured, "I've got that covered, babe," then sealed his mouth over hers. It was much later before she made her way home, leaving him to wish that she never had to leave.

19

"Allie, honey, are you sure you're okay?"

"Mom, I'm fine." She heard the snort on the other end of the line and couldn't hold back her own giggle. "Okay, okay, I know *fine* is a ridiculous word that truly means nothing. But other than being busy, there's nothing happening that I can't handle or is upsetting."

Busy was also a word that barely described what the last few days had been like. She'd risen early on Monday morning to get to Luke's apartment before the kids awoke. Anticipating they might be nervous about a new school, she'd hoped to ease the transition by helping Jessica get dressed and get her hair fixed, giving them breakfast, and accompanying them to school early so that she'd have time to assist with registration before getting to her class. Everything had been easy until Jessica, grinning ear to ear, mentioned that she'd never had her hair fixed before going to kindergarten. At that, Allie's heart clenched at the thought of the little girl who'd never had something so simple. Of course, Jessica went on to say that Jeremy always made sure to brush her hair, but he didn't know how to put in bows. Then, Jeremy mentioned that they usually had breakfast at school because there was nothing to eat at home. Once again, her heart clenched, and she'd glanced up to see a muscle in Luke's jaw tic. She'd seen that expression so much over the weekend she wondered how his molars didn't crack under the pressure.

Registering them for school had been much easier than she'd anticipated. With Luke's guardianship papers and their school in Richmond forwarding their records, they had no problems. It didn't hurt that Jeremy was placed in Emily McFarlane's class with Jade, giving him someone he knew right away. Jessica hung back, clutching Luke's hand until she made it into her kindergarten classroom, where the other children rushed up and greeted her with smiles.

Luke had bought the appropriate car seat for Jessica and booster for Jeremy, stopping to see Zac at the Baytown Fire Station to make sure they were properly installed in his SUV. The kids had been excited, having never had car seats before.

On Tuesday after school, she'd taken the kids with her to the municipal parking lot, where Luke had permission to leave early. It was on that day they'd realized they needed a second set of car seats for when they were with her. She'd tutored while he took the kids home, then she stopped by his apartment to make sure all was well in the evening.

On Wednesday after school, she'd kept the kids until Luke got off work, and they took them to the clinic. The doctor, Judith Coates, was so patient and kind with them, and it was with a sigh of relief that she'd pronounced them healthy.

Thursday, with the second set of car seats in her small car, they'd managed the transfer in the jail parking lot, and once again, she'd tutored then went to his apartment to spend time with everyone before going home. Luke had begged her not to run herself ragged, but she'd shushed him, telling him she was right where she wanted to be. And her heart sang when he admitted that he loved her being there also.

Granted, by the time she got to her house each evening, she was exhausted, barely having time to enjoy her new home before falling into bed. Now, it was Friday afternoon, and the kids were playing on the playground after school before they met with Luke to go shopping for more clothes.

"Well, your dad and I want to come to visit soon. We'd want to do that anyway, just to see you. Now, to find out that you're dating someone seriously, we would absolutely want to come to visit. On top of that, throw in two children that you're helping to take care of... well, let's just say that we are already planning on coming up. Your father's got the church event this weekend, but we'll be up next weekend."

"That would be great, Mom. I can't wait to see you and introduce you to Luke, Jessica, and Jeremy."

"Just make sure to take care of yourself, sweetheart," her mom said. "We love you."

With an 'I love you, too,' she disconnected the call just as Jessica and Jeremy ran over to her. She couldn't remember the last time she'd been so grateful for a weekend. She wanted to invite Luke and the kids over to her house so they'd have her fenced-in yard to play in. And, selfishly, she could enjoy some time there, as well.

"Hey, guys. Did you have a good day?"

"Yes!" Jessica shouted, bouncing over to give Allie a hug.

She wrapped her arms around the little girl, loving the feel of her body vibrating with exuberance. Lifting her head, she looked at Jeremy standing nearby and smiled. "What about you? Did you have a good day, too?"

He nodded, holding her gaze. "We had a spelling test today."

Her heart pitter-pattered, knowing the evaluations were necessary but uneasy with him being tested so soon after starting a new school after the trauma they'd had.

His lips curved upward as he said, "I got them all right. I aced it."

Not caring if he was too old for a hug, she lifted her other arm, and he hurried forward, allowing her to hug both at the same time. Feeling tears prick the back of her eyes, she breathed in deeply through her nose and let it out. "Okay, kiddos, we've got to get to Luke, and then we're heading to BigMart."

"Yay! New clothes!" Jessica shouted, letting go of Allie to twirl around.

She stood and tousled Jeremy's hair. "Don't worry. I'm sure Luke hates looking at clothes, too. You two can find man-things to do while we shop." She knew she'd said the right thing when Jeremy's face brightened. He was much slower to smile than Jessica but touched her heart just as quickly.

Leaving her car at the jail parking lot, they loaded into Luke's SUV after lots of hello hugs from Luke to the kids and a quick hello and kiss for Allie.

Driving down the road, Jeremy piped up from the back seat. "Allie says you and me can do man-things while they look for clothes."

Luke chuckled, glancing to the side as Allie grinned. He looked into the rearview mirror and nodded. "Absolutely. Of course, I think we'll have to pick up a few clothes, but then you can show me what games you like and if there's anything you need for school. We can also hit the food section, and you can show me what you and Jessica would like to have."

Jeremy agreed readily, and Allie figured he didn't care what he and Luke did as long as they did it together.

Luke dropped the girls off at the front door, saying that he and Jeremy were going to put gas in the SUV and then they'd be in. Leaning forward, she kissed him lightly, then hopped out and unbuckled Jessica. They waved as the vehicle drove off. Looking down, she held out her hand and asked, "Ready to go find some clothes?" With the excitement she expected, she and Jessica headed to the children's clothing section.

It didn't take long to discover that Jessica had never been shopping, certainly not at a store where she could look for her own clothes. She raced from one rack to the other, her little fingers barely reaching out to touch the colorful clothes.

Twisting her head around, she looked up at Allie. "Can I pick out something?"

"Of course, you can. You pick out what you like, and I'll make sure it's in your size and will fit."

Sucking in her lips, Jessica whispered, "Allie, you are so nice."

Kissing the top of her head, she easily said, "I love you, sweetheart."

"Mama never bought me clothes." Her voice was small, and Allie's heart felt shredded.

Kneeling so that she was at Jessica's level, she said, "Honey, I know your mom loved you. And I know this because you're the most lovable little girl I've ever met in my life. But your mom had some problems showing you how much she loved you. But never think that she didn't care." Trying hard not to cry as she thought Jessica's chin quivered, she brightened her voice and added, "Let's find some pretty things to wear to school, and maybe a couple of things just for fun. Then, we might need to shop for Jeremy because I don't know if he gets as excited about new clothes as we do."

Swiping at her face, Jessica nodded, her little smile returning. "I want to get something nice for him 'cause he's always nice to me."

Crisis avoided for now, she and Jessica shopped to their hearts' content. They were soon joined by Luke and Jeremy, who both made a great show of complimenting Jessica on her choices of all things pink and purple that filled the cart. Grateful that Luke commandeered Jeremy for his shopping, she watched them have fun and realized that Jeremy had never had this experience with his own dad. When the opportunity presented itself, she lifted on her toes and whispered to Luke, "This is a first for the kids."

"I figured as much," he acknowledged. "I just can't believe Larry and Chelle sold most of the clothes that I bought for the kids. Especially now that I know that he was probably dealing drugs. That meant there was money, even if it was dirty money."

"Maybe he didn't share it with Chelle," she surmised. Before they had a chance to talk further, the kids rushed over, showing them what each had picked out. With their purchases made, they stopped for pizza on the way home. Once again, the kids excitedly took in the whole experience, their eyes bright as they looked around the restaurant, both wolfing down pizza slices as though someone might take the food away. The dark thought crossed her mind that maybe that had happened before, and a side glance toward Luke gave evidence he had the same thought. Placing her hand on his thigh, she gave a little squeeze and mouthed, "They're going to be fine."

"When you get married, can I be one of the little princesses?"

Jerking her head around, she stared wide-eyed at Jessica, who was smiling with a pizza-mouth grin. "What?" she and Luke asked at the same time.

"I saw a show on TV, and this man and woman got married. The woman got to wear a pretty dress, and there was a little girl who got to wear a princess dress, too. So, when you get married, I want to be the little princess."

Stunned silent, Allie glanced at Luke, now bug-eyed.

Clearing his throat, Luke said, "Well, I think that whenever the time is right, then you can be a little princess."

"And wear a princess dress?"

Glancing toward Jeremy, Allie noticed he was sitting quietly but watching her and Luke intently. She offered him a smile, but his gaze moved to Luke.

"Yes, sweetheart, you'll get to wear a princess dress at the right time," Luke agreed.

Jessica, now completely satisfied that she'd get to be a princess, continued to slurp her soda and eat the large pizza slice on her plate. Jeremy held Luke's gaze before his lips quirked ever so slightly, and he turned back to his food, as well.

Luke winked at Allie, but she made bug eyes at him again although glad he'd kept his answer to Jessica vague. The last thing she wanted was for the kids to be disappointed with expectations that might not come true. By the time they'd finished and piled back into the SUV, the kids' smiles offered evidence they'd enjoyed the experience and their worries were finally easing, and she sighed in relief.

An hour later, it was as though everything was falling apart, and her heart pounded as she listened to the woman standing in Luke's living room.

"Mr. Purdue, while I certainly appreciate the clothing that you have bought for the children that are filling the bags in this room, I have to wonder where you're going to put them. There is only one bedroom with one closet, and it is filled with your clothes."

"Mrs. Nicholson, I've already told you that I'm in the process of cleaning out the coat closet in this room so that I can put my clothes in here and the kids can have that closet. Plus, I'm buying another dresser so that they can have one all to themselves."

"That's admirable but hardly addresses the fact that there is still only one bedroom. The children may have been used to sharing a bed in their former home, but they need their own space."

"I agree. I have a friend that's offering me bunk beds that I can put in there. Plus, I plan on moving us all into a larger place soon. Surely, you appreciate that we've had less than a week together, and I feel as though we've done very well in that time."

Allie felt her insides quiver, her pizza threatening to come back up. When they'd arrived back at Luke's apartment, they'd discovered Mrs. Nicholson standing outside his apartment. A sharp-edged woman with an equally sharp tone, she'd informed them that she was from the state, and it was her duty to make an unannounced visit before turning the children's welfare over to Luke. She'd also informed him that a local social worker would receive her report, as well.

Feeling the tension pouring off Luke, the kids began to fret, and Allie kept them on the landing one floor below. She noticed that Luke did not close the door all the way and had a feeling that he wanted a witness to what was being said. Leaving the kids on the landing so that she could keep an eye on them, she tiptoed back to the top of the stairs so that she could listen.

The longer the conversation went on, the more she could tell Mrs. Nicholson had a problem with a single man in a small apartment trying to raise two children.

"And furthermore, Mr. Purdue," Mrs. Nicholson said, "while I have looked in the refrigerator and pantry and certainly found healthy food, and the clothes and linens appear to be washed and clean, I would advise that you move up your accommodations search pronto. This is simply too close an environment for these kids and you to live in."

"And I will remind you, Mrs. Nicholson, that the environment the kids have been raised in by their parents was a neglectful environment and a squalor compared to this. I will do everything I can for these children, make any sacrifice I can, but do not walk in here and make veiled threats to take them away."

"They are not veiled threats, sir. You do realize that when their mother recovers and their father gets out of jail, they could have all parental rights restored—"

"I doubt he gets out of jail, and if he does, I'll fight him for custody of these children."

Unable to contain herself, Allie pushed the door open and stepped in. Crossing her arms over her chest, she leveled a hard stare at the other woman. "I assure you that these children are well-looked after. Luke is not alone in this endeavor."

"And who are you?" Mrs. Nicholson sniffed, haughtiness dripping from each word.

"I'm Allison Simpson, a teacher at the children's school. They're already doing very well academically and seeing a counselor, also."

"And you're here because…?"

"I'm also his girlfriend," she replied, stepping closer to Luke.

"Girlfriend?" Mrs. Nicholson parroted, her brows raised.

Allie had never heard the word *girlfriend* pronounced with such disdain. She opened her mouth to refute whatever notion the woman had, but Luke beat her to it.

"Fiancée. She's my fiancée."

The oxygen left the room as Allie's head felt as though it was spinning. *What did he just say?* He reached over and grabbed her hand, squeezing. Glancing to the side, she could feel panic swirling off him. Wanting to do anything to make it better, she gasped, "Ye… yes. Fiancée."

Mrs. Nicholson's gaze narrowed and dropped to Allison's hand. "And your ring?"

Luke once again jumped in. "It's being resized."

Unable to speak, Allie just jerked her head up and down a couple of times, focusing on sucking air into her lungs so that she wouldn't pass out in the middle of the floor.

"And when is the wedding to take place?" Mrs. Nicholson now seemed interested.

"This spring. We were going to get married in the

spring," Luke said, his voice sounding strangely steady in light of the situation.

"I'm not sure that will help your situation—"

"But we moved it up because of the kids. We just have to get the license, and then we're getting married in a couple of days."

Looking around the small apartment, Mrs. Nicholson turned back to them, but once again, Luke anticipated her complaint about four people living in the space.

"Allie has a house."

At that, it was evident that Mrs. Nicholson's attention was grabbed.

"A house?"

"Yes, plenty big for the kids and us," Luke continued to fib his way through.

Allie's chest heaved. *Oh, God, he's lying for the kids.* Steadying her breathing to keep from giving away her panic, she forced a stiff smile onto her face, feeling sure the dour social worker would see right through their bluster. Having no choice but to blunder along with Luke, Allie nodded. "I have three bedrooms and two bathrooms. Um… a yard. A fence. Um…"

"Well, that certainly changes everything," Mrs. Nicholson said, nodding. "I'll put this in my notes and turn it over to the local social worker for North Heron County. I'll give you her information, and you'll need to contact her this next week after you're married. She'll want to make an inspection once everyone is settled in the house."

Mrs. Nicholson moved past them to leave, and Allie

looked over at Luke, her fake smile now wobbling, her breathing shallow.

Before she had a chance to register the noise behind her, the sound of small footsteps running up the stairs caused her to whirl around as Jessica and Jeremy rushed in past Mrs. Nicholson. Jeremy hurried to stand next to Luke, lifting his hand and placing it in Luke's much larger one. Jessica wrapped her arms around Allison's leg and looked up.

"She's Allie. She's Uncle Luke's girlfriend. They're getting married, and I get to wear a princess dress."

20

Luke stood in the living room of his apartment, staring out the window at the street below. His mind swirled with the shitstorm that had started the minute Mrs. Nicholson had opened her mouth. Unable to have a moment alone with Allie, he listened as she read a bedtime story to the kids. As soon as Mrs. Nicholson had left, Allie had stayed busy, barely looking at him as she helped with bath time, putting away all their new clothes, and doing a load of laundry.

And what the fuck did I do? Just stayed out of her way. But the truth was he had no idea why he'd said what he had other than panic had struck him the minute he realized Mrs. Nicholson had the power to take the kids away from him. Gripping the windowsill, he fought to catch his breath at the thought. *Jesus, how do I make this right?*

A new type of panic set in, this one from the idea that he'd irrevocably harmed his blossoming relationship with Allie. *And how could I blame her for walking out the door?*

"Luke, the kids are ready to say good night."

He turned and spied her standing in the bedroom doorway, her knuckles white with her hands tightly clasped in front of her. Her chin was down, but she glanced up as he passed her, her lips sucked in and pressed tightly together. Stepping inside the room, a smile curved his lips as he looked at the two cherubic faces peering up at him from the large bed. Bending, he offered hugs and kisses, wishing them sweet dreams.

"Uncle Luke?"

Jeremy's voice was so tentative Luke could feel the emotion pouring from his nephew. Sitting on the edge of the bed next to Jeremy, he gave his full attention. "Yeah, buddy?"

Licking his lips, Jeremy glanced toward Jessica, but she was busy patting her stuffed cat. Keeping his voice low, he asked, "The lady that was here today. She's not gonna take us away, is she?"

"Absolutely not," Luke said, his voice firm. "There's no way anyone's taking you from me."

Jeremy held his gaze for a long moment, then his small shoulders sagged, and he smiled. "Good."

Kissing them once again, Luke walked out, closing the bedroom door after making sure the nightlight was on. Allie was now where he had been, standing in front of the window looking down on the street. Walking straight to her, he didn't hesitate. "Allie, I'm so fuckin' sorry. Never in my life have I lied. But that woman... I was terrified... I can't have those kids going into the system because of me. But don't worry, I'll find a place big enough and will tell the social worker that it was all a misunderstanding and—"

"Maybe we should do it."

Not sure he heard her correctly, he stammered, "Wh... what? Do what?"

She remained facing the window, but with her head lifted, he could see her eyes reflected in the glass as they held his gaze.

"Mrs. Nicholson said she was going to check on us. What if she finds out that we lied?"

"I'll deal." He dragged his fingers through his hair, grabbing the back of his neck and squeezing in a feeble attempt to stop the fear coursing through his body.

"How?"

"I don't know," he admitted, his jaw tight.

She turned slowly to face him, the foot of space between their bodies seeming like a chasm. "I looked when I first came to the area. There aren't a lot of apartments. I don't even know of any apartments that have three bedrooms. You'd have to find a house to rent and the rental market around here is horrible unless you're looking for an expensive temporary beach rental. Even Hannah's little cottage only has two bedrooms. I'm sure you could probably get away with the kids having bunk beds and sharing a room for another year, but what if that's a dealbreaker for the social worker?"

"I don't know," he repeated, the words growling up from deep inside. He still wasn't sure what she'd meant by *'Maybe we should do it,'* but his mind raced in too many different directions to focus.

"What about Larry? Is he getting out of jail soon? And what's the latest on Chelle? Will they want the kids back?"

"Right now, Chelle's facing medical issues as well as possible charges considering the amount of drugs she had in her possession indicated dealing and not just using. She hasn't got the ability, money, or resources for the kids, so I'd say the answer is 'no.' Larry? He was always useless and isn't about to be tied down with them."

"And a foster home?"

He shook his head vehemently. "I've wasted enough of their years not doing more. I'm not giving them to someone else." He sighed, his shoulders slumping. "That's why I made up the story about us getting married. It seemed like the most expedient way to get Mrs. Nicholson to back down and accept what I wanted to do for them."

She reached out and gripped his forearms, sucking in a ragged breath as she shook her head. "But what would make it certain that they would have what they need and satisfy the state? Us together, right? Isn't that what she implied? Married? In a home?" She swallowed deeply, her gaze not wavering, penetrating the cold shell that had surrounded him for several hours. Continuing, she said, "I know it's antiquated that a man can't do this on his own or that a non-married couple can't, but that's what she seemed to want. And she's got the power to make things difficult for you." Her gaze shot to the closed door of the bedroom, a pained grimace crossing her face. "And difficult for them."

He felt her anguish as much as his own. "I don't know what I can do, Allie, but just keep trying to give them what they need."

"It wouldn't have to be real. I mean, it would be, but it can be whatever it needs to be."

He blinked at her softly spoken words. "Babe, I'm not sure I follow what you're trying to say."

She pressed her lips together, then nodded. "I'm talking about getting married."

His eyes bulged, a gasp slipping from his lips at her offer. "No, Allie, I wouldn't have you—"

She hushed him with her fingers against his lips. "We need to do this, Luke. It can be a pretend marriage. Or a real one. I mean, it's not like we don't care about each other. It's just that... well... we'd just started dating. But I've got a house for all of us. It could work. Maybe." She suddenly jolted. "But not in a church. We'll do it at the courthouse—"

She was babbling, her nerves evident, but he knew her offer was sincere. Wrapping his arms around her, he tucked her head underneath his chin and held her close. Her cheek rested against his chest, and he whispered, "Do you hear my heartbeat?"

She nodded, her face rubbing against his T-shirt.

"I've been alone for a long time. But right now, I have three people in my life that have come to mean everything to me. Those two beautiful kids sleeping in the other room and you. You're right, we just started dating. And I opened up my mouth in panic earlier, and my lies now affect the ones I care about. Allie, honey, your offer to see this through is appreciated more than you'll ever know. But I care too much about you to follow through with this scheme where all of us move into your brand-new home that you haven't even had a chance to enjoy. I'm not going to force you to be inconvenienced, put out, have your space invaded, put you in a role that isn't right for you. I opened my fuckin' mouth and screwed up. And I'm going to be the one to make it right." He sucked in a deep breath and let it out slowly, glad that he'd pronounced his decision, hoping she'd now be able to relax.

With her arms encircling his waist, she leaned back and peered up at him, her gaze pleading. "Luke, think about this logically. What's the worst that can happen if we go to the justice of the peace and get married? We'd be going in with our eyes open. We'd do everything we could to provide a stable home for the kids during this transition. We'd consider it a true marriage and honor the vows. And if we got to a point where we decided it was no longer right, we'd dissolve it in a way that would make it the easiest for the kids. The best that can happen is that the kids have a happy home at a time in their life when they really need it." Shrugging, she added, "And for us? We might find that it works."

Barely able to breathe at what she was offering, he was humbled to his very core. "Allie, you can't possibly mean—"

"Yes, I can. We need to apply for a marriage license tomorrow. I happen to know the courthouse has morning hours on Saturdays."

His mind raced with all the implications, something that hadn't happened when he'd mouthed off to Mrs.

Nicholson. "Babe, I never want you to resent me. I never want you to look at me and think I've ruined your life. What you're offering is amazing, but this isn't a decision that should be made so quickly. This is a sacrifice for you to even consider it."

"Luke, honey, what you're doing for those kids is a sacrifice." She looked down, her gaze focused straight ahead at his chest before tilting her head back and holding his gaze again. "If you'd asked me if this was the way I wanted to get married, of course, I would've said no. But then, there are all sorts of reasons people get married. To me, doing this for those kids is as good as any."

They continued holding each other's gazes, silent for a long moment. Almost afraid to ask, he finally worked up the courage. "Allie, do you care for me?"

Her lips curved upward, and she nodded. "Yes. I care a great deal for you. But then, I told you that the night we slept together."

Feeling as though he was standing on a precipice, ready to take the plunge and spread his wings and fly or fall crashing to the rocks below, he drew in a ragged breath. "Then I only have one more question. Allie, will you marry me? I promise I'll be true to only you. I promise I'll do everything I can to make it a real marriage. I promise to do everything I can to give you what you need and what you want."

"That's all anyone can hope for," she said, lifting on her toes to press her lips to his.

He took over the kiss, pouring every ounce of emotion coursing through his being into their connection. Holding her tightly, he thrust his tongue into her warmth, his body vibrating with need for her. Every sense was filled with her. The delicate scent of vanilla. The soft curves pressed against his body. Her silky hair tickled his arm where it lay against her back. Her own special taste that he'd grown to love as his lips devoured her. The low moan from deep in her chest that he swallowed. The light in her eyes as she yielded all to him. The deep-seated understanding of what she was offering to him.

And he fell off the edge of the precipice with her and flew.

Finally, dragging his mouth from hers, he tried to ignore his aching cock. She grinned as she slid her hand between them, her fingers tracing the bulge pressing against her tummy. "Oh, babe," he groaned, no other words coming forth.

"I know," she replied, her words husky. She loosened her grip and stepped back, creating the necessary—but hated—space between them.

Sucking in her lips, she sighed. "I need to get home. We've got a lot to do tomorrow."

"I'll find out what we need—"

"I googled it earlier."

"You did?" he asked, his head jerking back slightly in surprise.

"No blood test required. No waiting period. We apply for the license together and pay the nominal fee. Then we can get married."

They stood apart, staring at each other in silence, both breathing heavily. Finally, she added, "But, um... I need to find something to wear… and I need to get a princess dress."

A chuckle erupted from deep within him, and he reached out to take her hands in his. "We're really doing this, aren't we?"

"Yeah, we are," she whispered, her lips curving, her gaze never wavering. "Are we crazy?"

"Yeah, we are." He grinned. "But then, some of the best things created have started out as crazy ideas."

21

Leaving Luke's apartment, she pushed aside doubts, worries, concerns, and rational arguments and focused on the most important task at hand: finding a princess dress. Instead of driving to her home, she headed back north to the BigMart, thankful that it was an all-night establishment.

Armed with determination and the kids' sizes, she grabbed a cart and headed straight to the children's clothing section. Jeremy was easy—a pair of khaki pants, a light blue shirt, and a clip-on tie. Grabbing a pair of navy socks he could pair with his dark sneakers, he'd be fine.

Then she headed to the little girl's section, where she became overwhelmed with pink ruffles and frills and tutu skirts. Just when she was ready to grab anything in Jessica's size, her gaze landed on a perfect outfit. Pale pink satin bodice that fell into a full skirt of satin covered in pink gauzy material. Tiny, embroidered flowers were stitched around the waist. She instantly fell in love. Black ballet-type slippers and pink tights completed the outfit. Well, almost. Hurrying to the section of the store that was already starting to stock Halloween costumes, she found a delicate princess tiara.

The next stop was the women's section, where she'd simply hoped to find anything new, even if it was from a big-box discount store. As long as it didn't look like her typical teaching clothes, she'd be satisfied. The wedding gods must have been with her because, just like with Jessica's outfit, there was one shining, perfect dress, and it was in her size. Exhausted, she ran to grab a few more items, then pushed her cart to the checkout line, trying not to think of the reason for her late-night shopping spree.

Driving back to Baytown, she left the children's bags outside his door. Lifting her hand to knock, she chickened out. *What if he says we can't do this? Then what? We let the kids flap in the wind when storms are all around?* Sneaking back out to her car, she sat for a moment, trying to calm her nerves. *We have to do this. We have to do this for them.*

She leaned forward and lightly banged her head on the steering wheel. *I'm considering marrying someone I'm just getting to know.* The reality was she did know a lot about Luke. And what she knew, she liked. A lot. A whole lot.

She stopped headbanging before her forehead accidentally hit the horn and she drew attention to the fact that she was in a parked car on a town street in the middle of the night.

What if we'd kept dating? Would we be making marriage

plans eventually? Sitting up straighter, she flipped down the visor and stared at her reflection. Her gaze offered no answers, but the resolute expression on her face gave credence that she'd already made up her mind and wasn't turning back now. *I'll face tomorrow, and the day after, and the week after, and for however long we can make this work and do it with a man I care about deeply. And maybe love will follow... but at least the kids will be safe.*

Pulling out her phone, she sent a text to Luke. **Open your door to find my gift for the kids for tomorrow.**

Her phone dinged an incoming message, but she didn't dare look at it until she made it back to her house. Then, still sitting in her car in the middle of the night, only this time in her driveway, she read it.

As crazy as this is, I have no doubts because I'm falling for you. Meet you on the steps of the court-house tomorrow at 10 AM.

Unable to sleep and unwilling to lay in bed with the crazy thoughts making her doubt her sanity, she cleaned the house until the wee hours. She had a guest bed in one bedroom but added a camping air mattress in the other, hoping Jeremy wouldn't mind *roughing* it until they could purchase a bed for him. She made sure the hall bathroom had towels and the small step stool she'd purchased so Jessica could reach the sink.

Falling into bed, she managed to sleep for a few hours before her alarm sounded. Leaping from bed, she was determined to keep her thoughts from sliding into doubts, so she focused on each task. Once showered, shaved, and moisturized, her hair curled and makeup applied with a bit more care than normal to cover the dark circles from lack of sleep, she managed to maintain her sanity.

Sliding the dress over her head, she zipped the back and then slid on her heels. Standing in front of the mirror, a grin spread over her face as she stared at her reflection. The ivory dress was made with a satin-sheen material and an overlay of ivory lace. The bodice was fitted with a V neck, giving only a hint of cleavage. The skirt was fuller, swirling slightly as she twirled in front of the mirror. In many ways, it looked like a grown-up version of Jessica's princess dress. *Not bad for a discount store.*

With a final spritz of perfume, she grabbed her purse and drove to the courthouse. Arriving early, she fretted at the thought of Luke having to get the kids up and into their outfits. Just as she was going to call to see if he needed help, the sound of a little girl's squeal came from the side of the building.

Her gaze shot to the sidewalk, and she spied Jessica skipping in her ballet slippers, perfectly dressed in her beautiful princess outfit, the glistening tiara tucked on top of her dark hair. Jeremy had a wide grin on his face, and his fingers kept reaching up to fiddle with his tie.

Then her gaze landed on Luke.

The world fell away as she stared at this man she was getting ready to marry. His beard was neatly trimmed, his dark hair combed. With his dark pants, he paired a light blue shirt and tie, similar to what she'd chosen for Jeremy. His blue eyes were pinned straight on her, and his smile pierced her heart. She was struck with the familial similarity between him and his niece and nephew and realized that anyone around would think he was their proud dad.

And right then and there, on a sunny fall Saturday, with white clouds passing through the blue sky, on the courthouse steps, it struck her that with the vows they were getting ready to promise, that beautiful family would be hers, as well. She hesitated for a second, waiting for the panic to consume her, but it never came. Her lips curved, and she beamed down toward them. All three rushed up the steps where they became a tangle of arms, embraces, kisses, and laughing.

Thirty minutes later, Allie's body hummed with vibrations as she stood in front of Minnie Fabor, the bespectacled, silver-haired, smiling court clerk. Holding the silk roses she'd bought in the hobby section the previous night, she faced Luke. Jessica, for once not bouncing in excitement, stood next to her, holding a smaller bouquet of silk roses. And next to Luke was Jeremy, his face filled with an emotion that was hard to define, but it almost looked like hope.

But it was when she faced Luke and stared up into his eyes that her heart, already filled to the brim, spilled over. However impulsive their decision was, she felt to her very core that it was the right thing to do.

Repeating the vows given by Minnie, they held each other's hands. She'd wondered if his might shake, but they'd never been more steady. Not having planned anything special, she blinked in surprise as he spoke.

"Allison, I've never met anyone so caring and selfless in my whole life. But I promise to be there for you no matter what life throws at us. I promise to be faithful. I promise to do everything in my power to take care of you. And I promise to spend every day of my life appreciating the gift of who you are and thanking God you're with me."

Her breath caught in her lungs, and she wasn't sure there was enough oxygen in the room to keep her standing. His gaze never wavered, and his hands clasped hers tightly. Her lips curved as she said, "Luke, I knew you were special the first minute I saw you. And every minute I've spent with you since then has only solidified that knowledge. I promise that I'll be at your side as we travel along this journey together. I promise to be faithful. I promise to take care of you, Jeremy, and Jessica. And I thank God that you're with me, too."

He turned toward Jeremy and winked, and she jolted as Jeremy, grinning widely, handed a thin gold band to Luke. He slid it onto her ring finger and said, "With this ring, I thee wed."

She glanced down at the small circle of gold on her finger. Of everything they'd done up to then, it could have almost seemed like playacting. But the ring was real. What they were doing was real. Her body quivered, but she still felt nothing but content. No panic. No doubts. No second thoughts.

Suddenly, it hit her that with all the preparations she'd done, she'd never once thought about a ring. Gasping, she looked up to see Luke's smiling face. He winked toward Jessica, who giggled as she handed a ring up to Allie. Glancing down, she could see it was a man's gold wedding ring. Having no idea where the rings came from, she took it from the beaming little girl's hand and slid it onto Luke's finger. "With this ring, I thee wed." She blew out a shaky breath and smiled.

Minnie grinned over the rim of her glasses. "By the authority given to me in the county of North Heron, I pronounce you husband and wife."

Allie sucked in a quick breath but barely had a chance to prepare as Luke let loose of her hands, wrapped his arms around her, and pulled her in tight, his lips sealing over hers. She melted against his body, giving in to the tingling sensations flooding her veins. He lifted his head, and she grinned, now aware of Jessica's squeal of delight.

Captured by the twinkle in his blue eyes, she clung to his shoulders. He leaned closer, his lips now right at her ears. "Christ, you're beautiful. I promise that I'll never make you regret this decision," he whispered. At that vow, she shivered, overwhelmed with emotions.

The kids were jumping up and down, but Minnie managed to get them to sign their marriage certificate. Standing together, Minnie then snapped pictures with Luke's phone before handing the certificate to him. With that all-important document tucked into Luke's pocket, they linked fingers, and with Jessica holding her other hand and Jeremy at Luke's side, the four of them walked out of the courthouse and into the sunshine.

Stopping at the bottom, she cast her gaze around the area. On a Saturday morning, there were a few people going in and out of the courthouse, several glancing at the new family all dressed up. For a second, Allie wished there had been friends and family to throw rice, snap pictures, or call out congratulations. But other than the sounds of a typical Saturday morning, it was quiet.

"I wish we didn't have to drive separately," she said, more under her breath than to speak out loud.

"I know, and that's why I made a call."

She turned as Wyatt and Joseph walked toward them, an almost identical smile on the brothers' faces. Jerking around, she squeaked, "You told them?"

"Babe, people are going to find out. This isn't something we're going to be able to keep a secret, but then, I hope you don't want to."

She hated that her surprised reaction might mar the day. Squeezing his hand, she shook her head. "No, not at all. I just wasn't expecting anyone, so it caught me off guard. But don't doubt that I'm in this all the way, Luke."

His smile of relief warmed her heart. "Good. Plus, I didn't want us to spend our entire wedding day having to move things, so I started out with a couple of friends who would help."

She held his gaze, trusting him completely. Nodding, she smiled as the two brothers approached. She'd never formally met either of them but had seen them at the AL ball games. Both in law enforcement, she knew Wyatt had gained notoriety when a few months earlier he became involved with Camilla Gannon, America's sweetheart actress who was hiding out on the Eastern Shore, and now lived there with him. Joseph had gone out with a couple of teachers she knew but so far had never been pinned down by any woman. Both turned their affable grins to them, offering cheek kisses to her and handshakes to Luke.

He handled his car keys to Joseph, making sure they had Allie's address. As they headed out, he turned to her and the kids with a wide smile on his face. "Who's ready to go take a look at our new house?" With Jeremy and Jessica's shouts and cheers ringing in her ears, she squeezed Luke's hand, and they buckled the kids into their seats. Before she could open the passenger door, Luke pulled her gently to the side. He lifted his hands and cupped her face, and her breath caught at the sight of his pained expression.

"What is it?"

"We haven't had a moment alone," he began, his thumb sweeping over her cheeks. "There's so much I want to say, Allie. And I don't… I'm not sure… it's just that… oh, fuck, I'm fucking this up."

"Luke, honey, you're not effing anything up. Just talk to me."

His lips curved, and she knew it was from her abbreviated version of cursing. He'd never asked her about it, but working in an elementary school, she was too afraid if cursing was her habit, she might say the wrong thing in front of the kids. Now, she was just glad for the little smile gracing his face.

He sucked in a deep breath, then said, "The last twenty-four hours have been a whirlwind, from celebrating the start of us as a couple to deciding to get married to make sure the kids can stay with me… now with us. You spent the night shopping for the kids to make sure this day was special for them. You look so gorgeous, and I stood there saying those vows, meaning every word, knowing I'm the luckiest man in the world to be in the presence of such a kind, giving beauty."

If she'd thought it was hard to breathe from his earlier expression, his words stole the air from her lungs. But it seemed he wasn't finished.

"I know this wasn't the day of your dreams. I know this wasn't the wedding you'd always imagined. I know we just started dating, and you'd never even considered that we might eventually marry down the road, much less right now. I'm so humbled and awed that you're making this sacrifice for me and Jessica and Jeremy. Opening your new house that you just bought and opening your heart. And I am so fuckin' terrified that you'll wake up tomorrow morning and hate me. But my vow to you in there was true. I promise to do everything I can to never make you regret this."

Her hands were clinging to his shoulders, and she wasn't sure if she let go that her legs would hold her upright. Dragging in a shaky breath, she smiled, wanting to erase all doubt from his beautiful blue eyes. "Luke, you're right. This wasn't the wedding I'd always thought I might have, but that doesn't make it wrong. And yes, we've just started dating, but we care for each other, and marriages have started with less. And I'm humbled and awed at the sacrifice that you're making for those kids, and believe me, the risk isn't all on me. You're taking a risk marrying me, as well. My house is big enough for us and will be a great place for them. And I'm also effing terrified that you'll wake up and hate this decision." She clutched him tighter, lifting on her toes to place her lips near his. "But I also promise to do everything I can to make you not regret this."

"Christ, I'm falling for you," he breathed just before he kissed her.

The kiss didn't last nearly long enough before Jessica shouted from inside the car, "Uncle Luke! Aunt Allie, come on!"

They separated, breathing heavily. Grinning, she said, "The princess commands our presence at the new home. I think we should obey."

Laughing, Luke let her go to open her door. "Then your carriage awaits."

The mood lighter, the four smiled all the way to her house.

22

During the drive, Luke continued to glance to the side, unable to believe this day had actually happened. Unable to believe he'd created such an outlandish lie to hopefully keep Mrs. Nicholson from having a reason to take the kids away, he'd been ready to beg Allie's forgiveness and admit to the social worker what he'd done. But when Allie had suggested they go through with it, as crazy as it was, he'd wanted to shout. For Jessica. For Jeremy. For himself.

When he'd looked at the bags she'd left outside his apartment, he was gutted at her thoughtfulness and knew his niece and nephew's luck had finally changed in a way they'd always remember. And when he and the kids had walked to the bottom of the courthouse steps and he'd looked up to see Allie in a lacy ivory dress with her makeup highlighting her beautiful face and her long hair in waves down her back, he knew he was the luckiest man in the world. Now, driving to her house, he could only pray that he was worthy of her.

"Are we there yet?" Jessica asked, bouncing in her seat.

"Almost, sweetie," Allie replied. She glanced toward Luke. "I'm nervous," she whispered. "What if they don't like it?"

"Babe."

She laughed. "Is that one word supposed to convey an entire answer?"

He chuckled, letting go of some of his own nervousness. "Yes. But in case you need more, just remember that my place seemed like a castle to them. This place will rock their world."

They turned onto her driveway, and the kids had fallen silent while their energy still vibrated inside the car. Stopping outside the house, he looked into the rearview mirror as Allie twisted her head around. "We're here, guys. Let's go explore your new home."

As soon as they were unbuckled, Jessica walked in her princess dress toward the porch then stopped, staring open-mouthed at the house. Jeremy followed his sister, then turned and looked over his shoulder.

"Who else lives here?"

Allie had been walking in front of Luke but halted, and he had to throw his hands up to her shoulders to keep from running into her back. He knew what Jeremy was asking and had just warned Allie that her house would seem huge to the kids but now realized he should have prepared them a little more. Allie looked over her shoulder, tears threatening to spill down her cheeks. Pulling her in tightly to his side, he guided her over to the kids. Placing his hand on Jeremy's shoulder, he replied, "No one else lives here. This is Allie's house, and she wants us to live here as a family."

The kids' eyes bugged out as they looked up toward the house and then around the yard. "We can play here?" Jessica asked. "Just like at the park?"

"Absolutely, beautiful girl," Allie answered.

Jessica clutched her silk flowers that she hadn't let go of since the wedding. "And we can stay here with you and Uncle Luke?"

Her little voice trembled, and Luke felt each shudder hit. Before Allie could move, he dropped to his knees and gathered her in his arms. Pressing her little head to his chest, he said, "Yeah, baby, this is your home now. Me and Allie got married and are living here now, so we all have this home together."

Allie squatted next to him, now on their level. "You know, this has been an exciting morning, with a lot of new things happening and a lot of changes. Let's go inside, and I'll show you around. You can see your rooms, and I'll fix some lunch."

With the kids now giving in to the excitement, Jessica bounced up and down and Jeremy's smile grew wide. Luke stood and gently pulled Allie to her feet. She led them into the house, and Luke followed right behind. After the tour downstairs, they went upstairs, where she opened one of the bedroom doors. "I haven't had a chance to fix anything up in here, but Jessica, this will be your room."

"But what about Jeremy?" Jessica asked.

"He'll be in the room next door." She turned to Jeremy and grimaced. "I feel really bad, but I don't have another bed right now. For tonight, I've put an air mattress in here, but as soon as we can, we'll get you your own furniture."

Luke hated that Allie had to apologize. "Don't worry about it, sweetheart. Jeremy and I have already talked, and he knows something for him is on the way."

Jeremy stepped into the room, his eyes wide and his smile bright as he turned around in a circle. "Yeah, Allie, don't worry about it. I can't believe this is all for me!"

Allie sidled over to Luke and whispered, "Are you bringing some furniture over for Jeremy?"

Praying his plan was going to work, he turned and wrapped his arms around her, pulling her close to his front. Dipping his chin, he held her gaze. "I've made some arrangements. Last night, when I called Wyatt and Joseph, they had a few ideas, and I thought they were good ones. Any other time, Allie, I would have talked it over with you first, but you had too much on your plate. I don't want to overwhelm you, so I'm asking for your trust."

Her head tilted to the side as she pressed her lips together, her gaze searching his face. Finally nodding, she smiled. "Okay, I trust you."

She showed them the bathroom they would share and then took them into the master bedroom.

Out on the small deck, Jeremy leaned over the rail, his eyes bright. "You could totally climb down that ladder with the plant growing on it."

Laughing, she shook her head. "It's a trellis, and while it looks like a ladder, I'm not sure it would hold my weight. It's built so that the pretty vines and flowers can grow upward."

Jeremy twisted his head to look upward, then asked, "Wow, it keeps going up to that window. What's up there?"

"I have a secret attic," she said. "Want to see it?"

Both kids shouted with excitement, and she walked them to the door next to the bathroom at the end of the hall. Opening it, they peered up the stairs.

"Is it scary up there?" Jessica asked, her eyes wide.

"No, it's actually very light. And I can turn it into a bedroom sometime for guests." She led the way and grinned as the kids walked around and Luke stood with his arm around her.

"Whoa... this is so cool," Jeremy said, his voice full of awe.

The sound of crunching tires on her oyster shell driveway met their ears, and she startled. Giving her a squeeze, Luke said, "Okay, it's go-time."

Her eyes widened, but the kids had already rushed down the stairs. "What's happening?"

"Me doing everything I can to take care of you." He turned with her in his arms and guided her down the stairs after the kids, hoping the plans he'd set in motion early that morning weren't going to backfire on them.

Three hours later, he and Allie waved goodbye to the group of friends who'd stopped by to help. Not only did Wyatt and Joseph go by Luke's apartment to load up his bed and bring it since it was larger than Allie's and had a new mattress, but they'd also moved her bed into Jeremy's room and put Luke's in the master's bedroom.

He'd called Joseph late last night and filled him in on the crazy plan, not sure if he wanted his friend to talk him out of the madness or offer support. He should have known that Joseph would listen, then simply say, "Whatever you need, man, I'm here." And then the two had planned on what needed to be done and how to make it work.

Zac and Maddie stopped by to bring food, and while Zac assisted with moving furniture, Maddie took Allie and Luke aside to talk about the decision to marry. Luke could see that Allie was anxious, but Maddie assured them that the kids were resilient and would adapt to the changes readily. She also reminded them that the most important thing right now was stability and that, in her opinion, the kids needed to be with them, not jerked out of a loving environment just because a state social worker wanted to throw her weight around.

Then Maddie walked to the side with Allie, and their heads bent together in softly spoken tones. The women's conversation made Luke nervous, but he breathed easier when they turned back to the house, both with smiles on their faces.

Before the gathering descended into madness, Luke handed his phone to Maddie and had her take so many pictures of them that finally, Jeremy declared, "Enough!" and ran to his room to help the other men put the bed together.

Aiden and his wife, Lia, brought their daughter, Emily, over, and she played with Jessica in her room once Joseph dropped off the toys and clothes from Luke's apartment. He'd kept an eye on the kids, but they seemed to have immediately adjusted to having a home and a yard.

It wasn't a huge gathering like the moving party that Allie had hosted, but it was perfect. Now, he turned and took a moment to hold her in his arms, loving the way she felt, the way she fit with him. But he was also scared shitless… *What if this goes south? What if she regrets our decision? What if she gets tired of—*

"I can hear you thinking," she said. Leaning back, she smiled up at him. "In fact, I can hear you *over*think."

He chuckled and squeezed her tighter. "Oh, you can, can you?"

"You're worried. But don't be, Luke. Not on my account." Her smile slowly faded, and she sighed. "Let's get the kids settled, and then you and I can figure some things out, okay?"

"Sounds like a plan, babe."

He hated that she was the one to offer reassurances when it should have been him, but just like he was learning about Allie, she didn't shy away from the tough conversations.

They headed inside, not having to look far for the kids with the laughter coming from upstairs. Earlier, the kids had raced around the backyard, ran in and out of the house for snacks, and gone up and down the stairs dozens of times as they tried to keep up with everything that was going on.

Now, they discovered both kids in Jessica's room. She was still in her princess dress, but her tiara was on top of the nightstand next to her bed. Lia had assisted Allie in getting the kids' clothes put away in their dressers and closets so that task was complete. Luke tousled Jeremy's hair, then snatched Jessica up from the bed, held her close, and gave her a twirl around the room.

"What kind of day did you have, princess?"

She threw her arms into the air and shouted, "The bestest day ever!"

Allie laughed and shook her head. "I can't imagine how you're not exhausted. And as much as I hate to make you take off your dress, it's time for a bath."

Jessica wrinkled her nose, but Allie promised more bubble bath, tempting her. Luke set her feet on the floor, and Allie grabbed pajamas and clean underwear before leading Jessica by the hand to the bathroom at the end of the hall.

While the girls were gone, he took the opportunity to find out how Jeremy was doing. "Let's go into your room and see what you might need."

Jeremy looked up in surprise but followed Luke into the next room. "Uncle Luke, there's nothing that I need."

"You and I can go shopping some time and get some posters to go on your walls, a few more games, a baseball and catcher's mitt if you like. You definitely need a bookcase." Smiling down, he said, "Anything you want or need, just let me know." Jeremy nodded, then climbed onto the bed, sitting cross-legged. Luke sat on the bed with him, wrapping his arm around his shoulders. "It was a busy day, bud. You okay?"

He sucked in his lips and nodded, but his brow was furrowed. "Ms. Maddie said that it was okay if we were worried about all the changes happening, but what if I'm not worried? Does that mean something's wrong with me?"

Luke's chin jerked back in. "Not at all. You can feel whatever you want to feel. I think that's what she meant." Jeremy nodded again, and Luke pressed, "So, you're okay with everything?"

A little smile curved Jeremy's lips. "Yeah." He glanced around the room, and his grin widened. "I've never had my own room before. Or a bed all to myself." Suddenly, he jerked around toward Luke. "Do you think that Jessica will be okay by herself?"

Luke chuckled, his heart warmed by Jeremy's concern. "She'll be fine, and Allie and I'll be right across the hall."

Jeremy's shoulders relaxed, and his grin returned. "You know, Uncle Luke, you don't have to buy anything to fix this room for me."

He wondered how often Chelle and Larry complained about the kids costing money. *When they were wasting what they had on drugs.* "Don't worry about it, kiddo. Whatever you and your sister need, we'll take care of it."

The sound of laughter in the hall captured their attention, and a freshly-washed and sweet-smelling Jessica bounded into the room. "I had a bubble bath!"

Luke gathered her in his arms, nuzzling her belly,

making her laugh even more. "You smell so sweet, I might have to eat you."

"No, Uncle Luke! You can't eat me."

Allie walked into the room, her smile landing on the others. "Did we interrupt man-talk?"

Jessica giggled as Luke said, "I think we finished our man-talk for one night, didn't we, Jeremy?"

"Yeah," Jeremy grinned, hopping from the bed.

She caught him by the shoulder and bent to kiss the top of his head. "Your turn for a shower, sweetie."

Luke's breath caught in his throat as he witnessed Jeremy's wonder-filled gaze hold on Allie. His nephew had never felt a woman's loving touch... a mother's loving touch. He set Jessica on the floor after another tickle and then nudged Jeremy. "Come on, bud. Let's get a shower over with."

As he guided Jeremy out the door, his hand caught Allie's, and he brought it to his lips, kissing her fingers. She graced him with a smile, and not for the first time, he hoped to God he would witness that smile every day for the rest of his life.

23

Allie quietly closed Jessica's door after the little girl finally crashed when the excitement of the day had completely exhausted her. The princess dress was hanging in the closet, but Allie planned on washing it before it was worn again. *Well, maybe. If Jessica will give me the* chance. She smiled as she tiptoed to the room next door. Looking down at Jeremy, her smile stayed firmly on her face. Leaning down, she kissed his forehead as he slept. Turning, she startled, spying Luke standing in the doorway, his gaze warmly resting on her. She moved directly toward him, and he shifted at the last second to allow her to pass.

He closed the door behind her, and she waited as he wrapped his arm around her shoulder, leading her into the hall. "They find sleep okay?"

She nodded and smiled in spite of the exhaustion pulling at her. "I think they finally dropped from all the excitement. That, plus warm bubble baths, and showers, and you reading a story."

"They've never had a day like this," he said as he guided her into the master bedroom.

"None of us have," she reminded.

Once inside, he closed the door, and she hesitated, suddenly having no idea what she was supposed to do. So tired she could fall asleep standing up, the idea of her wedding night loomed large in her mind. She'd taken off her dress earlier in the day and managed to grab a shower while Luke had read the kids a story. Now in her comfy yoga pants and a slouchy top, she wondered if she should put on something a little more alluring but doubted she had the energy.

Luke wrapped his arms around her as they stood in the middle of the room. "Babe, we've had a full, emotional day after neither of us got much sleep last night. And we've got a lot to talk about, most of which we won't get to tonight because we're both wiped."

She leaned back and looked up into his face, then smoothed her fingers over the lines in his forehead. "What are you saying?"

"That the idea of making love to my wife is tempting, but everything about today was so crazy that I'd rather just lay in bed and hold you while you go to sleep, knowing there will be lots of tomorrows for everything else."

She sucked in her lips for a few seconds, his words washing over her. There was a lot packed into the words he'd said, and she loved how he acknowledged their exhaustion and wasn't totally focused on just sex. And yet one word hit her, catching her by surprise. "Wife," she whispered.

His gaze zeroed in on her face. "What?"

"You called me 'wife.' I know that sounds silly to notice that over everything else you said. But I suppose it's just hitting me that I'm your wife. I haven't heard that word since Minnie pronounced it so clearly this morning just before you kissed me."

A chuckle erupted, and he shook his head before bending to take her lips in a soft kiss. "Wife... I like that." Lifting his head to peer into her eyes again, he sighed. "But the last twenty-four hours changed your life completely."

She knew that as tired as they were, some things needed to be said now. Stepping back, she linked fingers with him and led him to the bed. Crawling up to the head, she leaned back against the pillows and patted the mattress beside her. He kicked off his shoes and didn't hesitate to join her.

Settling her head on his shoulder with his arm wrapped around her, she closed her eyes and breathed him in. Her hand splayed over his abs underneath his T-shirt. Warm skin over steel muscles.

"What's on your mind, babe?" he prodded.

"I was thinking last night... or rather, in the early hours of this morning, after shopping and cleaning, that there are lots of reasons why people get married. Sure, falling desperately in love is the main one, but some people get married because they got pregnant. Some people get married because it's financially advantageous. Some people get married because they've confused lust with love. Some people get married when they find what happens in Vegas doesn't stay in Vegas

—" That earned her a chuckle, and she loved the sound. Loved that they were lying in bed, just talking. Loved that she felt so comfortable with him. She peered up and held his gaze. "And some people get married because they want to take care of their ready-made family."

"Like us," he said, his fingers linked with her again.

"Yeah. So, while our beginning wasn't planned, that doesn't make our feelings any less real. We just happen to be married while we discover more about each other."

"And if you don't like what you discover?"

She shook her head. "I might not know what your favorite food is, or which Lord of the Rings movie was the one that moved you the most, or the names of all your friends... but I had already discovered what kind of man you are."

"And what kind of man is that?"

"A man who'd give his life to protect those he loves. A man who'd fight to keep his family safe. A man who'd change his world to offer it to those kids. And that's the kind of man I married. That's the kind of man I always wanted to marry. So, stop worrying that I'll wake up and decide it was all a mistake. Just let me travel this journey with you and have you take it with me, as well."

"Christ, Allie, you take my breath away." His smile widened as he shifted their positions so she was straddling him. Their mouths sealed, their kiss flaming. His tongue swept through her mouth, the velvet strokes sending electricity straight to her inner core.

Suddenly not as tired as she thought she was as she

felt his cock swell against her sex, the desire for friction took over, and she rubbed herself along the thick ridge.

His hand moved to her shirt and whipped it over her head, their mouths barely separating for the thin material to pass between them. She'd slipped on a stretchy bra after she showered, and it quickly was pulled over her head, as well. His hands slid to her breasts, his thumbs and forefingers rolling her nipples.

Her fingers bunched and clutched the material of his T-shirt, trying to work it up his torso, but she made little progress with his back still against the pillows next to the headboard. A growl erupted, and she was startled to realize it came from her until he chuckled.

He pushed her back gently so that he had room to lean forward, snatching the T-shirt over his head. With his torso on display, the war between wanting to drag her tongue over his smooth skin or finish getting naked was fought and then decided when she threw her leg over to the side, shimmying out of her yoga pants and panties before kneeling in front of him completely naked.

"Shit, the door!" she whisper-cried.

"I locked it," he quickly assured. "I knew we were tired and wasn't going to try for anything, but I felt it was best in case we woke in the middle of the night feeling the urge. And hell, seeing you there, I would definitely have felt the urge."

She grinned and shook her head. "I thought we were too tired, but now I can't imagine not doing this."

He cupped her cheeks and held her close but didn't kiss her. Instead, his gaze roved over her face as though memorizing each inch. "I didn't allow myself to think that we'd do anything tonight. I'd vowed to give you whatever time and space you needed. If you'd wanted me to sleep on the sofa tonight, I would have."

"If you'd tried to sleep on the sofa, I would have dragged you back here and tied you to the bed."

His brows lifted, and he grinned. "Now, there's a game I'd like to play."

Laughing, she rolled her eyes, glad that they had slid into a comfortable mood, heavy conversations finished. Glancing down, she said, "As much as I love staring at your torso, touching your muscles…" for emphasis, she dragged her fingers along the ridges of his abs, loving the hiss that escaped his lips, "you do seem to be still overdressed." Her fingers now landed at the waistband of the sweatpants he'd put on after he'd showered. Easily able to slide her fingers down the front, she wrapped them around his erection, earning a growl that rumbled from deep inside his chest.

He shifted to his knees and jerked his sweatpants and boxers down, rolling his hip to the side as he tossed them over the edge of the bed before returning to his previous reclining position. Once again, she threw her leg over his thighs and lifted it so that her sex was directly over the head of his cock. She hesitated, then asked, "I'm assuming you're clean."

His eyes widened, and his fingertips pressed into the flesh of her ass. "Yeah… checked at work."

"Me, too. On birth control, as well."

"Babe, I've got condoms. And I haven't gotten you ready. We don't have to do this—"

"We're married. And I'm already ready. I trust you with my heart and my life."

He blinked, then his chest depressed as the air rushed out. "Christ, Allie, you completely undo me."

She said nothing but held his gaze as she sank onto his cock, his girth stretching her. She hadn't come first but was already so primed, her slick walls surrounded him. But even with the first stroke, she knew she wouldn't last long. With him reclined against the head-board, his knees cocked to cradle her ass from behind, and his hands guiding her up and down his shaft, she fell into the rhythm with abandon. Her breasts bounced, and while she controlled her movements with her thighs, her hands gave her leverage as they held onto his shoulders. He lifted a breast to his mouth, sucking deeply.

So much of the day had simply happened... barely planned for, mostly just going along with whatever needed to be done to get married, get moved, and make sure the kids were settled into their new home. But this... this was Luke giving her control. Luke giving her the position of power. Luke giving her the chance to take what she needed. And she loved him for that.

Blanking her mind of everything other than the feel of his cock dragging her inner walls, she closed her eyes and felt the coil tighten inside. Close. Closer.

"Allie," his guttural voice called out.

She jerked her eyes open, seeing his intense gaze on her. He didn't say anything else. She understood that he was begging for her eyes to be on him. Her fingers dug into his shoulders, and she smiled. The truth was she didn't need her eyes to be closed to focus on the swirling sensations deep inside her body nor the swirling emotions deep inside her mind. This man, her man, her husband. For better or for worse, she'd rushed into this union with her eyes open, no regrets.

As she fell over the precipice of her orgasm, she watched the beauty of him as his own release slammed into him at the same time. The vibrations fluttered inside as his erection had swelled even more. His face reddened, his neck muscles were tight with bulging veins, and they both choked back the roars that threatened to erupt. She fell forward, her face planting against his neck, her breasts crushed against his chest as he held her hips, still pistoning upward until she felt sure every last drop must have left his body.

Finally, his hands left her hips, and he banded his arms around her, holding her tight. Their sweat-slicked bodies slowly cooled as their breaths mingled, their breathing returning to normal. When she thought she could move, she pushed away and peered at him, gracing him with a contented smile. "Well, *husband*, it looks like we just consummated the marriage."

He burst out laughing, and after lifting her off his cock, he rolled them together so that his welcomed weight now pressed her into the mattress. He angled his head and kissed her long, hard, and wet... and if she wasn't mistaken, there was a bit of possessiveness in the kiss as well, something she didn't mind at all.

Thankful the next morning was Sunday, Allie still rose early to be ready for the kids when they awoke. Jessica bounded downstairs, talking a mile-a-minute, planning what she was going to wear today, and begging Jeremy to play outside with her.

Jeremy followed more slowly, his wakeup obviously on a slower pace than his sister's. Nonetheless, Allie noticed he was patient as always, taking care of Jessica as he'd obviously learned to do over the years.

Realizing she and Luke needed to have a conversation about the kids, she also knew that would have to wait… breakfast first. Taking orders, she fixed pancakes decorated with chocolate chips to make smiley faces, scrambled eggs, bacon, and sausage, and poured tall glasses of orange juice and milk.

The kids reacted with exuberance, but it was Luke's wide eyes and humor-tipped lips when he spied the smiling pancakes that made her glad she'd added the cute twist. He shoveled in a bite along with the kids and muttered, "Never ate smiling food before, but this is good."

Jessica giggled with her mouth stuffed full of syrupy goodness. Jeremy's gaze was pinned on Luke, mimicking his lip-quirk appreciation. Allie rolled her eyes but smiled, just glad to see everyone had survived the previous day without any meltdowns, tantrums, or tears.

As she finished, she asked, "Okay, what's on the agenda for today? And just to say, it will be great if you say nothing special is happening."

Luke chuckled, then said, "Allie's right. Today is

about everyone taking it easy. Play, rest, get used to your rooms, take time to enjoy the yard, but don't go outside the fenced area, and the only chore will be to find everything you'll need for school tomorrow before dinner so that there are no problems in the morning. And maybe if we're up to it, after lunch, Allie can walk with us down the road to the beach."

The kids' eyes bugged at that idea, both eagerly agreeing they wanted to see the water. Allie nodded, then started to collect their plates to rinse when Luke continued.

"There's one thing we need to make sure we do today, and we'll do that as soon as you two wash your hands and faces and brush your teeth. Take care of that and meet Allie and me in the living room. We need to make sure you understand what's happening so you have no questions."

Realizing Luke also saw the need to talk to the kids, she made big-*eek*-eyes at him, wishing they'd had the conversation first. He simply nodded until the kids thanked her for breakfast and then ran upstairs, ready to start their day. Her gaze followed them, her heart twinging.

"Babe?"

She turned to see Luke staring at her, questioning in his eyes. "That's probably the first time they've really been excited about a new day filled with new possibilities."

He slid off the stool and walked around the counter, caging her in with his hands on either side. "You're right. And I could tell from your expression that you're uncertain about us talking to them."

Shaking her head, she rested her hands on his arms. "No, not at all. I just... well, I just thought maybe we should talk first."

He lifted one hand from the counter, scrubbed it over his beard, then nodded slowly. "You're right, and I'm sorry."

She leaned forward, so their faces were closer. "Let's face it, we've only been married one day, and I have a feeling there will be a lot of things we have to learn to do together. And while you and I haven't discussed co-parenting the kids yet, I trust you."

He closed the distance and kissed her lightly. She fought the urge to melt into him, not knowing when the kids might rush back downstairs. He lifted his head and stared deeply into her eyes, opening and closing his mouth a couple of times as though starting to say something and then changing his mind. Before she had a chance to ask, the sounds of little footsteps on the stairs could be heard. Instead, she squeezed her fingers around his arms and smiled. "First true family meeting?"

His smile met hers. "Yeah, and I've got to say I like the sound of that."

With his arm wrapped around her, they walked into the living room.

24

Luke recognized that he'd screwed up on his first day as a husband. Allie was right, they needed to talk and agree on things with the kids before he made unilateral decisions for all of them. But he'd wanted to allay the shadows in Jeremy's eyes and make sure the kids knew that they were important in the building of their new family. He just hoped that as he spoke, what he said was what Allie felt as well. Looking at her sitting next to Jessica on the sofa with Jeremy on the other side of his sister, he felt her smile right to his very marrow. He sat on the coffee table facing them, wanting to be as close to them as possible.

"Okay, guys, yesterday was full and kind of rushed, so Allie and I wanted to make sure you two know why we're doing what we're doing and how that affects all of us."

Jessica stared at him, her little legs swinging, her stuffed cat in her lap. Jeremy's back was ramrod straight, his gaze not wavering, and Luke could swear he could feel his nephew's nerves vibrating from where he was sitting. Chancing a glance toward Allie, her encouraging smile gave him strength.

"You know the reason that you came to live with me was because your mom and dad are both unable to take care of you. And I'm sorry for the choices that they made, but that means that I was able to step in. Allie and I had started dating, and we care a great deal about each other. We hadn't talked about getting married yet because we were still very new at being a couple. When the social worker came the other day to check out where you were living, she wasn't happy that the space was really small. So, while we hadn't talked about it before, Allie and I decided to get married and move in here. That way, each of you has a room, and you now have a nice house with a yard."

"I like my room," Jessica pronounced. Her nose scrunched. "Do you think that lady will like my new room?"

Nodding, Luke replied, "Absolutely. Whether she or another person comes by to check out where you're living, I think they'll be very happy with us all being together in this house." Jeremy appeared thoughtful, and Luke turned toward him. "Do you have any questions so far, buddy?"

"Dad's in jail. Mom had told me that. Is that where she is, too?"

Jessica's eyes widened as though it was news to her. "Jail?" She turned to Jeremy and blinked. "That's where bad people go."

Jeremy's face hardened, and Luke jumped in. "Yes,

but it's also where people go who make bad choices and they have to spend time there to learn to make a better choice."

"And Mom is there, too?" Jessica asked, her eyes still wide.

Glancing toward Allie, he waited until she slowly nodded. Taking a big breath, he said, "I think it's important for you two to know the truth. Your mom is in the hospital because she took some drugs that weren't good for her. And when she gets better, she'll probably spend some time in jail, also."

"When they get out, do we have to go back?" Jeremy asked, a now-familiar wariness in his eyes.

Luke knew that living with Larry and Chelle as parents, Jeremy had worries that no eight-year-old should have to deal with. And it was obvious that Jeremy still had concerns. "I don't know what's happening with your parents other than they're not going to be around for quite a while. I'm going to talk to a judge to get permanent guardianship for both of you. I know that's a big word, but what it means is that your parents will let me and Allie raise you. When you become an adult, you can see them and talk to them, but for now, you need to concentrate on being kids and let your parents learn how to take care of themselves."

Jessica's face scrunched as her legs continued to kick back and forth. She twisted around to look at Jeremy, and Luke knew she was taking her cues from her older brother.

"What if I don't want to see them again?" Jeremy asked, his voice still hard.

"That'll be up to you."

"They always acted like we were in the way and didn't want us… don't know why I'd want them, either."

Jessica's shoulders slumped. "Don't be mad, Jeremy. Uncle Luke is gonna make it all better, and Allie makes happy pancakes."

At that, Jeremy's lips quirked upward slightly. "Yeah," he muttered.

Luke blew out a long breath, uncertain the family talk was going as well as he'd hoped. But too late to stop then, he continued, "Now, I don't want to dump too much on you all at once, but I want to make sure we all understand what's happening. Allie and I are married. And we're going to take care of you. There will be some house rules but nothing you can't handle, and mostly to make sure you're safe. But you need to do what Allie says just like you do for me. And what we really want is for you to have fun, be kids, do your best in school, and enjoy being a family."

"Are you our new mom and dad?" Jessica asked, her eyes wide, and as Luke peered at her, he could see hope reigning in her expression.

Looking toward Allie, he watched as she bit her lip in hesitation. Her gaze met his and she cocked her head to the side. Nodding, he was relieved when Allie took over. She smiled at Jessica and said, "In many ways, yes, beautiful girl. Families come in all different ways. You still have your mom and dad, but while we're your aunt and uncle, we're kind of like a mom and dad. The most important thing for you to remember is that we love you very much. And that's never going to change."

"And you want to keep us?" Jeremy asked, swallowing deeply.

"Yes," Luke replied without hesitation. "We want to stay a family and think that's best for all of us." Thinking their family meeting had been emotional enough, he plopped his hands onto his knees and stood. "Okay, first family meeting is over. Now, you two can have fun for the rest of the day."

Jessica hopped up from the couch, already twirling with her cat in her arms. Jeremy stood more slowly, then quickly wrapped his arms around Luke's waist. "Love you, Uncle Luke." One hand immediately went to Jeremy's back, and the other cupped the back of his head.

"Right back at you, Jeremy."

Faster than he thought possible, Jeremy let go and whirled to throw his arms around Allie. "Love you, too, Aunt Allie."

Her arms gathered Jeremy close to her, but her tearful gaze shot up to Luke's. "I love you, too, sweet boy." She bent her head closer to Jeremy, but Luke could still hear her whisper. "The time for you to worry about everything is over. Now, you just focus on being you."

He nodded, the top of his head bobbing into her chin slightly, but she didn't appear to mind. Then he let go and ran into the backyard, where Jessica was already calling for him to come to play.

Luke turned and plopped down on the sofa next to Allie, pulling her into his arms. Neither spoke for a moment, then finally, he asked, "Did I do okay?"

She twisted so that her gaze was on him, leaned forward, and kissed him lightly. "You were perfect."

"Were you nervous?"

She bit her lip while scrunching her nose. "Yeah, a little. In the future, we probably should talk first together when we need to have a family meeting. You and I are so new, Luke. We're not used to each other's thoughts ahead of time. Not tuned in to each other the way couples get when they're together for a while before having kids. But I was impressed... you told them exactly what I thought they needed to hear."

"You're absolutely right, babe. I should have talked to you first." He squeezed her shoulder. "I probably jumped the gun because I was worried about Jeremy."

"Me, too," she agreed, twisting to face him more fully. "I think we should continue to have him meet with Maddie. He holds a lot of resentment toward Larry and Chelle, which is understandable. They failed him as parents, and he knows that. He's also used to taking care of and shielding Jessica. And while that's a wonderful trait, he didn't learn it from watching a good man, he learned it from growing up in a neglectful home."

"I agree with him continuing to see Maddie. I want him to start relaxing and just be a kid. I want him to know that we're here for him and Jessica and that all this doesn't fall on his shoulders anymore."

They sat quietly for another moment, then he jumped into the next thing on his mind. "You need to let me see the expenses for the house—mortgage, electricity, cable, insurance."

She twisted around, her brow furrowed. "The expenses?"

"I know we haven't had a chance to figure out anything, but we are married and that means we need to take a look at income and expenses. I'll take care of the mortgage, the kids' expenses, the insurance, the—"

"And just what am I supposed to do?"

"I'm not going to have you pay for us—"

She shifted in her seat. "*Us*? *Us*? Just who makes up this *us*? Because I thought we were all now part of this *us*!"

"That's not what I mean, Allie. But you've given up so much, and I want to take care of the family. And that family includes you."

"We have to do this together," she huffed, crossing her arms over her chest.

He realized he'd stepped into another landmine. Choosing his words carefully, he said, "I'm sorry. I didn't mean to come across as caveman-ish. But you put the down payment on this house, so I want to help with the mortgage payments since there are now four of us here. I want to take some of the burden off you."

"Luke, it's not a burden." She squeezed her eyes shut and blew out a long breath, her shoulders slumping. "There really is a lot to figure out, isn't there? And doing it when we're tired probably isn't a good time."

He pulled her closer. "It's not like we can't make it all work, sweetheart. Tell you what, we'll look at all our expenses together. House, cars, kids, groceries… everything. Then we'll figure out how to combine and cover everything. Good?"

She nodded and lay her head back on his shoulder. "Yeah, good."

They stayed wrapped in each other's arms for a few minutes, hearing the children playing in the backyard, taking time to just enjoy a few minutes of peace.

It was later that afternoon that the shrieks of the children reached Luke's ears, and he laughed watching the kids running along the beach. When they'd walked down the road, they passed two other houses before coming to the cul-de-sac that had a sandy path leading over the dunes to the beach.

Both kids had come to a sudden stop, staring with open mouths, neither speaking. Allie and Luke had turned to watch joy and wonder fill their faces before Jeremy threw his arms into the air as he ran toward the gentle bay surf. Jessica, not to be left behind, followed, her little girl squeals ringing out as she chased her brother.

They'd walked along the sandy coast finding oyster shells and razor clam shells and watching the gulls dive into the water and little sand runners race along in front of them. After a while, Allie and Jessica sat in the sand to work on a sandcastle while Luke and Jeremy walked further before coming back to them, their pockets full of shells.

"Look what we found," Jeremy said, his eyes bright as Luke held out his palm, displaying a piece of green glass.

"Oh, no! Someone broke a bottle!" Jessica cried.

"This is sea glass," Allie said, reaching out to take the glass in her hand. "See? It's smooth and won't cut you."

The kids bent their heads over as she pulled out a few more pieces from her pocket. "It comes from the boats in the water."

"Huh?" Jeremy looked up at her.

"Those big boats will toss out some of their glass bottles, and then when the glass breaks, it gets tossed and turned by the waves and sand on the bottom of the ocean. All that churning makes the sharp edges nice and smooth. Then it washes up on shore, and we call it sea glass."

"Can we keep it?" Jessica said, her eyes wide as though Allie held magic in her hands.

"Absolutely, sweetie. The shells and sea glass you find out here can be yours to collect and keep if you want."

"I've never seen anything so pretty in my whole life!" Jessica vowed. "And I can keep it in my room and it won't get taken away!"

Allie's little gasp sounded and her gaze jerked over the kids' heads toward Luke. He pressed his lips tightly and sighed.

"Our parents were jerks," Jeremy bit out, his eyes on his sister.

"Jeremy," Luke said, his voice soft. "I know you feel it and that's cool. You can talk out those feelings with me or Allie or your counselor, but let's be careful around your sister."

His little-boy shoulders slumped as he held Luke's

gaze then nodded. Looking back toward Jessica, he smiled. "Let's go find some more sea glass for you."

As though her world just turned brighter than ever, Jessica smiled widely and jumped up, racing along the sandy dune with her brother.

Luke stood with Allie wrapped tightly in his embrace, and he loved the feel of her in his arms. If he'd had any idea what was coming, he would've held on a little tighter for a lot longer.

25

RICHMOND REGIONAL JAIL

Larry sat in the cafeteria, his wary eyes all around as he ate. He couldn't believe he was still in jail. *Fuckin' Chelle.* If she hadn't overdosed, the police would have never gotten involved. He'd been arrested before he'd had a chance to clear the drugs out of their apartment but had trusted Chelle to keep them safe. *Hell, I should have known she was too fuckin' weak to not take more than she could handle. And with the kids around.* The last thing he'd ever wanted was kids taking up time, space, and money. *Christ, I should have insisted she have abortions.* He snorted, remembering how Chelle had claimed she wanted to be a mom. *Yeah, right. She was as worthless as a mom as she was a wife.*

A couple of inmates sat down in front of him, and his gaze jumped to them, careful to make sure no one was trying to give him shit. They seemed to be just interested in eating, so he continued with his meal, his mind buried under his own thoughts.

One of the men finally looked up at Larry. "Word is you got a brother that works in the North Heron jail."

Larry's gaze jumped to the man, and hiding his fear, he nodded. While Luke had never helped him out before, he still liked to tell people that he got special privileges because of his brother's position. "Yeah, yeah. He works in the clinic. With all those drugs, you know. He's gonna try to get me transferred there so he can hook me up."

"Don't bullshit me. You aren't going anywhere. From what I hear, you pissed all over Stepanov."

Larry paled, his food now turning into a stone in his stomach. Thomas Stepanov was the supplier Larry moved drugs for. Heroin. Cocaine. Even Fentanyl. And getting caught, having his supply confiscated by the police, then having Chelle OD and what was in the apartment confiscated as well, the powerful cartel boss was not happy. Swallowing deeply, he blustered, "I'm gonna get out and make it all okay. We'll make more than before."

"I've got a message to pass on to you from Stepanov."

Trying to keep from hurling the lunch he'd already eaten, he just stared.

"Convince your brother to take care of things."

"Huh?"

"Stepanov's brother, Ivan, is currently stuck in the same backwater fuckin' jail your brother works in. But that puts your brother in a position to help him out."

"But he won't... I mean, he's not... I'm not sure I can..." Larry's breathing became shallow, but the thought hit him that if he didn't get Luke to do whatever these guys wanted, Larry might not keep breathing at all.

"Just do it. Tell him he'll be contacted. Tell him to follow directions." The man chuckled. "We'll keep it all in the family, right?" Then his face hardened. "Do this... and Stepanov will consider your debt partially paid. Fail? And you won't like the results."

The man stood, picked up his tray, and walked away, leaving Larry blinking in his wake. No longer hungry, he sat, mind racing. For all his bravado to others, he knew he was fucked. His brother would never agree to anything a drug cartel wanted him to do. He squeezed his eyes shut, desperate to find a way to get Luke to help him. *It would just be this once. I can act like I didn't know what he was being asked to do. Or I could tell him I'd be killed if he didn't handle this.* Shoving his tray to the side, he dropped his head into his hands. Luke would never agree, and Larry had absolutely nothing to coerce him to help.

Or do I? Standing quickly, he grabbed his half-full tray and dumped the contents into the garbage can and the tray onto the counter where the men on kitchen duty would rinse it off. The cafeteria was too noisy, and he needed to think.

Lining up with the first group to be taken back to their cells, he breathed easier when the sounds receded and he made it into the quiet of his cell. His roommate wasn't there, and he sat on the bottom bunk, toying with the idea that had struck him.

The kids. Luke wanted the kids. Luke wanted them so bad he had me sign papers that he could take care of them. He rubbed his hand over his chin, wondering how deep Luke's feelings for the kids ran. They'd never meant much to him, and it used to bug him when Luke would spend money on them but not give him or Chelle anything. *Luke would do it for them.*

His brow furrowed as he continued to plot. *But I'm fuckin' stuck in here, and he's already got them. Shit, if I'd only known this was going to happen before I signed that paper.* As he thought back to what he'd signed, he knew it was only temporary guardianship, and his lips slowly curved upward. *Chelle and I are still parents. In the eyes of the law, we're still in control. And if I want Luke to dance to my tune, I'll dangle full custody in front of him.* Finally satisfied that he had a way to coerce Luke into helping him out, he flopped back onto the bed and breathed easier.

26

Allie rose early the next morning, wanting to make sure that everything went smoothly for the first work and school day as a new family. She and Luke took turns taking a shower and getting dressed. Then she helped get Jessica up and dressed while he handled Jeremy.

She'd already fixed their lunches the night before and had the lunchboxes now next to their backpacks near the front door. Breakfast was oatmeal with apples, cinnamon, and a swirl of syrup on top. With orange juice and milk ready, she greeted the kids as they bounded down the stairs. Luke walked directly to her, bent, and offered her a light kiss which she eagerly accepted. As she turned back toward the kitchen table, she spied the kids grinning at them while spooning oatmeal into their mouths.

Breakfast was quick, then after a check to make sure they had everything for school and teeth were brushed, the kids piled into her car after kisses and hugs with Luke. He wrapped her in a hug while she stood at the driver's side of her car, and he whispered, "Are you sure you don't want me to come this morning when you talk to the principal?"

"It's okay, honey. As you said, people are going to find out soon enough that we got married. I just need to let him know that I'm now responsible for the kids, as well."

With a last kiss, they climbed into their separate vehicles, and he headed to the jail while she went to Baytown Elementary. The principal took the news of her marriage with barely a raised eyebrow. With as many responsibilities as he had, she assumed the marriage of one of his teachers wasn't big news. And since she was already taking the kids to and from school, nothing had really changed.

The teacher's lounge at lunch was a different matter.

"You did what?" Shonna asked, her eyes bugging.

Jade laughed softly, shaking her head. "I have to confess that the grapevine was already starting to chatter about the two of you. While I didn't know for sure that you'd gotten married, a couple of people saw you at the courthouse on Saturday, and then Millie knew that Wyatt and Joseph had gone to help Luke move his and the kids' things to your house."

She shook her head. "I know this sounds like I have doubts since I wasn't announcing it to everyone right away, it's just that I wanted the kids to have a chance to get settled before everyone descended upon us with the reaction like Shonna just had."

"Hey, girl," Shonna protested. "I'm just sorry you

didn't come ask me to be a witness! But please, please tell me you've got some pictures."

She grabbed her phone and began flipping through the pictures that Minnie had taken and then the ones that Maddie had snapped at her house. The exclamations immediately came as soon as her friends saw her dress, Luke and Jeremy in their dress clothes, and, of course, Princess Jessica.

"You got that at BigMart?" Shonna asked, her eyes wide. "Girl, you're the only person I know who could buy a dress there and make it look like it came from an expensive shop!"

One of the aides popped her head into the teacher's lounge and told Shonna that the nurse needed to see her about a student. When it was just Allie and Jade in the room, Jade turned to her.

"Please don't take this the wrong way, Allie, because I'm not trying to rain on your parade, but—"

"But you're wondering if I know what I'm getting into, right?" Seeing Jade nod, she said, "I'm not offended because you're simply voicing what most everyone will think. Luke and I had already officially become a couple when life threw him this curve. But instead of the kind of curve that knocks you down, Luke completely stepped up for those wonderful children. And everything I saw just made me care for him that much more. And when the state social worker implied that if she wasn't satisfied with where he lived and what he could provide for the kids then she might suggest they go into the system, I knew I needed to step up, too. Did we have to get married? I don't know. But am I sorry that we did?" Her smile curved her lips as she held the gaze of her friend. Shaking her head, she continued, "Not at all."

Jade's smile widened. "Then I think you all make a lovely family, and I predict that you're going to be one very happy lady who also makes those three very happy, as well."

Leaning toward each other, they hugged, and Allie felt a weight lift off her at the knowledge that her friends were going to be supportive.

She and Luke fielded a few more calls from friends during the week as news of their marriage and new family leaked out, but just like with Jade, no one seemed to think they were doomed just because they'd rushed to get married.

The week was busy, but the kids seemed to fall into the rhythm of their new family easily. It helped that they'd already learned to go with Allie at the end of the day, and on Tuesday and Thursday had the handoff in the municipal parking lot as Luke took over and she went into the jail to tutor. She'd informed Warden Neely that she would no longer be able to come on Saturdays, but he was fine with what she had accomplished so far and easily acquiesced.

The one hiccup was on Wednesday. Luke came home irritated although he hid it well from the kids. It wasn't until they were in bed that they were able to talk.

"Honey, what is going on?"

"Larry."

At that one word, her heart lurched. "What about him?" she rushed.

"I don't know what his fuckin' game is."

And at that, her heart lurched even more. "Game?" she croaked.

"Don't worry about the kids, babe. Believe me, the last thing he cares about is them. He wants to see me but wouldn't tell me why. My guess is that he needs money."

"What does he need money in jail for?"

"Inmates can have an account so they can buy things. Extra toiletries, cigarettes, things like that. Of course, we all know they use it for illegal shit, as well."

"What did you tell him?"

"I told him I have a job and can't just drop everything and come to him, but he said it was of absolute importance that he talked to me and can only do it in person. I told him that I had plans for Saturday that I wasn't going to break, but I could go see him on Sunday."

Her face fell at the idea that they wouldn't have a full weekend together.

He tucked a strand of her hair behind her ear and leaned forward to kiss her forehead. "I know, but they have morning visiting hours on Sunday. I'll leave before sunup and should be able to get there in a little over two hours. I'll give him about twenty minutes max and then I'm heading home. With any luck, I should be home by lunchtime. And while I'm there, I'll make sure he understands that this will be the last time I'm doing this."

She nodded, hating that he had to put up with Larry. Deciding to take his mind off his impending visit with his inmate brother, she threw her leg over his lap, straddling him. Leaning forward, she bypassed his lips and nuzzled the edge of his beard near his ear. She felt his fingers digging into the soft flesh of her ass and heard the hiss when she rocked against his cock. "Anything I can do to make things better?"

He flipped her quickly, settling his hips between her thighs, holding her hands pressed above her head, and kissing along her neck and down toward her breasts. Lifting his head, he wiggled his eyebrows. "Oh, babe, I think there's a lot of things we can do to make it better."

She laughed, loving the feel of him on top of her. His lips landed on her mouth, and she forgot everything but the way he made her feel, hoping she was doing the same thing for him. And if his actions were anything to go by, the way they made love, she'd accomplished her feat.

"Oh, my goodness, this home is lovely," Mrs. Gillis said, walking down the stairs, having inspected Jessica and Jeremy's room.

It was Friday afternoon, and they'd all just gotten home and were just walking through the door when a car drove into the driveway. The local social worker who'd been given their case was there for her surprise inspection. Allie's stomach had dropped, and even though she knew everything was well in order, fear scored through her.

Luke had grabbed her hand, linked fingers with her, and whispered, "It's all good, babe. Relax."

She'd stared up at him, wide-eyed. "Are *you* relaxed?"

she whispered in return, incredulity dripping from her question.

He shook his head. "No, but it won't help if both of us are freaking out."

She pressed her lips together, offering a little smile. Mrs. Gillis had sat in the living room and asked several questions, talked to Jeremy and Jessica for a few minutes, then was given a tour of the house, where she continually checked boxes and made comments on her tablet. Allie had the desire to rip the tablet from the woman's hands and discern what was being written in the report. Fighting that idea, she plastered a smile onto her face, praying that nothing would go amiss.

Finally, Mrs. Gillis encouraged the kids to play while she asked Luke and Allie to accompany her to her car. Allie, fear clutching at her heart, reached out and grabbed his arm. Once outside, the friendly social worker's face showed concern and she lowered her voice, "I wanted to let you know that I received word this morning that Chelle Purdue was charged with multiple drug charges and was taken into custody as soon as she was released from the hospital."

Allie squeezed Luke's hand but remained quiet, glancing his way to see his eyes flashing.

"And in front of the judge, she relinquished her parental rights, saying she didn't want to be bothered with them anymore."

"What?" Luke asked, his body jerking.

Mrs. Gillis offered a sympathetic nod. "The judge questioned her, but she remained steadfast. I'm having the papers she signed sent to me, and I'll have them in the file."

"That—"

"Luke," Allie interrupted, wanting to make sure that Luke kept his comments PG.

"Now, of course, their father is still their legal guardian although you have temporary guardianship. But it was important that you know what their mother's decision was."

Luke thanked her, and she soon waved goodbye after assuring them that she agreed, as long as Jessica and Jeremy's father was incarcerated and unable to care for his children, they were best with their uncle and his new wife.

As soon as she drove away, she and Luke slumped onto the top step of the front porch. Feeling as though every ounce of energy had just been drained, she looked to the side and could tell Luke felt the same.

"What are you thinking, honey?" she asked.

Luke swiped his hand over his face. "I think as pissed as I am at Chelle for being such a selfish bitch, she has unwittingly just given the kids their freedom from her toxic neglect."

Nodding, she replied, "I was thinking the same thing. We need to protect Jeremy and Jessica from knowing, though."

"Agreed. We can let Maddie know, and she can help us decide what to tell the kids and when."

"What about Larry?"

He shrugged. "I think we might be a step closer to making our family official."

"So, a silver lining."

He chuckled and she leaned her head on his shoulder. "It was a great fuckin' week and ending with a silver lining is a good way to kick off the weekend."

"I was going to fix supper, but now I think we're going to have to call for pizza."

Luke pulled her in closer and nodded. "I think it's definitely a pizza night."

The sound of tires on the oyster shell drive caught their attention, and they sat up in unison, their backs ramrod straight. Luke groaned, "Fuck. Tell me Mrs. Gillis didn't forget to inspect something and is back!"

27

As the car came into view, Allie gasped. "Oh, God. Oh, God. Oh, God." Luke jerked his head around to stare at her, but all she could manage was, "I forgot my parents were coming."

Wide-eyed, he asked, "Please tell me you got a call off to them this week and explained the situation."

Shaking her head slowly from side to side, she felt as though no oxygen could enter her lungs.

Her parents parked the car and climbed out, huge smiles and waves as they looked at her new home. "Allie!" her mother cried as she rushed forward, her arms extended.

Standing, Allie met her mom at the bottom of the front porch steps, and the two women hugged. Looking over her mom's shoulder, she could see her dad's appreciative gaze as he turned in a circle to view the house and yard.

"It looks like you're just a little way from the beach, Allie girl," he said, moving in for a hug, as well.

Luke stood off to the side, but her parents had immediately noticed him and smiled, waiting for an introduction. She stepped over and linked fingers with him, clutching so tightly she was afraid she might cut off his circulation but was unable to loosen her grip.

"Mom, Dad, I'd like you to meet Luke. Luke, these are my parents, Agatha and Richard Simpson."

"How nice to meet you," her mom said, smiling and shaking his hand before stepping back to let Richard greet him as well.

"The pleasure is all mine, Mr. and Mrs. Simpson."

"Oh, you can call us Agatha and—"

"Uncle Luke! Aunt Allie!" Jessica and Jeremy came running around from the backyard, laughing as they chased each other. Coming to a halt, they both looked up at Allie's parents.

"Oh, my, and who do we have here?" Agatha asked, her eyes alight and her smile wide.

"I'm Jessica, and I'm five years old. And this is my cat. And this is my brother, Jeremy. Did you come to see our house? If you want to, I can show you my room! And Aunt Allie says I can buy a pink bedspread if I want to."

"That sounds... um... very pretty," Agatha said, her smile dropping slightly as she turned her questioning gaze up to Allie.

"Mom, Dad, there's been a lot of things that have happened that I haven't had a chance to tell you about. This is Jeremy and Jessica. I had told you about them. They're Luke's niece and nephew."

"Of course," Agatha said, nodding.

"Yeah, we live here now since Allie and Luke got married last weekend," Jeremy pronounced, his eyes sparkling with pride.

"Married?" her parents said in unison, smiles gone and eyes wide in shock as they jerked them to Allie.

Luke looked down at the kids. "Jessica, Jeremy, how about you come with me, and we'll run out to get some pizza for everyone." Turning to Allie, he reached out and took her hand in his, keeping his voice low. "Is that a good idea, sweetheart? I don't want to abandon you, but maybe all this will be better without the kids around."

Panic threatened to choke her, but she stared into his concerned face and absorbed his warmth. Her shoulders sagged as her tension eased. Smiling, she nodded. "Yeah, that'd be great. That'll give me a chance to... um... explain, and then you guys come back and we'll eat." Looking down at Jessica and Jeremy, she cupped their faces. "Pick out enough pizza for everybody, and here's a hint... my dad likes pepperoni, and my mom loves extra cheese."

"Me too!" Jessica shouted, jumping up and down.

Allie kissed the top of her bouncing head before moving to place a kiss on Jeremy's forehead. "And I've got some ice cream we can have for dessert."

In her typical exuberance, Jessica threw her hands into the air and shouted, then grabbed Jeremy by the hand and began pulling him toward Luke's SUV. He went along with his sister but looked over his shoulder several times. As Luke buckled Jessica into her car seat, Jeremy asked loud enough for everyone to hear, "Is Allie okay? I don't want to leave her if she's not okay."

As Luke knelt to assure his nephew, tears hit Allie's eyes, and her heart melted a little more. Waving good-bye, she turned to her parents, seeing moisture in her mom's eyes. "Let's go in. I want to show you my house now that I've moved in and fill you in on the last week. I know you might not agree with the decisions I've made, but I hope by the time I finish, you'll understand."

Richard walked over and wrapped his arm around Allie. "It sounds like quite a tale to tell. Your mom and I can't wait to hear it." Pulling Agatha in with his other arm, the three of them went inside.

They sat in the living room, her parents on the sofa facing her and she in the overstuffed chair that didn't feel its usual comfort, and she launched into her relationship with Luke and then their decision to become a couple. Blowing out a breath, she plunged into the explanation about Jessica, Jeremy, their parents, the situation, what she and Luke had been doing to make things good for the kids, and then the visit with the state social worker that forced them to take the drastic step of deciding to get married.

Swallowing deeply, she held her parents' gazes, seeing mixed emotions flitting across their faces as they glanced at each other before turning back to her.

"Honey," her mom began, "everything you've told us makes sense. Perfect sense. Until the part about getting married. Could Luke not find a different place to live?

Or could you have invited them to stay with you for a while? Or..." Agatha sighed, her hands lifting to each side. "I don't know... just something other than getting married."

"Unless there's more you're not telling us," her dad said.

Her gaze jumped to his. "I don't know what you mean. I really told you everything there is." Like her mother, she sighed heavily. "When I say it all together like I just explained it to you, it sounds nuts. And it is. It's not the way I ever thought I'd fall in love. It's not the way I ever thought I'd get married. I never expected a ready-made family. I'd only lived in my house barely enough time to get the furniture moved in when suddenly, I have a ready-made family."

Her father nodded slowly, then said, "I think you've just admitted the one thing you'd left out. Only I'm not sure you even realize it."

Both she and her mom looked toward her dad, brows lowered. "What did I say?" Allie asked.

"You said it's not the way you ever thought you'd fall in love."

Agatha gasped and nodded as she looked toward Allie. "You're in love with Luke."

Shaking her head slowly, ready to deny that emotion, she felt her breath catch in her throat. "I... it's just that..." She closed her eyes for a moment, giving over to the images that rushed through her mind like flipping the pages of a photo book. Luke hugging the kids tight, playing ball with Jeremy, and letting Jessica climb him like her own personal jungle gym. Making sure the kids knew they were loved. Luke holding her hand, pulling her close. Moving slowly inside her, both knowing they were making love and not just screwing around. Tight hugs and soft kisses. For a man who'd grown up in a home where love wasn't often shown, he had no problem showing it to others. Opening her eyes, a smile graced her face as she stared at her parents. "Yes, I'm in love with Luke, and I haven't even told him yet."

Her mom reached over and clasped Allie's hand. "Tell us about him, sweetheart."

And so, she did. All the images that had moved through her mind—with the exception of their intimacy —she shared. Finally, when she'd finished, she added, "Outside of you two, he's the best man I know. And when the social worker scared him into thinking the kids could go into the system, knowing that we can give them so much love, he'd blurted that we were getting married and moving into this house. I could've said no. I could've turned away. But even though it wasn't planned, I knew it was right."

Finally, Richard smiled. "I raised a smart, thoughtful daughter. As strange as the last week has been for you, there's nothing you've told me that makes me doubt that you're still the daughter I raised."

"Thanks, Dad," she said, tears threatening once again. Turning to her mom, she waited.

"You know, Allie, no one knows how marriage will turn out. Many people are completely in love, and their marriages don't last for lots of different reasons. Other people work to make the relationships last a lifetime.

And I agree with your father. As different as this last week has been, you're still the girl we raised. And that tells me that Luke is a man worth being with. And I can't wait to get to know the children."

Dragging in a breath that hitched several times, she finally lunged toward them, her arms spread wide. Feeling her parents embracing her, their heads pressed together, she let out a sigh of relief. Finally, leaning back, she grinned. "Who's ready to see the rest of the house?"

She gave them the grand tour, then belatedly realized she no longer had a guest room. "Luke and I can sleep on the sofa—"

Agatha shook her head. "While you and your dad were looking at the backyard, I called the Sea Glass Inn in Baytown and booked a room for us tonight."

"Mom, are you sure you don't mind?"

"Mind? A chance to stay at a lovely inn that's right on the beach? I wouldn't call that hardship!" her mother laughed.

Luke and the kids came back with pizzas, and in her typical little-girl happiness, Jessica bounded out of the SUV when he unbuckled her and ran to Allie, throwing her arms around her. Jumping up and down, she said, "We got three pizzas! Three! And they're all huge! And one of them has pepperoni, and another has extra cheese so your mom and dad will be happy!"

Jeremy hustled to the front porch also, his wary eyes taking in the gathering, his shoulders relaxing when he saw the smiles on everyone's faces.

Richard walked over to Jeremy and said, "I hear

you've got a baseball and a glove. After dinner, if you'd like to toss a ball with me, I'd really enjoy that."

Jeremy looked to Allie first, and after she nodded, he did, as well. Jessica, not about to be left out, ran over and grabbed Agatha's hand. "I'm not good at ball. But we can play with my dolls!"

Kneeling, Agatha smiled. "Sweetheart, I think playing dolls with you after we eat pizza and have ice cream would be the best ending to this day."

The kids led the way into the house, followed by her parents. Luke reached out and snagged Allie's hand, pulling her close. Bending low, he whispered, "Is everything okay?"

She wrapped her arms around his neck and stared into the face she now knew she loved. It wasn't the right time to tell him, and considering she had no idea if he loved her also, she simply smiled. "I explained everything. They had questions. They had concerns. None that you and I haven't already thought of and talked about. But in the end, they could see that I was happy and what we're doing with our little family is right for us."

His smile melted the concern on his face, and he wrapped his arms around her, pulling her close. Leaning together, their mouths met in a soft, gentle kiss. Wanting more, she angled her head and opened for him, offering an invitation that he accepted as he swept his tongue through her mouth.

"Allie! Luke! Come on! It's pizza time!"

Separating, they pressed their foreheads together and laughed. She stepped back but kept her fingers linked with his. "Our presence for pizza is demanded by the princess."

He laughed as well, and they opened the screen door, letting it snap behind them as they headed into the kitchen.

28

Luke pulled into the parking lot of the Richmond Jail and sat for a moment, trying to get his mind on the task at hand. During the drive, he'd replayed the visit with Allie's parents and had to admit it went much better than he'd anticipated. After pizza and ice cream, her parents played with the kids before heading to the inn they were staying at. Allie had given him a play-by-play of their conversation, but he couldn't help but feel that she was holding something back.

On Saturday morning, they'd met her parents for breakfast at the Diner, and then her parents took Jessica and Jeremy to BigMart. There, Agatha commenced buying pink and purple sheets, pillowcases, a bedspread, and curtains for Jessica's room, and Richard headed to the game and sports section with Jeremy.

It seemed that as long as Allie was happy and no one, not even her parents, were upsetting her, Jeremy was happy. Luke was glad the kids were settling well but still wanted to get Jeremy to relax and enjoy being a kid more. *He's had way too much on his shoulders and has now seemed to take on worrying about Allie.*

And while the kids were with Agatha and Richard, he and Allie had gone back home and tangled in the sheets for a full, uninterrupted hour, discovering more about each other's bodies and celebrating being married without any kids across the hall.

By the time the kids got home with their bounty, Allie had fixed a picnic, and they walked down the street to the beach.

Before her parents left, Luke found a moment to chat with her parents alone and held their gazes as he said, "I know this weekend has been a shock, but you have my promise that I'll do everything in my power to take care of Allie."

Agatha had pulled him in for a long hug, whispering how glad she was to know him. Richard had shaken his hand and smiled warmly. "Son, if you care for her the way you do for those precious children, then I can leave my daughter confident in the knowledge that she is truly loved."

The kids rushed out to say goodbye, and then a flurry of bedtime activities began, keeping Luke busy. But not so busy that Richard's words didn't replay over and over in his mind. *She is truly loved. Loved.* He'd never told her how he felt about her. With so much going on, he hadn't allowed himself to define his feelings. *But love?* He'd lain awake for hours with her in his arms, and the knowledge moved over him that he *did* love her. *But how does she feel about me?*

Now, movement in the parking lot pulled his attention away from those thoughts, and instead, he was filled with irritation that he had to see what in the hell Larry wanted. Going through the security, he was finally escorted into a large room with multiple tables and families visiting. In a few minutes, Larry came in, his eyes darting around until they fell onto Luke, and he hurried over to the table.

Luke took the opportunity to watch as Larry approached carefully. His brother had two moods: sullen, complaining that the world owed him, or cocky, bragging that he had the world in the palm of his hand. Neither was true, but as far back as Luke could remember, that was Larry. But now, Larry approached with a bit of smile, a gleam in his eyes that Luke couldn't define. But he didn't like it.

"Hey, Luke," Larry greeted, sitting quickly in the chair across the table. His gaze met Luke's for a few seconds before his eyes slid to the side, scanning the area.

"Okay, Larry, you dragged me here on one of my off days, so what's so important?"

"I, uh, wanted to talk to you about an opportunity that's come up. Something that will be good for both of us."

Luke blinked. Slowly. Then lifted his brows as he leaned forward, his forearms planted on top of the table. "An opportunity? Are you shittin' me?"

"No, no, man. Seriously. It's good. It'll be good for both of us."

"Good for both of us," he repeated, still not believing he'd hauled his ass down the highway for a couple of hours and given up a Sunday with Allie and the kids to listen to his dipshit, inmate brother try to drag him into some con. Because if there was one thing he knew about Larry, any *opportunity* he'd talk about had to be a con job. "Larry, I'm gonna say this once, and you need to listen. If there's an emergency, you can have the jail call me. Otherwise, don't waste my time." He flattened his palms on the table and began to push up.

"Wait, Luke. You need to hear this. After all, you've only got temporary guardianship. Just temporary."

Ice cold raced through Luke's veins as his gaze stayed locked on Larry's face, his brother's expression now harder with a tinge of desperation in his eyes. "Temporary?" The word erupted from Luke, feeling like sandpaper as it escaped his lips.

"Come on, man, sit down. Hear me out. I swear, that'll be good for all of us," Larry pleaded.

Moving in slow motion, Luke lowered himself back into the chair, his forearms still on the tabletop, but now his hands curled into fists. Not trusting his voice, he said nothing as his hard gaze never wavered.

Leaning forward, keeping his voice low as his gaze darted between looking around the room and Luke's face, Larry said, "All you gotta do is follow some instructions. That's it. Somebody at the jail you work in will meet up with you and tell you what to do. Simple, man. There's nothing to it."

Larry's tone had moved from fearful to hopeful, something Luke had witnessed many times growing up. Larry fuckin' up. Larry about to get caught. Larry conning someone into taking away the heat. *Christ, will things never change?* He remained silent, not surprised when Larry moved into fast-talking to get his way.

"You've always had it easy, Luke. You were older when Dad left. You left home after high school, and I was stuck there with a worthless mom. You came home a big shot, then got a cushy job." His face contorted in a grimace. "Look, I owe some people. You know I shouldn't be in here, but because I am and because Chelle fucked up and got the police finding things in the apartment, things are tight for me. So, I've got no one I can rely on but you. There's someone in your jail that's related to someone I owe. They'll let you know what you can do to help, and you do it. Easy! I mean, seriously, bro, it couldn't be easier. Then the people I owe will back off, and everything will be good."

"You are seriously fucked in the head if you think I'm gonna take instructions from an inmate. Christ, I can't believe you, Larry—"

Larry sneered. "You want the kids, don't you? I know you do. Hell, you were always buying shit. You couldn't wait to get here and have me sign papers so you could take care of them. You want 'em, you do what I need."

"I've got the kids, Larry. You can't use them as bargaining chips! I've already got them."

"Yeah, temporarily. Chelle signed away her rights, so it's all me. I still got rights as their parent."

"You had her sign the kids away?"

"Fuck, it was easy. I got a call to her while she was still in the hospital. Told her what to do, and I could make things easier for her. She didn't care. Said they'd been a pain to take care of anyway when I wasn't around. She wanted her freedom."

Shaking his head, he growled, "You two are such shits—"

"I can just as easily sign over temporary guardianship to somebody else, Luke, and they'll be snatched away from you. Fuck, I can make up shit about you and make sure you never even get to see them again."

Luke's gut clenched at the audacity and bullshit pouring out of Larry's mouth. "Yeah, see how that goes for you, brother. Your kids are clean, fed, safe, in school, and in a loving home. If you gave one shit about them, they'd be the last thing you'd try to dangle to get someone to go along with your fuckin' scheme. And you should know that social workers have deemed their situation good, so you've got nothing to try to scare me with."

"Okay, okay, but what if I could make that permanent?"

"Make what permanent, asshole?"

"You and the kids. Look, Chelle gave up her rights. What if I do, too, giving you full legal custody? You get 'em, free and clear. Works for both of us 'cause I don't need to be spending money on them, and if you want to do it, then you can have 'em." He leaned forward, perspiration beading on his forehead. "You do this one thing... swear to God, it's only *one* thing, and I'll sign anything you put in front of me to give you the kids. You'd never have to worry about anyone ever threatening to take them away again. But if you don't... it won't only be me you'd have to worry about, but the

people I owe. They can make things difficult for you...
and for them."

"Are you threatening them?" he asked, the air feeling
thick, making it hard to breathe.

"Not me, bro... but the people I owe. Do it, and all
our problems go away, and you get what you want. You
get full custody of them."

———

Luke drove home, his mind furiously turning over what
Larry proposed. *Shit, no way... there's no fuckin' way I'm
getting involved in any of this.* His jaw was so tight he
wasn't surprised at the headache pounding.

When he'd walked away from Larry, he hadn't
agreed to anything. He hadn't even indicated that he
would consider anything. He just wanted to get away.
Get away from his brother's toxic scheming and back
to the fresh air of the shore and home with Allie,
Jessica, and Jeremy. *Home. But temporary?* Fuck, when
he'd married Allie, it was to provide a stable environment for the kids. She was all in. She said it was what
she wanted, too. And now he knew he loved her and
just had to prove that her faith in him wasn't
misplaced and prayed that she'd fall in love with him,
as well.

*But what if the kids are taken? But what if on the slightest
chance that Larry is right and he has the power to take them
back if he gets out or gives them to someone else or puts them
into the system? What then? And what would that do to the
kids? Christ, how could I live with myself if I allowed that to*

happen? Will Allie hate me for letting the kids be taken away? Will she feel cheated that the reason we got married is gone?

For almost three hours, he drove home, no answers coming to him, but his mind churned over the situation as much as his gut churned at the idea that he was considering Larry's proposal. *Maybe it's not something too bad... maybe it's just slipping some extra money to an inmate. Or giving them extra OTC pain meds. Or pretending someone is ill so they can be put on light duties.* The more he thought about it, the more convinced he was that a simple request that could be easily accommodated could be considered.

Pulling into the drive, he looked toward Allie's house —*their house*—and spied the kids playing in the front yard while she sat on the porch swing, one leg tucked underneath her and the other foot pushing the swing back and forth. The kids were laughing as they chased each other around, and the expression of happiness on Allie's face crashed into him. He'd do anything... *anything*... to keep those three just the way there were in that instant.

"Luke!" Jessica screamed as she ran toward him, her arms windmilling, excitement pouring off her.

He scooped her into his arms, then held her high so that he could settle her on his shoulders. "Hang on, princess."

"Jeremy! Allie! Look how high I am!" she cried out.

"Hey, Luke," Jeremy greeted, his face relaxed in a smile.

Reaching out, he tousled Jeremy's hair as they walked toward the porch. Shifting Jessica to the ground, he climbed the steps and walked over to the swing. Allie's gaze was searching his, and he knew she was looking for clues to how his meeting with Larry had gone. Smiling while hoping she could not read his angst, he bent and kissed her lightly before settling next to her on the swing, wrapping his arm around her, and pulling her close. "Did your parents get home okay?"

"Yes. They called this morning and once again said how much they enjoyed meeting you and the kids."

"Good. I enjoyed meeting them, too, and I can't tell you how glad I am that you have their support." He twisted his neck and kissed her forehead.

The kids continued to play, and as they moved out of earshot, she whispered, "So, how did it go?"

Deciding to start with honesty, he said, "I don't know why I sometimes think my brother might change. He swung between whining about life not being fair, blaming me for getting everything, and then just being a general prick."

She laid her head on his shoulder and sighed. "I'm really sorry, honey. I'm sorry you have to put up with that and have for years. I'm sorry that you hoped it might be different today."

"Me too, babe, but mostly I'm sorry that because of him, I missed a good chunk of a free Sunday with you all."

"You know," Allie said, "I was thinking that we should try to get more than just temporary guardianship."

His body jerked, but he quickly locked it down. "Yeah?"

"I looked into it today while you were gone. Even if Chelle signed away rights, Larry could get them back if he gets out of jail." She sighed. "I still can't believe their mom did that, and yet, I'm glad she did. Does that make me a horrible person?"

"Not at all, sweetheart. She was never a good mom, neglectful and sometimes mean. She thought having the kids was a way to tie Larry to her, and he'd be her ticket out of the shithole she was raised in, but she blamed them when she realized Larry wasn't any better of a catch than her old man was."

"What I looked into on the Internet today was how to legally prove that Larry's not a good father. I would think that the detective's testimony along with Jeremy and Jessica's former teachers and even the neighbor you talked to would help."

Hope loomed in Luke's chest that unknowingly, Allie was finding a solution to the problem he'd been turning over in his head for hours. *We could get custody of the kids, and I would never have to do anything for Larry!*

She sighed heavily again and added, "But what I also read is that it isn't easy to do. The courts are very reluctant to take away parental rights, even for people who are in jail multiple times or for long sentences. It's almost as though being a parent that's little more than a sperm donor is more important than the well-being of children." Her shoulders sagged. "I can't stand the idea of them being forced to go back into a situation like they just got out of."

"Allie! Come fix my ponytail!"

She turned and smiled at Luke, kissing the underside

of his jaw. "I'm so sorry to be such a downer when you just got home. I promised the kids that we could have an early dinner and then have a popcorn movie evening. Is that okay?"

He forced his lips to curve, his heart aching. "I can't think of a better way to spend an evening than with the three of you."

He watched her stand and jog down to the bottom of the steps, run her fingers along Jessica's hair, and pull it back into a ponytail. Calling them to come inside for their baths, she reminded them of their evening plans, and the kids rushed onto the porch, huge smiles on their faces.

Jessica stopped and turned toward Luke, her eyes dancing. "Uncle Luke! Did you hear? We're going to have a popcorn movie night! I've never had one of those!"

Her words grabbed his heart and squeezed. He watched as she grabbed Jeremy's hand and hurried her brother inside, still exclaiming about what movie they were going to watch.

And he knew exactly what he had to do. *Anything to keep the kids safe.*

29

Allie grinned as Jessica and Jeremy entered her classroom at the end of the school day. Jessica bounded at her usual fast pace, and Jeremy walked behind her, his smile coming easier now that they had settled into a routine.

"Hey, guys, are you ready?"

"Sure, Allie," Jeremy said, keeping his backpack on his shoulders and bending to pick up Jessica's where she had dropped it just inside the room.

She gathered her satchel and purse, then guided the kids to her car. It only took fifteen minutes to arrive at the municipal parking lot. As they sat for a few minutes waiting for Luke to come out so that they could hand off the kids and she'd go to the jail's library for tutoring, Jeremy asked, "Is this like Dad's jail?"

Blinking, she twisted around to see his gaze pinned on the large, brick building at the end of the parking lot. There were other large, brick buildings around holding county offices and the courthouse, but he was locked on the building that Luke would exit from.

"I… well, honey, I don't know. I've never been there."

"I'll ask Uncle Luke. He'll tell me," Jeremy said.

"Why is Dad in jail?" Jessica asked, her face scrunched.

"He was doing stuff he shouldn't," Jeremy sneered. "I know what he had in the house. I know what he and Mom were doing."

She stared at the hard line of his young face, and her heart ached. Feeling like she was losing control of the conversation and seeing Jessica's eyes fill with tears, she rushed, "Let's not focus on that right now. Luke will be here in a few minutes, and you two need to get home, have a snack, do homework, and then tonight, after Luke and I have a chance to talk, we'll let you all know what we can about your parents. Okay?"

"Okay," Jessica said easily, her trust in Allie and Luke showing resolutely through and her almost-six-year-old mind back on happier thoughts. Jeremy's brow was creased, an expression she hated to see but couldn't think of how to erase with Jessica present.

"Luke!" Jessica called, and Allie swung her head around to see him walking toward them.

She climbed from the car as the kids scrambled from their seats. She twisted her head as she heard him greet the kids and click his keyfob to let the kids now reverse-scramble into his SUV.

She looked up and smiled as he approached, and she wrapped her arms around him, lifting on her toes. Kissing him in greeting, she took in his smile but couldn't help notice the way it didn't seem to fill his whole face. Wondering if he'd had a difficult day, she realized it must have been a difficult week since that same ever-so-slightly-off expression had been there since he'd returned from visiting Larry. *Larry!* Whispering, she warned, "Honey, the kids were asking about their dad being in jail just before you came out. I had no idea what to say, so I kind of punted the subject. I just wanted you to know in case they ask you."

His shoulders sagged. "We knew this would come up."

"Yeah, but I'll let you know that Jeremy is pretty pissed at his parents, and Jessica seemed like she was more upset at her dad being in jail. I hope I didn't make it worse by deflecting, but I didn't want to tell them anything without you with me." His gaze hit hers, and she continued, "We're in this together, right?"

A flash of intensity hit her as his blue eyes lit from some inner fire. He kissed her firmly, then mumbled against her lips, "You bet we are, babe. Christ, it sounds good to know we're together."

"For better or for worse," she smiled.

"Come on, Uncle Luke! We need a snack!" Jessica called out.

Separating, she smiled and jerked her head to the side. "Hungry bellies are calling. I'll be home in a couple of hours."

With another touch of lips, she waved and headed into the security checkpoint, ready to work with her pupils. The women she saw on Thursdays were making excellent progress, and two were ready to take the GED as well as one of the men she worked with on Tuesday. She had talked with the warden the last time she was in, and they were planning to give her a few more inmates as soon as she was ready to dismiss those already showing success.

An hour later, she leaned back in her chair as the men were now working independently, and she had a small breather before she checked their reading comprehension. Glancing around, she smiled at Everett. He nodded politely, his lips curving slightly. She sighed. He'd cooled considerably since she'd married Luke. Casting her mind back, she'd never encouraged anything with him other than professional friendliness, but it seemed he took the news of her marriage as a disappointment.

One of the guards in the library was smirking at her, something he did whenever he saw her, which, thank God, wasn't often. She'd seen his name tag when he was standing with Everett and left the same time she did one evening. Officer Perkins. She'd meant to ask Luke about him but kept forgetting. A smile crossed her lips. *By the time I get home and see Luke, I have more important things on my mind!*

An inmate walked in, his gaze drifting slowly over the room before he made his way to the bank of computers that they were allowed to use. She'd had the opportunity to see inmates as individuals. Some looked like anyone you might see on the street, and others had a hardened expression that made her know she might walk the other way just to avoid their glare. This inmate had that hardened appearance, and yet, there was a control about him in the way he held his body, the way he scanned the room.

"Ms. Simpson… I mean, Mrs. Purdue…"

She smiled at her pupil. "Either name is fine. Truthfully, I'm still getting used to the married name."

He chuckled and asked his question, and she spent the next several minutes working over specific words he had difficulty with. After checking the other men's work, she was thrilled to give them the good news that they were all making huge advancements in their grade levels of reading. With hearty thanks and goodbyes said, they walked out with one of the guards.

As she packed up, she noticed the inmate at the computers had finished and was walking out with Officer Perkins just ahead of her. Deciding to give herself an extra moment, she stopped to chat with Everett, both hoping to let the smirking guard and the scary inmate move out so that she wouldn't be leaving at the same time and to see if she could salvage the friendliness with Everett that she'd had before Luke.

He smiled as she approached the desk, and she relaxed. They chatted as he shut off the computers and lights, then locked the library, and they walked out together. As they headed toward their cars, he said, "I was… um… surprised when you got married. I didn't realize you and Luke had been together for so long."

"I suppose you just know when it's right." She kept her response vague, not wanting to encourage a conversation about her and Luke. Glad that she'd reached her vehicle, she wished him a good evening and climbed inside. Sighing heavily, she started her car and began the drive home. While walking out with Everett had accomplished the goal of not being in the hallway at the same time as the men she would have preferred to avoid, she hated feeling that she needed to defend her choices to him.

At least their friends had all seemed truly happy if somewhat surprised that they were married. They'd fielded multiple calls from well-wishers and invites from friends who wanted to get together or arrange playdates with the kids.

By the time she turned into her driveway, the stress of the evening had faded away and was replaced with the excitement she always felt when she was coming home. Looking at her house, she couldn't imagine not having Luke, Jessica, and Jeremy there. Smiling, she hurried inside, greeted exuberantly by the family she loved.

Jeremy looked up from where he was bent over the coffee table, a new place he liked to do his homework, his face more relaxed than when she'd seen him last. Jessica raced from the kitchen to throw her arms around Allie's hips, giving a squeeze while shouting to Luke that Aunt Allie was home, then, like a whirling dervish, ran back to the table where she was helping Luke with dinner.

She stopped by the coffee table, squatted, and held Jeremy's gaze. "You good? Or at least better?"

His lips curved upward slightly. "Yeah. Me and Luke talked. He talked about their... um... addiction. I know Mom and Dad made bad choices. He said that's why they acted the way they did." His face scrunched, and for a few seconds, he looked so much like Jessica. Then he sighed, and it hit her that he looked so much older.

She nodded and cupped the back of his neck with her hand. "I agree completely, Jeremy. Your parents need to focus on their choices and how to live in a way that doesn't hurt others. And Luke and I want to take care of you and your sister."

"Yeah, that's what he said, too." He held her gaze, his eyes now hopeful. "He also said that he's looking into getting me and Jessica permanently..."

His voice trailed off, and she wasn't sure if it was because Jeremy didn't like the idea or was afraid to hope for it to come true. "Um... yeah... we've talked about it. Of course, making sure you and your sister are in the best place is what we—"

"I don't want to go back there to live, Aunt Allie. I want to stay here. Even if they get out of jail. They gotta take care of themselves, and me and Jessica need to be here, so it's better for us."

Smiling, she squeezed his neck, bent toward him, and kissed his forehead. "Totally agree, sweetheart." As she leaned back, his relief was palpable, and she grinned. "Now, let me go see what they're rustling up for dinner."

After complimenting Jessica on her beautiful table setting, she turned from the grinning girl and walked straight to Luke. He'd set the lasagna pan on a trivet, then opened his arms, allowing her to not stop until their bodies were connected, their arms wrapped around each other. With her cheek resting over his steady heartbeat, she relaxed. "You make me feel safe."

"Safe?" His mouth was near her cheek, and she felt the warm breath puff against the side of her face.

She hadn't meant to speak aloud but leaned her head back so that she could peer up into his beautiful eyes. "Yeah, safe. Probably a lot like how the kids feel. You're steady and real. You're a protector. You make us feel as though there's nothing bad in the world that can ever reach us." Lifting on her toes, she touched her lips to his, intending for the kiss to be light.

He had other intentions, and she realized that as soon as he angled his head and kissed her deeply. The timer on the stove went off, and he lifted his head. "I'd better get the rolls out, or they'll be burned."

Laughing, she released him and jerked her head toward the oven. "You'd better handle that. Jessica's got such a pretty table set, so we don't want burned rolls on the plates!"

While Luke finished dinner, she raced upstairs and changed into a sweatshirt and yoga pants. Sliding her feet into her sock-slippers, she hurried back downstairs just in time for the whole family to eat together.

After the kids had gone to bed, Allie ran the tub full and sank underneath the warm water with her head on her tub pillow. She'd lit a few candles, the lavender scent filling the air. The door opened, and Luke walked in, his eyes immediately sparkling in the candlelight as his gaze roved over her body. He closed the door quickly to keep the warmth in the room. He was already bare-chested, and the sight of his glorious naked torso had her press her legs together, the desire for friction creating a deep-seated need. Raking her gaze down his body, she noted his jeans were undone and his bare toes were peeking from the bottom. Something about his half-dressed appearance sent the air rushing from her lungs.

He squatted by the tub, dragging his hand along the water, his fingertips skimming her skin.

She smiled. "See anything you like?"

As his hand circled her chest before cupping her breasts, he leaned over the tub, his lips a breath away from hers. "Oh, hell yeah."

Before she could respond, his thumb swiped over her nipple, and she shivered despite the warm water. Closing the distance, his lips sealed over hers, his tongue immediately seeking entrance. She yielded instantly, opening her mouth, welcoming the onslaught of sensations that coursed through her. His other hand skimmed down her rib cage and over her tummy, cupping her mound as his forefinger slid through her folds. She opened her legs, inviting him to take what he wanted, offering him everything she had to give.

As his finger slid into her sex, then began thrusting in and out, he rolled and pinched her nipple with his other hand, his tongue still tangling with hers. Her body now on fire, she began to writhe, desperate for more and yet wondering if she could possibly take any more pleasure.

Just when she was sure she'd burst into flames even sitting in a tub of water, her inner coil sparked, sending vibrations shuddering throughout her body. Clinging to his arms, she cried out, thankful their bathroom was across the hall from the kids' bedrooms. Her legs felt like rubber, but as she regained control of her sated body, she managed, with his assistance, to climb from the tub. Dripping wet, she placed her hand in the unzipped waistband of his jeans and pushed them downward along with his boxers, freeing his erect cock. She dropped to her knees on the thick, soft bath mat and licked the length of him, her tongue swirling around the pre-cum drop on the head.

"Christ, babe," he groaned. His hands shot to her head, his fingers tangling in her hair.

Heady with power and the desire to give back some of the pleasure he'd just given her, she slid him into her mouth. With his hands slightly gripping her hair, she moved in a rhythm all her own, alternating between licking and sucking, taking him as deeply as she could then circling her tongue around him. His groans grew deeper, and with her hands clutching his bare ass, she worked him until she was sure he was going to come.

He pulled back suddenly, catching her by surprise. Moving faster than her sex-filled brain could process, he lifted her from the floor with his hands under her armpits, then turned her to face the counter. Shucking his pants and boxers the rest of the way off, he palmed her ass before sliding a finger through her wet folds.

"I'm ready, Luke, please. Take me."

As her hands clutched the counter and her gaze stared at their reflection in the mirror, he lined up at her entrance and plunged into her sex. She'd never watched herself have sex before but now found the experience totally erotic. Her breasts bounced with the rhythm of his thrusts. His hands held her hips, and she watched his face as the sensations crashed over them.

"Need you to come, babe," he grunted, his eyes staring at hers in the mirror.

"I'm close."

"Need you to come, now, babe," he repeated, his voice gravel deep. Sliding one hand forward, he pinched her clit.

Trying to keep from screaming out as another orgasm shook her body, she heard a strangled squeak and knew it came from her lips.

He dropped his head back, the corded muscles of his neck standing out, and groaned through his clenched teeth. Watching him come was so beautiful, so uniting. He continued to pump slowly, then finally pulled out, wrapping his arms around her with her back tucked to his front and their gazes pinned on their reflections.

Nothing about her relationship with Luke had followed a path that she once thought she'd follow. And yet, this man holding her filled her thoughts and her heart. As their chests heaved, their gazes never wavered from each other. Trapped in his blue eyes, she whispered, "I love you." The instant the words left her lips, her chest seized from fear that she'd spoken what he might not want to hear. Then his arms tightened around her. But the words were out, and she didn't want to pull them back. Continuing to hold his gaze steadily, she repeated, "I love you. It's okay if you're not there, Luke, but—"

"I love you too, Allie."

She blinked, her mouth open but no words coming forth.

"I was afraid maybe it was just me," he confessed. "I've never been in love with anyone before, so I was afraid to say it too soon, afraid it might not be right. And I know that there's not one thing that you and I have done that fits the concept of normal or what many others would have done. But I know what I feel when I'm with you. I know what I feel when we're all together. And I love Jeremy and Jessica. And I love the family we're making together. But it's important for you to know that I love *you*, too."

As much as she appreciated looking at them together in the mirror, she turned slowly in his arms so that their fronts were pressed together, her arms around his neck, staring up into his eyes. Her body felt weightless, as though if she weren't clinging to him, she would float off the ground. But his firm body with his arms wrapped around her kept her grounded. He bent, and they kissed lightly at first, then deeper, finally allowing their love to flow free.

30

Wednesday and nothing so far. The past couple of days had been a tumultuous roller coaster of emotions for Luke. From last Sunday's anger at Larry to the confusion of what to do about his request and subsequent promise to sign full guardianship while relinquishing his parental rights, to the acceptance that he'd do anything to keep his newfound family together. Each day of the week, he'd been anxious to see if anyone approached him, viewing every inmate who came into the clinic with suspicion. Add this to his and Allie's declarations of love which had sent his heart soaring, and he was exhausted. Even twenty-four-hour shifts in a medical tent in Afghanistan had not affected him this way.

"Are you okay?" Margaret asked as she and Jerika looked over the day's schedule for both the men's and women's clinics.

"Yeah, yeah. Just a lot on my mind."

Dr. Bailey looked up from his desk. "Taking on a

wife and kids is a lot to handle. I'm not surprised you've got a lot on your mind."

"Nothing I can't handle," he replied.

Margaret grinned. "You got that right, Luke. I've never met anyone so willing to change their whole life around to make sure those kids are taken care of. You and Allie make quite a pair."

As Luke finished the prep-work, Dr. Bailey answered a call then looked over toward the others. "Looks like it's all hands on deck today. Dr. Cisco has a bout of kidney stones. He's fine, but he's going to be out today."

"Whoo-wee," Margaret breathed. "We've got a packed day." Looking toward Luke, she said, "You'll be solo for part of the day while we work through the women's exams. You good with that?"

"Yeah, I'll be fine." The words had barely left his mouth when two of the female security guards began bringing in women inmates in pairs for their wellness exams. He walked back to the lab and into the men's clinic, arriving when their first patient of the day was escorted by one of the guards. By the time lunch rolled around, Jerika had taken her lunch break with Margaret, and Dr. Bailey left the clinic to meet with the warden.

"Got one for you."

Looking up, Luke spied Gary Perkins at the doorway to the clinic, an inmate sitting in the outer room.

"Complaint?" he asked.

"Says he's had the runs for two days. Don't know…

I'm sure as fuck not checking his shitter." Gary laughed over his attempt at sophomoric humor, but Luke just scowled.

Walking into the clinic, he recognized the inmate he'd met a few weeks past. Medium height but well-built as though he never neglected his workouts. Black hair. Dark eyes. Intense gaze. Remembering the inmate hadn't seemed thrilled with Gary, and now even less so, he jerked his head toward the exam room. "Go on in." Gary was about to follow the inmate when the inmate suddenly clutched his stomach and groaned, sending Gary retreating backward as fast as his feet could go.

"I'll just wait out here," Gary said, his nose wrinkling as his mouth twisted in a grimace.

"That's fine, Officer Perkins." Luke left the door open but noted Gary had backed almost to the outer door, diverting his attention to one of the other guards in the hall. Luke turned to his patient. Glancing down at the form, he lifted his gaze. "How long has this been going on, Ivan?"

Ivan glanced out the door, then turned. "Just keep acting normal."

"What?" Luke jerked his chin back.

"I've been waiting to get in here to see you. I figured the only way I could get rid of Officer Idiot was to give him a reason to stay away from me. Nothing like a hint of contagious diarrhea that'll keep a man away."

"What do you want?" Luke asked, his stomach dropping.

"You've got a brother that made a request of you."

Luke's gaze snapped to the inmate's face as the air rushed from his lungs.

"Saw your wife the other evening. Pretty thing."

Luke's eyes blazed. "How the fuck do you know—"

Ivan glanced toward the door where Gary was still gabbing with one of the female guards. "Not hard to find things out."

Luke felt his chest quiver with uncertainty. He wanted to call for Gary, send Ivan back to his cell, threaten him, hell... put his fist in the man's face. Swallowing deeply, he finally said, "I owe nothing to my brother."

Ivan snorted. "From what I hear, that shithead owes you. But then, like most shitheads, they manage to get others to sort their fuckups."

Luke remained quiet, hating but needing to hear what the man had to say.

Ivan held his gaze but, with another glance behind him, said, "You're smart. Nothing like your brother. So, here's the deal... you'll meet with someone, get a package from them, and bring it to me. Easy. Simple."

"What's in the package?"

Ivan just grinned.

"You seriously think I'll go meet someone on an inmate's errand, pick up a package that I have no idea what it contains, and bring it into this jail? How fuckin' nuts are you? If it's explosives, I could blow myself up, and I sure as fuck am not gonna bring something like that in—"

"It's not fuckin' explosives, not weapons. And keep your voice down if you know what's good for you."

"Are you threatening me?" Luke growled, straightening to his full height, knowing as tough as the man in front of him was, he could still take him down.

"Let's just say I'm looking after your best interests. There's something out there I want. Your brother owes my brother a debt. And we're going to see that debt paid, either by you, or your brother will fuck with you over those kids of his." A slow smile spread over Ivan's face as he lowered his voice. "It's a simple job, Medic Purdue. One job. One chance to make those kids yours permanently."

"I'm not doing it without at least knowing what's in the package." Luke's stomach clenched at the idea that he was even considering the demand.

The noise from the outer clinic sounded as though Gary was finished flirting with the female guard. Ivan whipped his head back toward Luke. "Medicine."

"Drugs."

Ivan grinned. "Medicine, drugs, what's the difference? Things that people will pay for that make them feel better… and keep coming back for more." The smile disappeared almost immediately, and his hard gaze hit Luke once again. "So, what's it going to be, Medic Purdue?"

"One time. That's what you said."

Ivan nodded.

"I have no reason to believe you, and I sure as hell have no reason to trust that Larry will keep his word."

Ivan's dark eyes flashed. "My family is honorable. Our word is law." He snorted, "I can understand your concern about your brother. But we will see the deed done. You complete the request, and your brother will sign anything you need him to sign. He will not renege. He knows what his life is worth if he doesn't."

"Where's the meeting?"

"One a.m. at the pier just north of the Creekside Campground. They'll be expecting you."

"What do I do with it? I'm not having it around my family."

"That pretty wife of yours works tomorrow evening... when there are fewer guards around. Just slip it into her bag. She'll never know anything. Someone will make their way into the library and take care of it."

"If you think for one moment that I'm getting her involved—"

Ivan lifted his hands to the side. "No harm will come to her. She won't even know what's happening. Your choice, of course. Think of the ramifications. Every man has a price. Yours isn't money, but I'll bet it's keeping that family together. And my family can make things very difficult or very easy for you."

Scrubbing his hand over his face, he grimaced, his mind racing and heart pounding.

A low growl erupted from Ivan, "I grow impatient, Medic Purdue."

Luke felt his chest quiver and seize, wondering if this was what a heart attack felt like. "Yeah... yeah."

"You finished in here?" Gary asked, walking toward them.

"Yes, sir, Officer Perkins," Ivan said, his voice conciliatory, his expression blank. "Medic Purdue is making sure everything is taken care of."

"Then let's go. I've got better things to do than hang around here with you," Gary ordered.

Ivan held Luke's gaze for a few more seconds, then, with a barely perceptible chin lift, turned and followed Gary out the door, leaving Luke to slump into the nearest chair. Bending forward, he placed his head in his hands, trying to still the shaking he felt throughout his entire body. *Jesus, what the hell am I considering?*

Allie watched Luke pace outside while she waited for dinner to finish. He appeared unable to settle down for what she thought would be a good, mid-week, fun family evening with dinner followed by a movie and ice cream sundaes since neither of the kids had homework. At first, she wondered if he didn't feel well, but when she asked, he just shook his head and said he had some things on his mind.

The mortgage payment was due the next week, and he'd said he wanted to transfer money into her account to pay half, but now she wondered if money was an issue since there were expenses with the kids. She didn't want to bring it up considering he'd been adamant after their last *discussion* about money. She'd talked to her mom after that conversation, and her mom had just laughed. *"Honey, you got married before you two had a chance to do much arguing. But it'll be all right. Making up is not a bad way to get closer between two people who love each other!"*

That was another thing... ever since they'd

confessed their love for each other last weekend, he hadn't missed an opportunity to tell her and show her as often as possible. But since getting home from work today, he'd been jumpy, irritated, and hadn't spoken of love at all.

Jeremy stood at the back door, his gaze following Luke as he paced, but said nothing. Jeremy's pinched lips gave away his worry, but Allie didn't know how to comfort either of them since she had no idea what was going through Luke's mind.

The kitchen timer sounded, and she hurried to pull the chicken out of the oven. Placing it on the counter, she turned to see Jeremy watching her.

"Should I call for Luke?"

She heard the hesitancy in Jeremy's voice and sucked in a quick breath. She and Luke needed to have words, but they would be after the kids went to bed. He needed to understand that while everyone had their own ways of working out stress and pacing in the backyard wasn't a bad way, he still needed to be cognizant of the kids watching him. Especially since she had an idea that Larry and Chelle's ways of handling stress weren't healthy or good for the kids. Forcing a smile, she nodded. "That'd be great, sweetheart."

Just as Jeremy turned toward the back door, Jessica had pulled it open and called out, "Uncle Luke! Come on! Dinner's ready!"

Jeremy looked over his shoulder toward her, and she laughed. "Guess that'll get his attention." Clapping her hands, she said, "Okay, dinner time!"

31

By the time the kids finally went to bed, Allie was furious. Luke had remained quiet during dinner, barely paying attention to her or the kids. He'd eaten quickly, then disappeared into the yard, supposedly to tinker with his vehicle. She'd made sure the kids were bathed and ready for bed then read to them, all the while getting more worried and admittedly pissed about Luke's strange behavior.

Jessica fretted as Allie tucked her in, her little face scrunched as she whined. "I don't feel good. My tummy hurts."

Allie ran her fingers over Jessica's forehead, detecting no fever. Since the little girl's behavior earlier had been fine, she had a feeling that the tummy ache was due more to worry and confusion over Luke's distant actions. Bending, she kissed her cheek and said, "Sleep now, sweetheart. Your tummy will feel better tomorrow."

Forcing a smile as she turned off the light, leaving

the room illuminated from the nightlight, she closed her door. *If I have to kick Luke's ass, I'll make sure your tummy feels better tomorrow!*

Moving into Jeremy's room, she found him sitting in bed reading, or at least pretending to read considering he was still on the same page she'd seen him read earlier. "It's time for lights out," she said softly, bending to kiss his head.

"Is Luke upset with us?"

She sat on the side of the bed near his knees. "No. Whatever is bothering him has nothing to do with you and Jessica."

"But maybe he feels trapped."

Startling, her chin jerked back. "Trapped? Why on earth would you think that?"

"Because Richie said that he overheard his stepdad tell his mom that he realized he wasn't ready to be a dad and felt trapped having Richie around."

Her chest depressed as a heavy sigh left her lungs. "Oh, honey, I'm so sorry that Richie overheard that, and even more sorry that now you're worried about our family. But I promise you that whatever is on Luke's mind, it has nothing to do with us. Sometimes grownups have bad days at work, or problems with friends, or just a day where they don't feel great. And your uncle handles those times by needing some time alone."

He stared at her for a long time as though weighing her words, turning them over in his mind. He finally nodded, sage wisdom passing through his eyes. "Even though it's kind of weird, that's better than what Mom and Dad used to do. Dad would leave for days, and

Mom would start yelling at me and Jessica, telling us that Dad was a dick for walking out and she was stuck with us or else she'd do the same. When he stayed gone longer, she'd just start drinking or doing whatever and end up sleeping for a couple of days."

Allie knew Chelle's *sleeping* was either passed out drunk or high, and her heart ached even more. "Well, you're right. Luke's way of dealing with needing to think through things is much healthier. And all you need to know is that you and Jessica are wanted and loved."

"That's right, bud."

She and Jeremy jerked their heads around toward the door at the same time, seeing Luke standing in the doorway. His face was partially hidden in shadow, and she had no idea how much he'd heard. Looking back toward Jeremy, she smiled as she kissed his forehead. Leaning to the side, she turned off his bedside lamp, his room also illuminated by a nightlight.

She started toward the door, uncertain how she felt about Luke suddenly showing up to say good night to the kids after having been so distant all evening. What she'd said to Jeremy about healthy ways to deal with stress was true, but she was so irritated that she found it difficult to simply wash away Luke's earlier behavior. Passing him as she walked out the door, she glanced up, but his attention was on Jeremy.

She headed downstairs, deciding that tonight was a glass-of-wine night, and was in the process of pouring a large glass when she felt Luke's presence in the kitchen.

With her back still to him, she gripped the counter, her emotions churning.

"You're pissed."

A snort erupted from her, and she whirled around. He was standing at the end of the island, his hands shoved into his jeans pockets, his chin lowered slightly, but his eyes were on her. "You think?" she snapped.

"Look, babe, I know—"

She threw her hand up toward him, palm out. It was a motion she abhorred and yet did it without thinking. Plowing ahead, she dropped her hand but started talking before he had a chance to continue. "I don't know if you overheard all of Jeremy's conversation, but he's worried. Worried that you might already be tired of having him and Jessica around."

"What?"

Allie stared. Luke's eyes were wide, his face pale. Sucking in a deep breath, she let it out slowly, determined to speak calmly. "I know that you're bothered about something. I explained that it's healthy for adults to work through stress, and sometimes being by yourself is a good way to do it. But Luke, you've got to think about how your reactions affect them. I'm not telling you not to have stress. I'm not telling you that you can't have a bad day. But just like I'm with a bunch of third graders every day, I often have to slap a smile on my face and learn how to hide things until I can deal with them on my own. Your behavior this evening and tonight, while not yelling and screaming or running away, was so different that the kids really noticed, and they were upset."

His shoulders slumped, and she wanted to go to him, offering comfort. But she hesitated before taking tentative steps toward him.

As she neared, he kept his gaze on her. "I'm sorry. I'm trying to work through something and didn't mean to upset everyone."

"We're all getting used to having a ready-made family. Let's face it, we're new to this. Marriage, guardianship. You and I have done everything we can to make sure those kids are in a good place while at the same time building our relationship, and maybe we just forgot to take time for ourselves."

"There were just some things that went down at work today. Some stupid shit that isn't over with yet, and I'm struggling with what to do."

She tilted her head to the side in silent question, but when he didn't expound, she asked, "Is there anything I can do to help?"

He held her gaze for so long she fought the urge to squirm with concern. Finally, he shook his head slowly. "No, it's something I need to take care of myself."

Closing the distance, she wrapped her arms around his waist and pressed her cheek against his heart. "Well, if you need me, let me know."

"I just… I just don't want us to change… any of this."

She felt his words as they rumbled from deep inside his chest. "Oh, Luke, I know. And I know you'll always do whatever you can to keep us together."

He didn't reply, but she felt his chest heave against her cheek as a heavy sigh left his body.

Luke lay in bed, unable to sleep, but it was just as well. At least he knew Allie was sound asleep when he slipped from underneath the covers. Padding to the bathroom, he quickly dressed and left a hastily written note on the bathroom counter that simply said, **I had to run out to check on something. I'll be back soon. Love, Luke**.

Praying that he got back before Allie woke and found the note, he carried his boots in his hand as he quietly closed the bedroom door behind him and tiptoed down the stairs. Once on the road heading north toward the campground, his stomach churned, the pain now making him wonder if it was possible to develop an ulcer in only twelve hours. That was about how long it had been since Ivan met with him. *Heart pain... stomach pain... this is a fuckin' nightmare!*

The entire situation was untenable, but Luke had never felt so stuck between two impossible choices. He was no stranger to difficult decisions, but agony speared through him. *Can I trust this guy? Will it really only be one time? I know Larry is not fuckin' trustworthy, but will these people force Larry to fulfill his promise? How big is this package going to be? Can I hide it until tomorrow? Is there any way I can keep from involving Allie?*

A few answers came to mind and he now wished that he had thought of them when Ivan was in the clinic. *Fuck, my head was so muddled then, I'm surprised I could think of anything!*

He quickly came to the turnoff for the campground, bypassing the registration office, which was now closed and dark. Driving past campsites, the road was lit only by the occasional lamp and his headlights. Coming to the small parking lot near the fishing pier, he looked around but saw no movement. He climbed from his SUV, his phone in his jacket pocket, his key fob still in his hand. Walking slowly toward the water, he spied a small boat tied to the edge of the pier, a single man standing on the wooden planks nearby. He had no idea how a deal like this was supposed to go, so he simply stopped, waiting for the other man to make the first move.

"Purdue?" the man called out softly.

"Yes."

"I have something for you."

The man's voice held a slight Slavic accent, but he didn't recognize him. Nodding, he remained quiet.

The man walked forward, and Luke was relieved that it didn't appear he was holding anything large in his hands. When they were several feet apart, the man, whose face was still mostly hidden in the shadows, reached into his jacket pocket and pulled out a small, brown paper sack. The top was folded over and secured with a strip of clear tape. It wasn't well packaged, obviously meaning they didn't care if he looked to see what was inside. He held it out, and Luke's fingers twitched as they hesitated. This was it, a moment in time, terror striking at him. With his hand reaching out, he took the package, its weight little more than what the kids carried in their lunch, and started to put it into his jacket pocket, then stopped. It was in his hand, but he didn't want it any closer.

The other man started to turn back toward the boat, but Luke called out, "This is it? All of it? The deal is done?"

The other man twisted his neck, his gaze boring straight into Luke's eyes. "Whatever bargain you struck will be honored." His lips curved barely upward, but he said nothing else before climbing back into the boat, starting the engine, and disappearing out over the water.

Luke stayed, making sure the man was gone before he jogged back to his SUV, the man's words—and smile—plastered in his mind. *Christ, I can't trust any of them.* Wondering about the ramifications of his decision, he tried to swallow down the bile that threatened to erupt from his throat.

Sitting in his SUV once he arrived back home, he considered what to do with the package. He toyed with the idea of opening it, seeing what was inside, but hated to know at the same time. *I just want this over.* Sighing heavily, he slid it underneath the driver's seat for safe-keeping until he needed to follow the rest of the directions given to him.

Once inside the house, he tiptoed up the stairs, first checking on Jeremy and then Jessica, his breathing easing as he discovered them both sleeping deeply. Moving across the hall, he entered the master bedroom, seeing the lump of Allie's body under the covers. Walking stealthily into the bathroom to undress, he spied his note still on the bathroom counter. He reached out to snatch it, wadding the paper before shoving it into his pocket. Stripped down to his boxers, he flipped off the light and made his way over to the bed.

Allie was on her side, facing away from him, a position he wasn't used to. When they slept, she usually curled into him, her slight weight pressed against his body. And he loved the feel of her in his arms. When he woke at night, just knowing she was embraced by him, giving him her trust and love, made him feel as though he could slay all dragons. But sometime in the night while he was gone, she'd rolled over.

Sliding under the covers, he realized how cold the sheets felt without her body next to him. He didn't want to wake her but needed to feel grounded by her, so he rolled toward her, his front curling around her back. She stiffened slightly. The change was almost imperceptible, but his breathing slowed.

"I went to the bathroom earlier." Her voice was as cold as his side of the bed.

Now his breath halted, his heart plunging.

"I don't suppose you're going to tell me where you went in the middle of the night."

He wrapped his arm around her waist, unable to stand having even the smallest space between them. "I... I needed—"

"Please don't lie to me. No matter what, don't lie to me," she begged.

Sighing heavily, he said, "I just went for a drive. I needed to get my head clear."

She said nothing, but at least she didn't start yelling or crying, for which he was glad. But then, after a moment of silence between them, a chasm opened up that seemed to grow by the minute. He couldn't think of what to say to make things better and hated not having the gift of glib replies or quick assurances.

Finally, he nuzzled her neck and whispered, "Sleep, babe. It'll all be fine. I promise." She still said nothing, and he had no idea if his words rang true or not, but at least she didn't pull away. Closing his eyes, he thought of Allie, Jessica, and Jeremy, and holding them tight in his mind, knew his decisions would affect them all.

32

Allie stood in the bathroom the next morning staring at her makeup job, doing a poor job of trying to un-poof her eyes that were still swollen from having cried in the night. When she'd found the note in the bathroom, she mentally cursed Luke for his secrets and then burst into tears as she lay in bed wondering where he was, what he was doing, and why he wasn't talking to her about whatever was bothering him. He had initially been the one who worried about their hasty decision to marry, but now she wondered if he had regrets.

She'd finally stopped crying, but hearing him get home and then enter the bed as though nothing had happened, she'd felt her anger rise again.

Not trusting that she might say something sharp, Allie stayed facing away from him but was still comforted by his warm embrace as she fell asleep again.

Now, staring in the mirror, she felt exhausted and wondered how she would manage to make it through the day and evening tutoring session. Blowing out a long breath, she stopped fussing with her makeup and walked downstairs. *I've got kids to get ready for school, so I'll deal with Luke later... tonight... sometime.*

He had already gone downstairs, and she was relieved to see that Jessica was sitting at the table with him, eating her bowl of oatmeal, a half-drunk glass of milk next to her. Jeremy was at the kitchen counter, busy spreading peanut butter on crackers. Winking toward Jessica, she walked over to Jeremy and kissed the top of his head. Peering down, she could see that he was also squeezing a small amount of honey onto the peanut butter before placing another cracker on top. "I've already got your lunch ready, sweetheart. If you'd wanted honey and peanut butter crackers, I could have made that for you."

He twisted his neck around and looked up at her, his smile a little uncertain. "These are for you, Allie. I know you'll get hungry before you get home tonight, so I wanted you to have a snack."

"Oh, how sweet. That'll be perfect." She inclined her head toward her school bag and purse at the end of the counter. "You can just put those in my bag if you want to."

His smile widened, and she moved to pour a cup of coffee. Once it was doctored to her taste, the microwave dinged, and she looked over in surprise as Luke pulled out another bowl of oatmeal.

"We made your oatmeal!" Jessica called out, her smile accentuated with a milk mustache.

Passing Luke, she walked over to Jessica and wiped her face. Kissing the top of her head, she glanced down and exclaimed, "Looks like you made a good breakfast. Your tummy must be feeling better."

Jessica nodded, then finished her milk, initiating another round of wiping the milk from her lips.

Luke approached from her side, placed the bowl of oatmeal onto the table, and rested his hand on the small of her back. "Here you go, babe."

She hadn't met his eyes since she'd walked into the kitchen, knowing it was childish but struggling to do so. But Jessica was staring at them, and a quick glance toward the kitchen counter showed that Jeremy was watching as well. She turned toward Luke and smiled. "Thank you." Sliding into the chair, she ate, forced lively conversation with the kids, and smiled at the appropriate times. Just like she told Luke she had to do at work sometimes, she hoped she could fake it until she could make it.

Hurrying through their breakfast routine, they all left the house at the same time. The kids clambered into their seats in the back and she tossed her bags into the passenger seat and walked around the front of her car to the driver's door where Luke was waiting for her.

Meeting his gaze, she tried not to melt but found it impossible. His blue eyes held hers, almost pleading. He hesitated, but she stepped forward and placed her hands on his forearms. "Are you okay, Luke?"

Breath rushed from his lungs, and it struck her that while she'd been irritated at his actions, her actions had caused him more stress.

"Yeah, Allie. I'm fine, and I promise that I'm going to take care of what's going on at work."

"I'm here, you know. You can talk to me."

He leaned forward and placed his forehead against hers. "I know. And as soon as I'm able, I will."

"Are we... are we okay?" She knew her voice was hesitant, but the question was weighted with emotion.

His head jerked back slightly, his gaze penetrating deeply into hers. "Fuck yeah, babe. Christ, we're fine. I promise... we're good."

His words eased the weight off her chest, and she nodded. Lifting on her toes, she kissed him lightly.

"Stop kissing, guys!" Jessica called out from inside the car, giggling.

Allie grinned against his lips. "It seems the princess is ready for her carriage to take her to school. I'll see you at the drop-off this afternoon." With another quick kiss, they separated, and she climbed behind the wheel. Waving, she drove off, seeing him standing in the driveway, staring at them until she could see him no longer. And while the kids chattered on the way to school, she could not help but feel the heaviness return to her heart. *Something's not right.* But with a sigh, she tried to push those thoughts aside as they arrived at school.

Luke spent the day edgy and irritable. He was never chatty with his coworkers or inmates, but today he was even more silent. Dr. Cisco was back at work, but Luke had no desire to listen to the description of the doctor's kidney stone passing although it seemed Margaret and Jerika were fascinated.

He saw no sight of Ivan but then didn't expect to. Still, he couldn't get the idea out of his head that Ivan would be the one in the library this evening with Allie. *Shit...*

But as he pondered the ramifications, he knew there was no way Ivan would be the one taking the risk. *No, he'll send a flunky.* Luke wanted to be there. Wanted to make sure that nothing went wrong. *But to deviate could mean disaster for everyone.*

He'd questioned Allie about her tutoring before, and she'd explained that she now spent most of the time with her students as they worked on reading programs on the computer.

Her bag won't be with her then. That's when someone will make a move.

"Medic Purdue?" Margaret called out. "You have a re-check that's just come in."

He looked up to see Ivan enter the exam room. Swallowing deeply, he stared at the inmate, barely keeping his anger in check.

"Good afternoon, Medic Purdue," Ivan said casually. "I just wanted to let you know that everything is fine with me today."

He nodded, not trusting his voice, but finally moved closer as he attached the blood pressure cuff to Ivan. Bending lower as he pretended to listen through the stethoscope, he asked, "No harm... she'll know nothing?"

"Absolutely. The last thing we want is for her to sound an alarm. She will have no idea someone is retrieving the package."

The assurance should have made him feel better, but in truth, he still felt like shit. Watching Ivan leave the clinic, he scrubbed his hand over his face, sighing heavily. Glancing at the clock, seeing he only had an hour of work to go, he tried to stay busy even if his mind wasn't on the job. *Let me just get today over with and get Larry to sign the fucking papers.*

When it was finally time to leave, he walked out of the jail, the tension threatening to make him burst into flames. Seeing Allie's car parked next to his should have sent joy throughout, but instead only made his task worse. Then, as she alighted, smiled, and waved toward him, he wasn't sure he could sink any lower.

"Hi, Allie!"

He jerked toward the left, seeing Hannah walking along the sidewalk. His heart jumped into his throat. Allie walked over to chat with Easton's police chief. Having no time to waste if he was going to accomplish what he needed to do, he jogged toward them. Tossing a wave toward Hannah, he unlocked his SUV with the pretense of getting it ready for the kids. Bending, he slipped the small paper bag out from under his seat and shoved it into his jacket pocket. Blowing out a breath, he stood and smiled toward the kids. He'd never allow them to be in a vehicle with drugs, but with the bag securely in his pocket, he tried to steady his breathing.

Jeremy had already jumped from his seat and headed toward the SUV, greeting Luke warily. Offering a smile that he hoped appeared genuine to his nephew, he caught Jessica as she jumped from her seat. Kissing her head, he inhaled deeply, finding a modicum of peace in the scent of her little-girl shampoo. "Go ahead and climb in, princess. I'll get your backpack."

With a quick glance over his shoulder, he watched as Allie said goodbye to Hannah before she turned toward his SUV to say goodbye to the kids. Acting quickly, he pulled the paper sack from his coat pocket and shoved it toward the bottom of her bag. Not wanting her to discover it before the recipient, he choked back his nerves at how many things needed to go right to pull this disastrous caper off.

Backing out of her car with Jessica's backpack in his hand, he watched as Hannah, still on the sidewalk, waved to the kids before turning to him. He tried to smile but couldn't help but feel as though her gaze was assessing. With a chin lift toward Hannah, he moved over to Allie. His wife was smiling, and the expression on her face reminded him of the first time he'd seen her on the pier in the sunset. Her face lit with an inner glow that he now knew was from pure goodness and happiness.

She turned and moved into his arms. He kissed her forehead, wishing he could confess all while praying that nothing untoward happened.

She leaned back and looked up, and fear shot through him that she was suddenly going to announce she knew what he'd been up to. Instead, she said, "Go easy on what you feed Jessica this afternoon, Luke. She said her stomach still felt yucky."

Clinging to a normal topic, he nodded. "Sure, babe. Absolutely. I'll make sure she doesn't eat too much. Any suggestions?"

"We've got some bananas, so I'd let her have them. Maybe some of the crackers. I think they were left on the counter from this morning. Depending on how she feels, we'll choose something easy for dinner."

He nodded, forcing a smile onto his face. "Sounds good."

She lifted on her toes, and he wasn't about to pass up the invitation. Kissing her lightly, his arms squeezed around her. "Please be careful," he said.

Her brow furrowed slightly, and his breath halted, hoping she wasn't going to ask about his warning. She then smiled before saying goodbye. She leaned into her car and grabbed her purse and tote bag.

"Wait!" he called out, then turned to look at Hannah. "Um… I forgot something in the clinic. Can you watch the kids for five minutes?"

Hannah smiled. "Sure."

He reached down and lifted the tote bag from Allie's shoulder. "I'll carry this in for you and then head to the clinic to get my phone."

She beamed again, and they walked back through the guard station and down the hall. They passed the clinic, and she looked up, but he quickly said, "I'll see you to the library, then come back."

"Wow, an escort all the way. How gallant!"

He hid the wince that threatened to mar his attempt to smile. At the door to the library, he entered and scanned the area. A few inmates were at the computers, and a few more were at the books. Everett looked up to smile at Allie, but it didn't pass Luke's attention that as soon as the librarian's eyes moved up to see Luke, his smile dropped. *Yeah, the prick is still into my wife.* In the middle of this shitstorm, he had no idea why that thought topped all others, but he was in the mood to put his fist through someone's face, and Everett's was as good as any.

"You can set it here, sweetie," Allie said, pointing down to the floor next to a chair at one of the tables.

He wanted to kiss her goodbye, stake his claim, beg for forgiveness, wrap her in armor, but all he managed to do was swallow deeply and reach out to clasp her hand. "Be safe," he said again. He glanced up to see one of the guards he knew he could trust and offered a chin lift. The guard acknowledged the silent request to watch over her with a chin lift of his own, giving Luke a modicum of comfort.

As he walked out of the library, his chest depressed as the inner battle waged. He made it back to his SUV. Once there, he forced a grin toward the kids still in their seats.

"You okay?"

He twisted his neck to see Hannah standing on the sidewalk.

"Yeah, yeah. Just… um… lost in thought. Thanks for this… um… watching the kids."

"Did you get what you needed?" she asked, inclining her head toward the jail.

He swallowed deeply, avoided her gaze, and nodded.

"Well, you've got some kids who look ready to leave," she said, smiling toward his vehicle.

Following her gaze, he spied Jeremy and Jessica grinning, ready to go home. *Home. Our home. Me, Allie,*

Jeremy, and Jessica. Holding on to that thought as his lifeboat in the storm swirling around him, he slid into the driver's seat and headed out of the parking lot. In the rearview mirror, he could see Hannah still standing on the sidewalk. But then she turned and greeted her husband, Dylan, another local police chief. They walked away together, and he released a heavy sigh.

33

Allie smiled at the three men sitting at her table. She couldn't believe how much progress had been made and felt a sense of pride at being part of their success. As they worked, she reached into her tote and let her fingers dig around until she encountered the lunch sack and pulled out her crackers. Nibbling, she offered the men a snack, but they politely declined. Too hungry to be embarrassed, she loved that Jeremy had been so thoughtful.

"Mrs. Purdue, the computers are ready whenever you are."

She looked over her shoulder to see Everett near the computer table, smiling. He'd informed her when she'd arrived that the warden was so impressed with the men's reading scores that they were looking to add one more to her schedule next week with the anticipation that at least one of the men tonight would hit his goal and be able to continue with computer lessons while she picked up another pupil. A few other men were at a different table of computers, their voices low, and she knew they wouldn't be disturbed.

Not wanting to have peanut butter and honey near the computers, she shoved her hand back to the bottom of her tote, feeling around for the paper sack. It felt like tape was stuck to something, so she quickly ripped through it and shoved the plastic baggie with the last few crackers into the sack. Embarrassed that she'd made so much noise in the quiet library, she hurried to wipe her fingers off on a tissue.

Turning to her group, she said, "Since you all aced those assignments, we'll move to the computers." They all stood, and she walked over, monitoring along with Everett as they logged on, making sure they were on the correct program. After a moment, Everett walked away, and she stood behind the men, watching carefully as they moved through the reading comprehension assignments.

Hearing voices, she glanced over to see Everett back at the counter, the smirking guard nearby, and another man she didn't recognize wearing a white lab jacket. She wondered if he was a doctor at the clinic, but her attention was soon drawn back to her pupils. Watching in amazement as each scored higher than they ever had on an assessment, she offered a heartfelt congratulations to the men, receiving their thanks in return. She looked up at the clock on the wall. "We only have five minutes left, so if you start powering down the computers, we should all leave on time."

By the time they'd accomplished their task, she had glanced over and noted the man in the lab jacket had left, the smirking guard was no longer there, replaced by someone who would take the men back to their cells, and Everett was waiting for her. Collecting her tote bag and purse, she and Everett walked out together. He was once again his chatty self, no longer seeming to hold any resentment that she wasn't interested in him other than friendship.

Pulling onto the oyster shell driveway, she smiled at the lights on inside the house and the sunset casting its glow in the distance. The days were getting shorter, the sun setting earlier. For a moment, she wondered what this house would've been like with only her. If she'd never met Luke. If she'd never met Jeremy and Jessica. She knew some might assume that she missed out on the opportunity to enjoy her first true home by herself. As she opened the door, she could hear laughter from the inside and smiled. *No, I didn't miss out on anything. Plus, if the kids are laughing, then Luke must be in a better mood.* With that thought, she hurried inside, wanting to take advantage of everyone's happiness.

Ivan worked in the cafeteria that evening for kitchen duty. Finishing the tray washing, he kept his face impassive, but inwardly his gut tightened at the menial labor. But he was not in this shithole jail in this shithole county for long, according to his attorney and his brother's promise. Another inmate passed him by, made eye contact, and nodded. Ivan's chin lifted almost imperceptibly. So... the signal had been passed along.

The sack had been delivered and placed in the designated safe place to be retrieved tomorrow. Finally, things were looking up.

Allie curled into Luke, her head resting on his pecs, his arms around her, her hand resting on his stomach. The kids were asleep, having enjoyed Luke being more like himself as he joked and played with them in the backyard after dinner. Both tired, they decided to head to bed early, and while he closed and secured the house, she took a bath. Now, with him propped up against the pillows next to the headboard, she reclined next to him, warm, relaxed, and ready to put the last few days behind her.

"I know I owe you a huge apology, Allie. And honest to God, I'm sorry, babe."

"Can you tell me about it?"

He sighed, her head moving with motion. She kept it resting on his chest.

"There was stress at work that just needed to be resolved. And this is no excuse, but I've always pulled inside myself when I needed to work through something."

She leaned up so she could look into his face. "There's nothing wrong with that, honey. All of this is so new to us. I guess we've just been riding the high of a happy family for weeks, and it was bound to hit a bump sometime."

He held her gaze and nodded. "It doesn't help that Larry's shit is still all over us."

She sighed, placing her head back on his chest. "He never wanted the kids anyway, so I don't know why he won't just relinquish parental rights. And it shouldn't be hard for us to convince a judge to approve everything. Right now, Chelle is out of the picture, and Larry is in jail, along with a history of neglect."

"I think we're about at the end of it, sweetheart. Larry indicated he's ready to sign. With any luck, our family will be free and clear soon."

"Good," she said, ready to move forward. She yawned widely, pressing herself tighter to his side.

"We're wiped, babe. Let's turn in."

Nodding, she slid down further under the covers. He turned out the lamp on the nightstand. Exhaustion pulled at her, her limbs feeling as heavy as her eyelids. Soon, sleep claimed her.

The door opened, jolting Luke awake. He'd been fast asleep but always slept light. Twisting his neck, he looked over his shoulder, seeing a small silhouette backlit by the nightlight in the hall.

"Jessica? What's wrong?"

Next to him, Allie jerked and partially sat up, blinking as she grunted, "Huh?"

"I don't feel so good," Jessica's small voice whispered.

He was already tossing back the covers, aware that Allie

was doing the same on the other side, but neither made it in time. Jessica bent over, throwing up what little she'd eaten for dinner. He reached her first and carefully picked her up, then rushed to the bathroom. Allie was just a few seconds behind him, already reaching for a bath cloth.

"Hold her next to the toilet," she said, wetting the cloth in the sink.

He settled Jessica between his thighs when she retched again. He hated the way her tiny body lurched, gasping as she emptied her stomach even though she'd eaten little that evening. Holding her hair back from her face, he felt Allie's presence as she leaned around him and pressed the wet cloth on Jessica's forehead.

"She feels a little warm," Allie said, "but not burning up. She's been complaining of a tummy ache for a couple of days."

When it seemed as though there was nothing else to come up, Luke settled his ass onto the floor, resting his back against the bathroom wall, and cradled her in his arms while Allie wrapped a blanket around both of them.

They sat together, quietly murmuring comforting words to Jessica as she sniffled against his chest. He was tired, but when he looked toward Allie, he could see dark circles underneath her eyes. He wanted to suggest she go back to bed but had just opened his mouth when he was interrupted.

"Allie? Luke?"

Their gazes latched onto each other as they heard Jeremy calling from the hall. Allie had just made it to her feet when the sound of Jeremy throwing up met their ears. "Damn," Luke breathed as he took to his feet with Jessica still in his arms.

She lifted her head weakly from his shoulder, her brow scrunched. "Did Jeremy get sick, too?"

"Sounds like it, baby," he said, stalking through the bedroom, making sure to step over where Jessica had thrown up. Once in the hall, he could hear Jeremy in the kids' bathroom still retching. Glancing down, he side-stepped Jeremy's sick on the floor and stood at the doorway to the bathroom, seeing Allie in a similar position as he'd been with Jessica, helping Jeremy as he bent over the toilet.

"I don't think it can be food poisoning," he said. "The kids had the same dinner that we did."

She looked up and nodded. "It must be a stomach bug. Hopefully, it'll pass quickly."

"As soon as they can tolerate liquids, we need them to drink a little bit." Then, as an afterthought, he added, "I've never treated kids before, but I figure it can't be much different than adults."

"When kids are throwing up at school, the nurse always calls the parents to come to get them, so I'm afraid my experience is also limited." She looked up again. "My thermometer is in the master bathroom. It's in the drawer to the left of my sink."

Still cradling Jessica in his arms, he turned and made his way back into the master bathroom. Using the forehead scanning thermometer, he could see Jessica had a mild fever. Handing it to Allie, she checked Jeremy's, finding it almost the same.

Since it seemed the kids wanted to stay together, she

brought Jeremy into Jessica's room, settling them on Jessica's bed. They stayed together, encouraging the kids to sip their electrolyte water, have doses of children's acetaminophen, and, when they were able, to nibble on a cracker.

An hour later, Jessica was tucked under the covers, her forehead was cooler, and she was sound asleep.

"How about we head back into your room?" Luke asked Jeremy, receiving a nod.

Allie had already cleaned up where the children had been sick, and Luke was thankful they didn't have carpet. Whatever she'd used had eradicated the smell. He tucked Jeremy into bed, soon joined by Allie as she bent to kiss his head.

They left the bedroom doors open in case the kids needed to get to the bathroom quickly again. Walking back into their bedroom, Allie looked as though she was barely standing. He herded her straight to their bed where they curled into each other once again. She found sleep immediately, but he lay for a few minutes with his arms around her, feeling the soft puff of her breath warmly against his chest.

As much as he hated that the kids had gotten sick, this was what he wanted. Home. Family. Committed people working together. *Larry and I sure as fuck never had this.* And with this thought, he was reminded about the difference between him and his brother. Somehow, he'd grown up with the desire to have everything their parents had never given them and was willing to work for it. Larry grew up wanting to take what he thought everyone owed him, the consequences be damned.

It's over. I did the deed. I did what was necessary. I'll get Larry to sign the paperwork. And this family will be mine to take care of.

Hours later, after little sleep, Luke bent over Allie's sleeping form, hating to wake her but didn't want to leave another note to remind her of the note he'd left the other night. "Babe," he said softly, shaking her gently.

She blinked her eyes then sat up quickly. "What time is it?"

"It's early, but I want you to stay home today."

Still blinking up at him, she shoved her hair out of her face and scrunched her nose. He watched the sleep clear from her tired face.

"Oh! How are the kids?"

"I just checked on them, and they're still asleep. I took their temperature, and they never woke up, but thank goodness, neither had a fever. I'll go to work, but you should stay home with them. Do you have to call in?"

"I'll log into the school's employee site." She tossed back the covers and climbed from the bed, straight into his embrace.

Closing his eyes, he held her tight, relishing the feel of her in his arms. He remembered his mother used to hold onto a mean grudge, but that wasn't Allie. She'd been upset with him, they talked about it, then she let it go. They still weren't in the clear yet, though. *Larry. I've got to deal with Larry. But I'll go to Richmond tomorrow.* He kissed the top of her head and mumbled, "I wish I could stay home, too, and let you keep sleeping, but I need to be at work. I won't be in the clinic because I'm serving on a committee for the warden, and he's got it scheduled for most of the day. But I'll have my phone with me. If the kids get worse or anything happens, you let me know."

She nodded, then gently pulled from his arms. She bent and snagged a large clip from her nightstand and fastened it around her hair to keep it from falling in her face. "I'll check in on the kids, then go downstairs and put in my request for a substitute." She glanced back toward the rumpled bed covers. "I'd so much rather be spending the day with you being here also." Lifting on her toes, she kissed him lightly. "But you go do your committee thing and come home as soon as you can."

With that, she turned and headed downstairs, leaving him staring at her. Scrubbing his hand over his face, he winced. *Committee... yeah, right.*

34

Allie showered while Luke went downstairs for breakfast. She wanted to luxuriate under the warm spray but quickly washed her hair and body in case the kids got up early. Dressed for stay-at-home comfort, she pulled on yoga pants, a camisole, and one of Luke's sweatshirts. With her hair towel-dried and braided, she moisturized her face, then headed to the kitchen.

He was at the counter and smiled as she walked in. Moving to him, she kissed him lightly, wishing he could take the day off, as well. As he filled his travel mug full of coffee, she heard the patter of little feet, and Jessica and Jeremy walked into the kitchen. She and Luke opened their arms, hugging the kids tightly while checking their foreheads. Looking at each other over the tops of the kids, they both smiled and nodded, acknowledging that the fevers seemed to be gone.

"Are we not going to school today?" Jessica asked, her nose scrunched.

"I'm hungry," Jeremy pronounced.

"No, you're going to stay home today until I'm sure you're over the stomach bug. I'm taking the day off to stay with you while Luke has to go to work," she replied to Jessica.

Luke, with his hand on Jeremy's shoulder, said, "And both of you need to take it easy today with what you eat. Lots of liquid. Allie's going to make some flavored gelatin. And make sure you check with her before you snack on anything. Deal?"

Jeremy looked up and smiled first at Luke, then Allie. "Deal."

"Me deal, too!" Jessica said loudly.

Luke lifted her in his arms, kissed her cheek, and set her into one of the kitchen chairs. He ruffled Jeremy's hair, bent and kissed the top of his head, then inclined his head toward the kitchen table, indicating Jeremy should have a seat, as well. Allie opened her arms as he walked toward her, lifted on her toes to accept a kiss, and felt his arms tighten around her.

"I love you, babe," he said softly, holding her gaze.

Drowning in his eyes as she almost always did, she smiled. "I love you, too." With another quick kiss, she walked to the door and said goodbye.

After he left, she fixed oatmeal with bananas for breakfast, giving them apple juice to drink. The kids seemed fine although tired, and she insisted they rest. Letting them pile up on the sofa, she put on a movie and headed upstairs to strip their sheets and carried them downstairs to throw into the laundry.

By then, she was already yawning. The kids clamored for her to join them, and she was more than happy to plop down on the sofa between them, put her feet up on the coffee table, and lose herself in the Disney movie.

Luke walked down the hall in the jail's administrative wing. Hesitating just outside the conference room, he swallowed deeply, steeled his spine, and then opened the door, entering the room, jolting at the sight.

His gaze landed first on Warden Neely, who nodded his greeting. Then he looked around at the other people circling the large table in the middle of the room. Sheriff Colt Hudson. Sheriff Liam Sullivan. Police Chiefs Mitch Evans, Hannah and Dylan Hunt. Wyatt Newman. Captain Ryan Coates and Joseph Newman. Another woman sat at the table. Her requisite dark suit and white blouse gave evidence that she was probably from the FBI. And two other men wearing jackets with DEA insignias on the front. He stood motionless for a moment, hating to have everyone's eyes on him. Finally, he nodded and said, "It's over. Hope like fuck you got it all on recordings because I want to be done with this shit."

"We got it," Colt said.

"You pulled it off perfectly, man," Liam said with admiration on his face.

Luke's jaw was tight. He didn't need the praise; he knew what he'd done. He was aware of all the steps these people had put in place to make sure Allie was safe, but he also knew it was his family on the line if something had gone sideways and fucked up.

"I was with the kids until you came back out of the jail," Hannah said. Her lips were pinched, giving evidence that she knew how he was torn up inside with worry.

"And we had her on camera from the moment she entered until she left," Colt said with Warden Neely nodding next to him.

"I followed her home when she left," Dylan said. "I watched her go inside your house where you were waiting."

Joseph left his chair and walked over to Luke, clapping him on the shoulder. Luke knew that Joseph didn't have the rank as the others in the room but had been brought in as Luke's friend for support. He appreciated that Joseph didn't offer platitudes but instead just held his gaze, let his fingers dig into Luke's shoulder, and then returned to his chair.

Luke had no official law enforcement position, but considering he was in the middle of this operation, they included him in their counsel. He'd recorded his meeting with Larry only because he didn't trust his brother but had no idea his brother would suggest something illegal to keep the kids. Driving home from Richmond as his gut churned, his head hurt, and his heart ached at the idea of giving in to Larry to get custody of the kids, he knew he had to do something.

He'd met with Colt and Warden Neely the next day, and after they'd listened to the recording, they made calls to the DEA and the FBI. It was arranged that Luke would agree to the demands and pick up the drugs while wearing a wiretap and knowing Wyatt and Colt were watching from the nearby woods and Ryan was watching from the water's edge. He was to follow the directions on how to get the drugs into the jail. After Ivan came into the clinic, they'd had him recorded, also. It didn't matter that Luke had protested using Allie, the FBI insisted they needed everything followed exactly to keep Ivan from becoming suspicious. But there was no way he was leaving her alone with the drugs.

The jail had cameras everywhere, including the library, and while Allie was in there the night before, Colt and Liam were just outside the room. Unbeknownst to Allie, Hannah was there to watch the kids, and Dylan had followed her through the parking lot until she got into her car when her tutoring session was over.

His head knew that everything had been in place for her safety, but his heart hadn't stopped pounding during the entire days that it took for everything to be set up.

"So, what's the deal?" he said, sitting down between Joseph and Mitch.

Colt held his gaze for a moment, then replied, "Everett is the one who took the sack out of her tote while her back was turned to help the inmates she was tutoring as they were on the computers."

His chin jerked inward, his back straightened, his eyes widened, and he didn't attempt to hide his surprise. "Everett? He's Ivan's errand boy? Jesus, you're shittin' me!"

"It surprised us, too," Warden Neely admitted. "I've

never seen Everett do anything that made me remotely suspicious of him."

"What did he do with the bag?" Luke asked.

"He immediately set it on the shelf behind the librarians' counter. It was hidden and yet not suspicious looking," Colt admitted, shaking his head.

"There was an inmate in the library who acted like a lookout," Liam added. "When the cameras followed him, we saw him go past Ivan in the cafeteria, and when their eyes met, the inmate nodded. That's nothing to get him on, but he may be somebody the FBI can use."

"Absolutely," the woman in the FBI attire said, her voice resolute.

"And today?" Luke asked. "What's happened so far today?"

Warden Neely inclined his head to the widescreen TV in the corner of the room. "The library opened, and Ivan had already requested several days ago to use the computers this morning. I gave permission, and he's already been in. He used the computers for approximately ten minutes, then Everett went to him. He leaned over while acting like he was trying to help Ivan with the computer, and believe it or not, just like some old movie, Everett handed him a book that had been hollowed out. The bag was stuffed inside."

Once again, not hiding his incredulity, Luke's eyes bugged, and he shook his head. "That's fuckin' nuts."

"Right now, the camera is still on them," Warden Neely said.

The room quieted, and Luke's gaze stayed pinned on

the sight of Ivan. While there was audio attached to the cameras, Ivan kept his face away and his voice very low. Everett appeared to startle but then quickly looked down. Everett fiddled with something underneath the counter and nodded. Ivan turned and spoke to the guard at the door and was escorted out, the book still in his hands.

Everyone's gaze followed the camera angle on Ivan, but Luke was so pissed at Everett his eyes never left the screen that showed the librarian. He watched as Everett grabbed a tissue from the counter and wiped his brow. "He's sweating," Luke mumbled.

"He's nervous and fuckin' well should be," Joseph noted.

"Something's wrong," Luke said, his heart starting to beat faster as his gaze now swung over to Ivan as he was returned to his cell. "I just know it. I can feel it." Looking over at Warden Neely, he said, "There are no cameras in the cells. How will you know—"

"It's taken care of."

Luke's gaze jerked over to the tight-faced FBI agent. "You put them there?"

"It's taken care of," she repeated.

Once inside the cell, Ivan, who obviously had no idea his cell now had a monitor camera, sat on his mattress and opened the book. He pulled out the contents and held the bag in his hand, staring down at it. He shoved his hand inside and pulled out several bottles, his grin evident. He stood, turned to bend to the far side of the mattress next to the wall, and slid them into what appeared to be a slit in the material. He picked up the paper sack and peered down into it again, then pulled out another plastic baggie.

"He's got more," the agent said, her eyes bright as she leaned forward.

Luke's heart lurched, recognizing the cartoon character on the side of the baggie. "Fuck no!" Jerking around to the others who were staring at him, he shouted, "That's a bag from home. She had a snack in it and must have shoved it in the bag when finished. He fucking knows she fucking had her hand in his drug stash!"

"She'll be fine," the agent said. "He can't contact anyone."

"No, but Everett can," Hannah said, her gaze on the other screen. "I think he was sending a message from his phone before Ivan left the library."

"You deal with this shit!" Luke shouted, heading toward the door. He looked over his shoulder. "You promised no blowback for my family, so there'd better not be any fucking blowback!" With that, he raced out the door and down the hall, pulling his phone out of his pocket while hearing boot steps in his wake.

35

"Okay, guys, let's take the clean sheets upstairs and make your beds," Allie called out, her arms filled with fresh-smelling linens.

The kids were feeling better and raced upstairs, ready to help. While putting the sheets on their beds involved more tug-of-war and playful grunting, they finally accomplished the task. "You can play up here while I go back downstairs and fix some lunch. How about chicken noodle soup and a grilled cheese sandwich?"

With four arms thrown into the air and shouts of glee filling her ears, she laughed and headed down to the kitchen. The soup was warming on the stove, and the sandwiches were almost made when a sound could be heard coming from the back door. Wiping her hands on a dishtowel, she turned and screamed at the sight of a man standing nearby, his face hard, his cold eyes pinned on her.

"Who are you? Get out of my house!" she growled, her hands clenched at her sides.

"You shouldn't have looked," he said, his fingers flexing.

"Looked? Looked at what?" She took a step back, wanting more distance between them.

"At what was in your bag. We can't have you know what was there."

She had no idea what he was referring to and at that moment didn't care. All she wanted was to keep him away from the children. Taking another step back, she shook her head. "I don't know what you're talking about, but I'm asking you to leave."

He stepped forward, his grimace replaced with a menacing scowl. Instinct took over, and she grabbed the first thing she could get her hands on. Slinging the hot soup toward him, his roar of pain belted out as he dropped to his knees, his hand holding his face. Taking the frying pan with the sandwiches, she swung it, hitting him in the side of the head, and he crumpled to the floor.

Screaming, she ran to the stairs but through the small window near the front door saw another man sitting in a dark truck. Racing upward, she was met at the top by the wide-eyed kids standing in the hallway. She snatched Jessica's hand and cried, "Come on!" She felt Jeremy's presence right behind her. "Good—stay with me!"

She ran to the door leading to the attic. "Take your sister up there." While Jeremy did as she asked, she followed, closing the door behind her. Once at the top, she reached her hand into her pocket. "I don't have my phone!" Turning to the kids now in the attic, she hugged them tightly, then ordered, "Stay here and stay quiet. I'm going to get my phone and lead the man away from the house."

"No," Jessica whimpered, tears forming.

"Baby, I have to protect you." She turned to Jeremy. "You stay here with her. I'll be back as soon as I can." She could see fear in his eyes but had no time to try to take it away. She ran back down the attic steps and opened the door quietly. Hearing some movement downstairs, she stepped into the upstairs hall then secured the door behind her. Dashing into the master bedroom, she hurried to the door that opened to the small deck. Now grateful for the vine trellis next to the deck, she swung her leg over the railing and scrambled down to the ground.

Once there, she flattened her back next to the house, having no idea what her next move should be.

"What the fuck happened?"

"The bitch hit me."

The sound of men's voices coming from the front yard jolted her into action.

She ran toward the back door, knowing if they were in the front, she had a chance to get back into the house. Slipping inside, she snagged her phone from the kitchen counter and hit the emergency button before shoving it into her pocket. Racing through the house to the front door, she could see they were looking toward the side yard for her.

"She must have run that way 'cause I could have seen

her if she'd gone out the front." One of the men started toward the trees. Careful to watch the man she'd hit, her heart nearly stopped as he turned to come back to the front porch as though he was coming inside. Seeing him stagger slightly, she took advantage of his weakness. With a flying leap, she jumped on him just as he entered the house, her fingers digging into the burned flesh on the side of his face and neck.

He cried out in pain, and she scrambled to her feet, landing a kick to his groin but wasn't sure she hit her mark. Jumping down the steps to the ground, she stumbled, then pushed herself back up. He rallied and flung himself onto her, cocking his arm with his hand in a fist.

"No!"

She jerked at the sound and gasped, seeing Jeremy swing his baseball bat, hitting the man in the back. He yelled as he staggered forward, barely missing landing on top of her. The man whirled around, his arm cocked, and his fist raised toward Jeremy.

Screaming, Allie forced her legs under her, ready to launch toward the man, when suddenly, in a flashing tangle of arms and legs, the man was knocked sideways, landing with a thud onto the ground, and Luke was straddling him, his hands around the man's throat.

She grabbed his arm and screamed, "There's another man! Heading to the woods!" Other people were running in that direction, and she glanced over to see deputies out in force, some running in the direction she had pointed. Hearing another grunt, she looked down to see Luke like a man possessed continuing to squeeze.

She tugged as hard as she could. "No, Luke! We've got to get to Jessica!"

That must have penetrated because he leaped from the man on the ground and, eyes wide, whirled around.

"She's in the attic," Allie said, running up the porch steps. Joseph was a step ahead, already inside and running up the stairs.

"No, Uncle Luke!" Jeremy called over his shoulder, racing toward the side of the house. "She's over here!"

Luke took off after Jeremy with Allie close behind, her mind closed to everything other than they had to get to her daughter.

———

As soon as Luke had pulled into the driveway, his gaze landed on Allie falling under the weight of a man in their front yard. His heart leaped into his throat, and he'd barely slammed on the brakes before bolting out of his vehicle. Jeremy was racing around the side of the house, his baseball bat in his hands. Luke was almost on them when Jeremy whacked the man on the back. It caused the man to let go of Allie, but he whirled around to hit Jeremy.

Seeing red and filled with the desire to kill anyone who dared to hurt his family, Luke leaped and slammed into the man, knocking him to the ground. Wrapping his hands around the man's throat, he squeezed. His face was turning purple, but Luke blanked everything, fury coursing through his blood. "…Jessica…"

At the sound of Allie screaming, the red veil lifted,

and he blinked, looking over to hear her cry, "... we have to get Jessica!" No longer caring about the piece of shit on the ground, he jumped up and raced after Jeremy, who was leading the way to the backyard, barely aware that Allie was on his heels.

Jeremy stopped at the bottom of the trellis. He started to climb up, but Luke stopped him. "Where is she?"

"Here! I'm up here, Uncle Luke!"

He nearly dropped to his knees seeing Jessica's face peering out the attic window, waving her arms. He started to climb, but Allie shouted, "You're too heavy."

Just then, Joseph's head popped out next to Jessica's. "Hey, sweetheart, can you come with me to get to your aunt and uncle?"

"Go with him," Allie called out, already running back toward the front of the house.

Luke started to follow but felt Jeremy running with him, reaching out to slip his hand into Luke's. He stopped and bent, scooping Jeremy up in his arms as he jogged toward the door, not worrying if his nephew would think he was babying him. He felt Jeremy's arms latch around his neck and his legs wrapped around his waist. Holding the little warrior next to his chest, he bypassed the others in the front yard and hurried into the house.

Joseph had made it to the bottom of the stairs, and Jessica launched into Allie's waiting arms. Luke shifted Jeremy to one hip and wrapped his arm around Allie, and in a tangle of arms and legs, they pressed closely together.

The next hours were spent in what Luke thought of as a nightmare and yet knew that things could have turned out so much worse. He'd managed to hold on to his temper in front of the kids but then let loose on the FBI and DEA agents who'd missed Everett making a call to someone outside the jail to get to Allie. "I put my family... my fucking *world* on the line to keep us all together, and you nearly had them taken out!"

The only thing that calmed him down was Colt, Joseph, and a few of the others taking him outside and saying, "Be pissed. Be angry. But not now. Right now, give your statement, support Allie as she gives hers, and then we'll all explain what the fuck happened."

His chest depressed at those words, bile threatening to rise up his throat. "Don't you see? This is on me. My actions nearly cost my woman and my children to be injured or worse. How the hell can she ever forgive that? I did all this to save my family and may have just torn us apart." His last words were a bare whisper, tears filling his eyes.

A soft hand landed on his back, and he jerked his gaze down to see Allie standing at his side. A tear slid down her cheek.

"Oh, babe," he choked out, "I'm so sorry."

She slid around to his front and pressed in tightly. "Honey, I still don't understand everything that went down, but I know anything that happened was because you were trying to give our kids the permanency that they need and keep us together. So, Luke... you've got nothing to apologize for."

He held her close, their bodies aligned, heartbeats

pounding together, and buried his face into her hair, breathing her in. They moved back inside the living room, finding that Hannah and Dylan had taken the kids upstairs to play. While sitting on the sofa with her tucked to his side, Allie gave her statement to Colt. Hearing about the pot of hot soup and the frying pan, Luke's arms tightened around her even more, pride soaring through him.

"Christ, Allie," Wyatt said, shaking his head. "As crazy as this sounds, that was a brilliant way to use what you had."

"Well, I can tell you it made a difference in slowing him down," Liam agreed. "He was burned, has a welt on the side of his head, scratches, and I'm sure a bat-sized bruise across his back."

"He deserves to not be breathing," Luke mumbled, but Allie pressed her palm over his chest, and he sucked in a deep breath to wipe his mind from murderous thoughts.

"I can't believe Jeremy crawled down from the attic window and got his bat," Allie said, her eyes filling with tears as she shook her head. "It was so reckless and so dangerous, but how can I fuss at him? He may have saved me!"

"I know, babe. We'll talk to him." Luke then twisted to face her as he explained what had happened ever since he'd talked to Larry. "I recorded my conversation with him using my phone because I've learned to not trust what he says. I wanted to play it back for him if he tried to deny whatever bullshit he wanted to ask me. I had no idea he was going to try to drag me into a drug deal before he'd sign the kids over to us. When I got back here, I met with Colt and Warden Neely the next day. From there, things happened quickly." He continued telling her every conversation, every action, every decision.

Her eyes widened as the story unfolded. "That's what had you so conflicted. That's why you walked me into the jail last night, so that I didn't have to carry the bag with drugs."

"I didn't want you to touch it. I didn't want it around you at all, but the agent convinced me we couldn't deviate from the plan. I knew once you were in the jail, someone would be watching over you, but I didn't want you to have that stain on you at all. There was a risk that you might find the bag before the person assigned to get it, but you'd mentioned that the men were almost always on the computer now. Hell, what are the odds that you'd have a snack in the same kind of paper sack? The plan the agent came up with had too many holes. Too many risks. I should've never—"

"Stop it, honey," she said. "What you did was so incredibly brave. Even if I'd found it, there were people all around who would have kept me safe. You kept this family together."

Feet racing down the steps had them swing their head to the side in time to see Jeremy, tears streaming down his face, running into the living room, followed by Dylan hot on his heels.

"I thought he was in the bathroom," Dylan said, wincing. "I'm sorry."

"I heard," Jeremy said, his gaze pinned on Luke, his

voice hitching. "Dad… he… he was going to… just for drugs…"

Allie choked a sob, her arms reaching out, but Luke got there first, sliding out from behind her and pulling Jeremy onto his lap. "Don't think that, bud. Your dad has problems and doesn't make good decisions. But that's not on you. That's on him. And he didn't mean—"

"Are you going to keep us?" Jeremy asked, another tear sliding down his cheeks.

"Absolutely," Luke vowed as Allie nodded next to him.

"I don't want anyone to take us away. I want you to be my dad, and I want Allie to be my mom." Jeremy lifted his arm and wiped his face with his sleeve.

"That's what we want too, Jeremy. And we're going to do everything we can to make that happen."

"You told Allie that Dad said he'd sign papers. He never does what he says he's going to—"

"He's going to this time. Believe me, he has no choice. I'm going to get them to take care of that tomorrow, and then Allie and I are filing for full custody. That means you and Jessica are ours, and we're yours."

Jeremy held his gaze for a long time, but Luke never wavered. Finally, his nephew dragged in a ragged breath and nodded. "That's why I had to help Allie," he said, his voice hiccupping. "That's what you would have done, and I want to be like you."

Luke opened his arms, bracing as Jeremy flung himself toward him. Wrapping his arms around him, he felt Allie press in tightly to his side.

Hannah walked down the stairs with Jessica's hand

in hers. Luke looked over, breathing a sigh of relief when Hannah offered a slight shake of her head, indicating Jessica hadn't heard anything. Other than being scared when Allie had to rush them into the attic, she hadn't seen the men or anything that occurred in the front yard. To her, it was a bit of an adventure when Jeremy had left the attic to climb down the trellis, and now, with people in the house, she smiled as though it were a party. She ran over and jumped into Allie's lap, and with his arms full of the ones he loved, Luke figured it was the best reason to celebrate.

Luke walked into the master bedroom, seeing Allie sitting up in their bed, her back propped against the pillows, the room lit by the lamps on the nightstand. They'd been concerned about the kids having nightmares, ready to let them sleep in the king-size bed with them, but each fell asleep in their own beds during storytime.

She looked up at him and smiled. "You'll wake them up if you keep checking on them."

"If they wake up, they can come in here."

She laughed softly and nodded. He walked over to the bed and slid under the covers, pulling her close to him. With her hand resting on his shoulder and her fingers splayed over his heart, he wrapped his arms around her, soaking in the warmth of her skin and the floral scent of her shampoo. For long minutes, they lay silent. Guilt still sat heavily on his shoulders. It didn't matter that the others involved assured him that he'd done everything right. The fact that his family was threatened was something he'd wrestle with for a long time.

He'd heard from Colt that while the investigation was ongoing, one of the other inmates had no problem giving Ivan and Everett's plan away. The drugs were stolen fentanyl, and Ivan's purpose was to get other inmates hooked so they'd continue to need more. Even once they left jail, they'd work for the Stepanov family's drug syndicate. Everett's deal was simply to make money. He'd facilitate giving the inmates a place to gather for a drug deal, earning a cut of the profit. And it turned out that the Stepanovs were running the same organized crime scheme in multiple jails and prisons.

"I know there's nothing I can say to make it better, Luke, but eventually, you'll let this go and realize that your actions gave us all that we need. Even the best-laid plans can go sideways. Focus on us being happy, healthy, and most importantly, together as a family."

She'd said the same thing numerous times during the evening, and he knew it would take time for it to completely sink in. But for now, with her in his arms and the kids sleeping across the hall in their beds, he allowed the sentiment to wash through him.

Her body relaxed, and he recognized that sleep was not far off for her. Curling into her, he pulled her close and whispered, "I love you."

He'd thought she was asleep, but her arms tightened as her lips touched his chest. "I love you, too."

They were the sweetest words he'd ever heard.

36

TEN YEARS LATER

"I can't believe I'm letting my daughter go out dressed like that," Luke grumbled under his breath, earning a soft giggle from Allie.

"Like what, honey? She looks like she stepped out of a classic Grace Kelly or Audrey Hepburn movie."

He scowled but said nothing. The truth was, sixteen-year-old Jessica was a beauty in every sense of the word. Long, dark hair that was now pulled back in a complicated twist with little sparkly clips in her hair. She'd gained height, and her figure was what he begrudgingly knew would turn any teenage boy's head. And while there wasn't a lot of skin showing in her long dress, it was off the shoulders, which set his teeth on edge. She was only a sophomore but had been invited to the spring dance by a boy in the eleventh grade, who was standing entirely too close to her while parents snapped pictures.

Turning his attention for a moment, he had to admit

that Jeremy in a tux was even more handsome than when he was in his Baytown Boys baseball uniform. And there was no doubt that the beautiful Emily MacFarlane on his arm thought so, as well. They'd stayed friends all through elementary and middle school, and while Jeremy had dated others in high school, he and Emily always found their way back to each other. And now, they'd dated during their entire senior year.

His yard was filled with Jeremy and Jessica's friends, all in their elegant attire, with parents mingling around taking pictures. His other two children with Allie, nine-year-old Jonathan and seven-year-old Jennifer, raced around the yard. They'd bought a new house when Allie was pregnant with Jonathan, wanting more room and also wanting to bury any lingering thoughts of that terrifying day.

As the teenagers began to fill cars and leave along with their parents, Lia and Aiden chatted with Emily, and Allie and Jessica had their heads together while her date waited nearby, laughing at Jessica's two younger siblings.

Luke straightened as Jeremy approached. His nephew that he'd called his son for ten years stood in front of him. The same height, they looked eye to eye, and although Luke had more weight, he knew Jeremy would finish filling out as he continued to mature. Jeremy had accepted an ROTC scholarship to Old Dominion University, and Luke was beside himself that he wasn't going too far away... for now.

After that day when Jeremy discovered the depths that his birth father would sink to, Jeremy called Luke and Allie his mom and dad. Jessica easily thought of them that way as well and was more than happy to follow her brother's lead.

Larry remained a guest of various jails over the years, finally landing in federal prison for drug trafficking. Luke had never spoken to his brother again. Larry had given up parental rights, easily approved by a judge. A few months later, they'd received news of Chelle's death, having never recovered from the effects of her overdose. They'd helped the kids grieve, making sure they talked to Maddie for more sessions, but found that there seemed to be a relief from them that their newly established family was finally settled. And they'd formally adopted Jeremy and Jessica.

Now, he waited to see what his oldest had to say. Jeremy didn't hesitate. Much like Luke, he might not talk a lot but had no trouble saying what was on his mind. "I know you're going to tell me that I have to be careful tonight," Jeremy stated, inclining his head toward Emily. "But you don't have to. I know I have precious cargo."

Luke swallowed hard, nodding.

"You taught me that, Dad. To take care of those you love."

"Then you learned well, and a father can't ask for anything more."

Jeremy grinned and then inclined his head toward Jessica. "I'll keep an eye on her, too."

Sucking in a breath through his nose, he chuckled ruefully. "Your sister likes to think she can handle herself, but I know you'll make sure she's safe."

Jeremy stuck his hand out, something Luke had noticed he'd been doing more often. He reached out, his fingers wrapping around his son's, remembering when the hand was much smaller. Pulling him in for a hug, he blinked at the moisture gathering in his eyes.

"I love you, Dad."

He wasn't sure how he managed, but he choked out, "I love you, too, son."

As Jeremy stepped back, he offered a chin lift, then turned and walked over to Allie, hugging her as well. They whispered to each other, and Luke felt sure that more words of love were being exchanged. From that moment when Jeremy had jumped in to save Allie, he'd been her special warrior.

He grinned as he walked to Emily, making sure he was directly in front of her so she could read his lips as he also signed, "Are you ready to go?"

She smiled and nodded, and Jeremy escorted her to his car, opening the door and giving her a chance to gather her gown before he closed her safely inside.

Jessica, a bright smile on her face, jogged over in her heels, and Luke wasn't surprised that she never wobbled considering she'd been trotting around in dress-up princess shoes for as long as he could remember. With her typical exuberance, she threw her arms around his neck, and he pulled her in tight. "I know, I know, Dad. Be safe. Be good. Don't do anything crazy."

Once again, with one of his children in his arms, he chuckled. "It's good that you have my lectures memorized."

She laughed, and her arms tightened around his neck a little more. "I love you, Dad."

He repeated the words he'd often said over the years. "I love you, too, princess."

She walked over to her date, who made sure to help her into his car much like Jeremy had for Emily. With a final wave, they drove off.

Allie moved straight to Luke, and he wrapped his arm around her, looking at his beautiful wife. He could still remember the first time he'd seen her, carefree, eyes bright, and with a smile that had rocked his world. Their marriage was unplanned but not unwanted. Their union started out as an arrangement that quickly grew into love. And for ten years, he'd considered himself the luckiest man alive.

Jonathan and Jennifer were laughing in the back-yard, playing on the swing set. A spring breeze was blowing from the bay, and the sun was setting over the trees, lighting the sky with pink and yellow, orange and red.

He dropped his gaze from the gorgeous sunset back to Allie's face, seeing her smile beaming up at him. He bent and kissed her, lightly at first, then taking the kiss deeper, drinking his fill, giving his all. It was a kiss of thanks for all they'd shared. It was a kiss that celebrated all they had. It was a kiss that vowed love and protection. It was a kiss that celebrated a future together.

It was the best kind… a sunset kiss.

Don't miss the next book in the Baytown Heroes
Finding a Hero (Joseph's story)

And if you missed it, here's the first Baytown Hero
A Hero's Chance (Ryan's story)

ALSO BY MARYANN JORDAN

Don't miss other Maryann Jordan books!

Lots more Baytown stories to enjoy and more to come!

Baytown Boys (small town, military romantic suspense)

Coming Home

Just One More Chance

Clues of the Heart

Finding Peace

Picking Up the Pieces

Sunset Flames

Waiting for Sunrise

Hear My Heart

Guarding Your Heart

Sweet Rose

Our Time

Count On Me

Shielding You

To Love Someone

Sea Glass Hearts

Protecting Her Heart

Sunset Kiss

Baytown Heroes - A Baytown Boys subseries

A Hero's Chance

Finding a Hero

For all of Miss Ethel's boys:

Heroes at Heart (Military Romance)

Zander

Rafe

Cael

Jaxon

Jayden

Asher

Zeke

Cas

Lighthouse Security Investigations

Mace

Rank

Walker

Drew

Blake

Tate

Levi

Clay

Cobb

Bray

Knox (LSI)

Lighthouse Security Investigations West Coast

Remember Love

Discover Love

Surviving Love

Celebrating Love

Searching Love

Follow the exciting spin-off series:

Alvarez Security (military romantic suspense)

Gabe

Tony

Vinny

Jobe

SEALs

Thin Ice (Sleeper SEAL)

SEAL Together (Silver SEAL)

Undercover Groom (Hot SEAL)

Also for a Hope City Crossover Novel / Hot SEAL...

A Forever Dad

Long Road Home

Military Romantic Suspense

Home to Stay (a Lighthouse Security Investigation crossover novel)

Home Port (an LSI West Coast crossover novel)

Letters From Home (military romance)

Class of Love

Freedom of Love

Bond of Love

The Love's Series (detectives)

Love's Taming

Love's Tempting

Love's Trusting

The Fairfield Series (small town detectives)

Emma's Home

Laurie's Time

Carol's Image

Fireworks Over Fairfield

Please take the time to leave a review of this book. Feel free to contact me, especially if you enjoyed my book. I love to hear from readers!

Facebook

Email

Website

ABOUT THE AUTHOR

I am an avid reader of romance novels, often joking that I cut my teeth on the historical romances. I have been reading and reviewing for years. In 2013, I finally gave into the characters in my head, screaming for their story to be told. From these musings, my first novel, Emma's Home, The Fairfield Series was born.

I was a high school counselor having worked in education for thirty years. I live in Virginia, having also lived in four states and two foreign countries. I have been married to a wonderfully patient man for forty years. When writing, my dog or one of my four cats can generally be found in the same room if not on my lap.

Please take the time to leave a review of this book. Feel free to contact me, especially if you enjoyed my book. I love to hear from readers!

Facebook
Email
Website

[f]

Made in the USA
Coppell, TX
21 July 2022